THE DEVIL IN LOVE

an Italian fairytale epic
by
Nick DiMartino

University Book Store Press
Seattle, Washington

THE DEVIL IN LOVE
Copyright © 2013 by Nick DiMartino

DRAGONWEED
First Version 25 May - 24 July 1981
Second Version 14-16 September 2013
Third Version 11-13 October 2013
SPELLBOUND
First Version 30 July - 12 August 1981
Second Version 24 October - 27 November '81
Third Version 16-19 September 2013
Fourth Version 13-18 October '13
TERROR ISLAND
First Version 28 August – 10 October 1981
Second Version 19-22 September 2013
Third Version 18-20 October 2013

Cover design by Jake Monderen
Cover photo by Noah Parrell
Michael Wallenfels, publishing coordinator
UNIVERSITY BOOK STORE PRESS
Espresso Book Machine
First Printing: November 2013

ISBN: 978-1937358341
All rights reserved.

UNIVERSITY BOOK STORE
4326 University Way NE
Seattle, Washington 98105
www.ubookstore.com
206-634-3400

THE DEVIL IN LOVE

BOOK 1 *Dragonweed*

BOOK 2 *Spellbound*

BOOK 3 *Terror Island*

BOOK 4 *The Prince Who Wept Jewels*

BOOK 5 *The Lucky Baby*

BOOK 6 *The Goose Boy*

BOOK 7 *Three Hairs from the Devil*

BOOK 8 *The Faithful Servant*

List of Chapters

BOOK ONE *DRAGONWEED*

1. A Stranger in the Garden — 13
2. The Secret of the Cottage — 20
3. The Prisoners of Fausto — 26
4. Death Comes to Bolgaro — 33
5. Noraldo's Mistake — 39
6. A Portrait of the Prince — 43
7. The Stolen Book — 47
8. "Do You Know This Man?" — 50
9. The Devil Laughs — 57
10. Dragonweed! — 63
11. The Conquered City — 68
12. Lightning Strikes — 72
13. "My Price Is Amalia" — 78
14. The Witch's Hoe — 83
15. The Profligate's Vow — 90
16. The Truth — 97
17. Ursula's Wish — 101
18. Shadows in the Castle — 104
19. Bells at Midnight — 108
20. The Devil's Land — 114

BOOK TWO *SPELLBOUND*

1. Late Knock at the Shoeshop — 119
2. Plans and Promises — 126
3. Into the Forest — 130
4. The Black Stag — 134
5. The Mysterious Palace — 138
6. The Invisible Guest — 144
7. "His Bed or Mine?" — 148
8. Spellbound — 152
9. Saved — 158
10. "What Really Happened?" — 163

11. Without His Book	169
12. Behind the Leather Mask	173
13. The Forbidden Chamber	178
14. The Wizard's Dream	182
15. Master of the Game	187
16. Running Out of Time	193
17. Sign of the Hanged Man	200
18. The Innkeeper's News	205
19. Desire and Treachery	211
20. Red Wine	219
21. White Wine	228
22. The Secret Watcher	237
23. The Wizard's Triumph	245
24. The Three Talismans	250
25. The Disenchanted	255

BOOK THREE *TERROR ISLAND*

1. Noraldo's Obsession	263
2. A Pool in the Forest	268
3. The Hermit's Search	272
4. Shoemaker's Holiday	276
5. Hour of the Assassin	281
6. Bargain with the Devil	285
7. Doorway of the Ancients	290
8. The Castaways	294
9. The Shores of Maligna	300
10. The Giant at the Bridge	305
11. Brief Reunion	310
12. The Riddle of the Sfinge	317
13. Zambardo's Net	324
14. Spiritual Consolation	332
15. Victims of the Cyclops	337
16. Dinner Fights Back	342
17. From Out of the Pit	349
18. The Jaws of the Skull	355
19. A Taste of That Water	359
20. The Devil's Doorway	363
21. The Kiss	369
22. The Child Bringer	374

INTRODUCTION

Thirty-two years ago, a little-known Seattle writer in his mid-thirties, a lonely, over-educated gay bookseller who loved epics and classic literature, decided to create a fairytale epic like the Ramayana or the Odyssey or the Arabian Nights, but entirely, defiantly gay. In 1981 there was no market for such an oddity. It was simply a lonely labor of love, his own mythology for gay people, an alternate fairytale world filled with all his favorite classic storytelling devices, but instead his epic would be the extravagant, guilt-free magical adventures of hunky young guys in love.

It became an interlocking chain of over 200,000 words that were stored in eight boxes and lost for thirty years called *The Devil in Love*. It's typed on engineering paper, and several chapters are still handwritten in minute, immaculate script. There's an innocent wholesomeness in this gay adventure unfolding in its own Wonderful Land of Oz, an erotic tale taking place in a world still naïve of the AIDS plague, with a last lingering flavor of the Sixties sexual romanticism, the idealism and horny recklessness of youth.

Like Elias Lonnrot gathering cycles of Finnish tales and weaving them together into a single epic, the *Kalevala*, so this lonely author writing for years braided together numerous tales of not only the Grimm brothers but also Boccaccio and Scheherazade, transformed them in the style of Tolkien and James Branch Cabell, along with a literary conglomerate from *Platero and I* all the way to *Bomba the Jungle Boy*, from *Treasure Island* to *Our Lady of the Flowers*, to create a monumental tale that was originally two smaller epics, *The Devil in Love* and *The Devil Goes Mad*, modeled on Boiardo's *Orlando Innamorato* and the greatest sequel ever written, Ariosto's *Orlando Furioso*.

I was that author a long time ago.

As with most of my writing projects, I lost faith in this one, too. After years of work, I put all that madness away inside a big cardboard box and lost it among dozens of other boxes in storage. The rain didn't get that box. The mice didn't chew that box. When my little cottage was doomed and I was forced to move, I found the box. It contained eight other boxes full of unnumbered typed and handwritten pages. The time capsule from another person with my name was called in big bold print *The Devil in Love*. I've now re-typed those eight boxes word-by-word into the book you now hold in your hands, reading it to myself as I typed, laughing and crying and gasping at my own surprises and forgotten set-ups, correcting a few slips, keeping the names consistent, cleaning up a few bad habits and a couple of the clunkier passages. Here's hoping I can finally share the delight of the Devil's Land not only with my gay brothers, for whom it was written, but with everyone who loves storytelling, the same way I've enjoyed heterosexual literature all my life.

And now here's the Preface I wrote thirty-two years ago.

FIRST PREFACE

The Devil in Love (*Il Diavolo Innamorato*) is my own personal version of a Renaissance fairytale epic, in the style of Boiardo and Ariosto – which is to say, multiple heroes in a multi-branching plot, swept up in a virtually inexhaustible current of enchantment, danger, and erotic adventure. Unlike my Italian masters, however, I have not drawn my plot elements from the Arthurian legends or the legends of Charlemagne, but from the fairytale world of the Brothers Grimm and Italo Calvino's *Italian Folktales*.

The eight books comprising this epic take place in an Italy which has never existed, a sensual, non-historical realm of the imagination called the Devil's Land. This cluster of small, independent kingdoms exists in a dimension which is comfortably similar to our own in most instances, but alarmingly different in a few areas of note. There are no wars in the Devil's Land, no tournaments or armor, no religion or sexual guilt. There are also, in short order, no women. Most of the men are good-looking and attracted to each other. Babies are delivered by a little old man riding a donkey. In many ways, it's a lovely, delightful place to live – with one shortcoming. The Devil is a perpetual nuisance there, always stirring up trouble. Against him no other god is pitted, only human ingenuity and men banding together in love.

I have tried to provide gay readers with the pleasure of a non-psychotic, non-tragic story about heroes of our own sexual orientation, in an action-packed fantasy adventure. At the same time, I have tried to write a story so full of humor, magic, suspense and surprises that it will also offer enjoyment to readers who are not erotically involved. The Devil of this tale is not to be confused with the Satan of Christian mythology. The absence of women does not in any way reflect anti-feminine feelings. I acknowledge an unrepayable debt to the magnificent Ariosto, as well as L. Frank Baum, George Macdonald, the Brothers Grimm, Italo Calvino, Federico Fellini, Pier Paolo Pasolini, and Jean Genet.

BOOK ONE
DRAGONWEED

CHAPTER 1
A Stranger in the Garden

With a rustling of leaves and snapping of twigs, a young man half-lunged and half-fell out of the forest, looking battered and thoroughly confused. One side of his shirt was torn, and edged with blood. Scratches on his cheek were still bleeding. Tucked under his arm was a large, leather-bound book. A travelling bag was slung over his shoulder. He had obviously been running for some time, and was taking deep breaths because of it. He was a tall, strapping fellow, not yet twenty, clumsy but solid, with vague, foggy eyes.

For a moment he simply stood there, staring.

He blinked. It didn't go away.

The Devil in Love

Before him was a small, thatched cottage in a glade, miles from anywhere, in the middle of the forest. Beside the cottage was a large garden laid out in orderly rows – round, full heads of lettuce, beanpoles, cornstalks, endive and parsley, carrot-tops and swollen zucchinis and big yellow sunflowers. There wasn't a weed in sight, and each of the plants had been carefully tended and watered.

In the midst of that plentiful yield of vegetables knelt a young woman. She abruptly stopped her work, scrambling to her feet with an uprooted weed still clinging to her apron. Reaching for her hoe, which she seized with both hands, the interrupted gardener stared back at him, clearly as surprised as he was. She was about twenty-seven, tall and straight as a tree, with long, straight hair that was golden-brown. There were earth-stains on her dress where she'd been kneeling by her weed-bucket, and her hands were brown with dirt.

Swinging his travelling bag down from his shoulder to the ground, the young man hastily brushed off his clothes, snatched off his hat, and bowed.

"Pardon me, good woman," he said courteously, "but I appear to have lost my way in the forest. My name is Noraldo. I'm on my way to my uncle's house in Bolgaro. I was walking down the old forest road, and somewhere I must have taken a wrong turn."

"That road is a good hour's walk to the west," said the woman, "and there are no turns in it." There was an unspoken accusation in her voice. She didn't acknowledge

The Devil in Love

his bow, or offer her own name in return. Her sharp eyes regarded him suspiciously, as he stood there shifting from foot to foot. She gripped her hoe more firmly, ready at any moment to use it as a weapon.

"It is?" said Noraldo, his voice sinking in gloom. "But it can't be! I was just walking on it a few minutes ago."

"Good evening to you, sir," said the woman coldly. "I have work to finish before nightfall." She made it clear that she was waiting for him to leave.

A third voice startled both of them, coming from the direction of the cottage. "Ursula, who's that with you?"

Another young woman approached the garden, shorter and several years younger, with a soft, delicate beauty – pale, blushing skin, sky-blue eyes, black hair. Her voice sounded uncertain, protective. She hurried closer, to stand beside and partly behind Ursula and her hoe. The younger woman wore an old gray dress, patched many times and splattered down the front with a rainbow of colors. In her hand was a paintbrush.

"He says he lost the road," said Ursula. "Don't worry, he's just leaving."

"Please let me explain," said Noraldo. He blushed. "You see, if I had been watching where I was going and not reading this book, I wouldn't be lost." And before either of the women had a chance to object, he began telling his story.

The Devil in Love

"I live in Valbrosa, with my father and two older brothers. Father owns a little shoeshop there – well, not so little anymore, we're the best shoeshop in Bolgaro, we've expanded next door. All three of us work for him. Last night after supper, while my brothers went back to cutting and sewing, Father took me aside and said he had to send me on a long journey.

"He'd just received a letter from his brother who lives in Bolgaro. Uncle Piero is very rich. My father comes from a wealthy family, one of the most powerful in Bolgaro, but he married beneath him for love when he was young. Grandfather disinherited him. Uncle Piero got everything. Father won't talk about it much. That's why he moved to Valbrosa and opened the shoeshop.

"Well, in the letter Uncle Piero said he was dying, and had a great longing to read one more time an old epic fairytale the brothers invented together when they were young. The three of them had kept adding to it throughout their childhood, and it had been written down by their older brother shortly before he ran away. My father and Uncle Piero had boxed up the book of their childhood nonsense, and when my father left Bolgaro it somehow came with him. Now all Uncle Piero can think about is wanting to read this old story one last time.

"'Just imagine,' laughed my father, 'with all his money he could have anything, and yet what he wants is that stupid

The Devil in Love

old thing. I'm not even sure I remember where it is. I might have thrown it out. Let's go see if we can find it.'

We searched the stockroom and the storage room. We searched the basement and every closet. We almost gave up. And then up in the attic, underneath some scraps of shoe leather and a mildewed old blanket we found it. This lovely book! Father took one look inside, actually blushed, and said we really should have thrown it away long ago, but since Uncle Piero wanted it, and he was dying, he should have it. Although he had tears in his eyes, Father insisted he had no interest in seeing his brother again, and couldn't spare anyone else from the shoeshop.

"That old bastard is incredibly wealthy," my father told me. "He almost inherited the Bolgaro throne once, you know. You came this close to being royalty, my boy. And he may repay you grandly for this old thing. I'll pack you a good lunch, and you'll leave tomorrow at dawn. Just one thing – no reading on the way. I know how much you love to waste time reading. You are not to open this silly book. Is that understood?'

"I should have listened to him.

"Instead, after walking for hours, I started getting bored. Bolgaro is a long way to walk. The book was making me curious. I didn't think it would do any harm to just peek inside long enough to find out the book's name. Do you know what I discovered? It hasn't got one. The title page has

The Devil in Love

been torn out. So has the first chapter. The story starts right in the middle of a sentence.

"I read a few lines. I read a few more. I couldn't stop. I tried to keep walking while I was reading, so I wouldn't lose any time, but I became so lost in the story that when I looked up a few minutes ago, the road was gone. I found myself out in the middle of nowhere. Then I came upon your cottage and this lovely garden."

"You are indeed far from the road," said the second woman with a sympathetic smile. "It's the Devil playing his tricks again. He just can't bear to let a traveler go by without causing him some mischief."

"Would you mind if I sat down for a moment, to catch my breath?" asked Noraldo.

"No, of course not," said the second woman. She gestured toward a nearby stump, upon which the young man immediately sank down with a sigh.

"Perhaps I could impose upon you for a drink of water, too?" asked Noraldo. "Perhaps, indeed, you would be kind enough to let me spend the night by your hearth?"

"There is a stream with good water on the other side of this glade," said Ursula. "When you have quenched your thirst, if you leave at once, you may be able to find your way back to the road again before it's too dark. Unfortunately, you cannot stay here. Five years ago, the two of us swore a

The Devil in Love

vow together never to let a man spend the night under our roof. That vow has never been broken."

At first Noraldo thought he was hearing things, but the look on Ursula's face assured him that she wasn't joking. He became very aware of the way she was gripping her hoe.

"I see," sighed Noraldo, rising wearily to his feet again. "What bad luck – and how ironic! I suppose it's useless to assure you that I mean no harm. I couldn't possibly – I mean – though I find that women are the kindest companions, I – actually..." He fumbled for words. "...it's just that all my pleasures have always been with men. I've never been with a woman. I'm still a virgin."

There was an awkward silence. He could tell that the women didn't believe him. "Oh, well," he said. "I'll just get a drink at the stream, and be on my way. Don't tell me what kind of animals are out there – I don't want to know." He gave an uneasy glance at the darkening sky and the sinister forest, gripped his book more tightly under his arm, shifted his travelling bag to a new position on his shoulder, and turned to go. "Goodbye, then."

"Goodbye," said the two young women.

He walked away.

Chapter 2
The Secret of the Cottage

"He does seem harmless," said the one with the paintbrush, as the two women regarded each other reluctantly.

"Nothing in nature is completely harmless," said Ursula. "Least of all a man. Do you really believe he's still a virgin, and only likes boys?"

"I suppose it's possible," said her friend. "I would certainly feel terrible if anything happened to him in the forest."

"I'll abide by whatever you think best," said Ursula. "But please think before you do anything rash."

They watched him trudging unhappily away from the cottage. He was almost across the glade now, fading into the gloomy shadows of twilight in the waiting trees.

"Noraldo!"

The voice of the second woman rang crystal-clear in the stillness of the glade. He stopped in his tracks and turned around, unable to conceal the flickering hope in his eyes.

She motioned him with her paintbrush to come back. "We have decided to trust you for just one night," she said as he approached. "Please conduct yourself honorably, for we

The Devil in Love

are breaking our vow in order to help you. My name is Amalia."

"How can I think you, Amalia?" exclaimed the young man.

"Give us nothing to regret," said Ursula, "and that will be thanks enough."

"Come inside the cottage with me now," said Amalia. "I'll put some balm on those scratches of yours while Ursula finishes her work."

"Then," said Ursula with some effort, "we would be honored to have you share our meal." She smiled thinly, to show she wished him no ill. "I hope you like vegetables."

"I'm starving," said Noraldo, with a grateful smile. "I didn't mean to invite myself to dinner."

"You may share our meal and share our home," said Ursula, smiling no longer, "on the condition that you sleep quietly by the hearth without disturbing us, and are gone by the first light of day."

"Thank you for trusting me," he said. "I promise to do exactly that."

"Go with Amalia, then," she said. "I'll be there shortly."

Ursula resumed weeding in her garden, while Amalia took Noraldo by the hand and led him toward the little cottage. Stepping aside at the threshold, she motioned him to enter before her. Two paces through the door, and Noraldo's mouth fell open in silent wonder.

The Devil in Love

The walls of the cottage, the ceiling, even parts of the floor had been painted with an intricate design of leaves, birds, flowers, and small forest animals. Every corner of the room was embellished with so many visual delights that, upon entering, Noraldo's eyes were drawn helplessly up, around, and in all directions, to find surprises hidden everywhere, just waiting to be discovered. He turned around slowly in circles, as he drifted in a larger circle around the room, in a trance.

Hung in various places amid this all-encompassing fresco were individual framed paintings of breathtaking beauty, all of natural objects and many of Ursula. The artist seemed able to paint in lifelike detail whatever she saw around her, finding in almost everything a radiance of balance and color. Those portraits of her companion in particular (Ursula at work in her garden, Ursula bathing in a stream, Ursula surrounded by her harvest) were visual poems of feminine strength and natural, undomesticated womanhood. An easel in the middle of the room supported a painting scarcely begun, in which Ursula's eyes alone looked out of an unformed whiteness.

"I must have interrupted your work," apologized Noraldo.

"It was growing too dark," said Amalia. "I was just preparing my sketches and colors for tomorrow." She smiled as she watched him examining the walls. "Besides my love

The Devil in Love

for Ursula," she said softly behind him, "I live for only one thing – to paint."

"So I can see," said the lost traveler. "Your skill amazes me."

She had been gathering up several jars of oils and creams, which she set on the rough, simple table. "Now, come over here and take off your shirt," she said, gesturing toward the bench beside her. "Let's see what I can do for those wounds of yours?"

Noraldo started to take off his shirt, but halfway out of it he stopped, wincing. Amalia had to help him. Dried blood pulled away with the shirt. The cut on his side started to bleed again. A red line crawled down over his skin.

"How did this happen?" she asked.

"A sharp branch," said Noraldo. He flinched as she dabbed it with water.

"Did you walk right into it?"

"Something like that," he said, with downcast eyes. "That's when I realized I wasn't on the road anymore."

"And look at this." She wet his shoulder, crossed by an ugly welt where his travelling bag had rubbed against it all day in the heat. Water dribbled down his back. "And here. Tip your head." She gently washed his cheek. "Looks like someone scratched you."

"Thorns," he said.

Gently her fingers applied the ointments, massaging herbal remedies into the torn skin, the sore and aching

The Devil in Love

muscles. Her salves at once brought a cool, healing comfort and relief.

"Thank you, that's much better," sighed Noraldo. His eyes continued to roam over the walls. "How long did it take you to paint this room?"

"Oh, it's not finished," said Amalia. "I'm always adding things to it. There are five years of memories on these walls. Five happy years. The love I share with Ursula is very rare, priceless. We're lucky to have each other."

"And the two of you manage, all by yourselves?"

"Happily so," said Amalia. "Her garden keeps us well-supplied with vegetables. There are plenty of wild foods in the forest. We spend our days washing clothes in the stream, sewing on the porch, gathering firewood, repairing the house. There's always plenty of work to be done, but I have such a pleasant companion to share it with."

Ursula entered the cottage, her hair damp from washing in the stream. Amalia at once seemed to forget Noraldo existed, and the two women began talking softly together and laughing amiably as they set about preparing supper. Ursula chopped up vegetables from the garden into a steaming soup over the fire, while Amalia made a salad out of a variety of greens, nuts, and tasty chunks of fruit. Both soup and salad they sprinkled with dry, grated cheese, and served them to their guest with hot, brown bread and wine. Noraldo was quite willing to eat as much as they put before him, and lick his fingers, too.

The Devil in Love

When they had finished and were sitting peacefully before the fire, he thanked them again heartily and then added, "Please don't take offense if I seem nosy, but how is it that two good and lovely women like yourselves have come to live out here in the forest, swearing a vow against men?"

"Our lives have not always been so peaceful," said Ursula, taking Amalia's hand. "To reach this moment of happiness here in the forest, we have both endured terrible suffering. Only patience and great determination helped us to escape a vicious man's cruelty five years ago with our love intact.

"That man," said Amalia, "was my brother."

CHAPTER 3
The Prisoners of Fausto

"If you knew him, you'd understand," said Amalia. "All his life, Fausto has lived for only one purpose – his own pleasure. It's the only thing that matters to him. Until five years ago, lack of funds always held him in restraint. My father was a wealthy merchant. He could see that Fausto's only ambition was to indulge himself. He made my brother work for his money. It merely drove Fausto to gambling.

"Then my parents died, both of the same fever, within a month of each other. Fausto inherited everything. I was left in his charge. How dear Papa could have abandoned me so completely to Fausto's mercy, I'll never understand! Perhaps he hoped that with age and the inheritance, his son would give up his wild ways and develop some responsibility, a little wisdom. He hoped in vain.

"At first, since Fausto and I had always gotten along so well together, I only worried about his drinking and his endless round of bed-partners. I never dreamed that, without my parents to interfere, my brother would ever try to make me one of them.

"It began three months later, at one of his parties. My brother's friend, Sergio, had drunk too much and was trying to kiss me. His hands were all over me. Fausto came to my rescue. My brother is very handsome and charming. We danced together. He became visibly – aroused. I couldn't help but see it. At the time, I blamed the party, the wine. I thought we were happy.

"Then one hot afternoon, while we were napping in the shade by the side of the pool, my brother's friendly caresses became more than friendly. He was on top of me before I realized it was no longer a game. When he wouldn't stop, I hit him and ran back into the house. He never treated me the same.

"Ursula came to stay with us shortly after that. Her father and mine had been business associates. We'd met each other several times before, but we'd never shared anything more than a few secret kisses. Ursula's father had sent her to us on a visit of several months, to keep me company. There could have been no better remedy. It was like finding the other half of my soul. I painted her portrait. With every stroke of the brush, I fell more deeply in love. We became inseparable.

"Sooner or later, my brother was doomed by his very nature to interfere. In the world of the senses, Fausto was never satisfied until he tasted everything. You can see her for yourself. Can a bee resist a flower? He was interested from the start. Ursula is three years older than I am, only a year younger than Fausto. He would talk to her as an adult, to me as a child. He was always loitering nearby, always courteous, looking his best. He was like a handsome spider, spinning his web, biding his time.

The Devil in Love

"His first tactic was interrupting us when we were alone together, asking me to do some favor for him. That left him alone for a few minutes with Ursula. I was unsuspecting. 'Amalia, where did you put my yellow shirt?' he would say, and away I would go to find it. 'Amalia, one of your flowerpots just fell off the balcony.' Now they seem so obvious.

"Ursula was too honorable to tell me the shameless ways my brother conducted himself while they were alone. Whenever I was around, he would treat us both like sisters. As soon as I left, he would begin rubbing up against her, trying to reach in her dress, trying to break down her resistance. Ursula wanted nothing to do with him. Finally she confessed to me in tears. The next time Fausto asked me to do him a favor, I told him to do it himself. He glared at us, and then grinned like a cat.

"The next morning I woke up and found myself locked in my room. After several hours of weeping and beating my fists on the door, Fausto came in and told me that he would let me out only if I stopped turning Ursula against him. He made me promise to plead his cause with her. 'Don't you understand?' he reasoned with me. 'If Ursula becomes my wife, the three of us will be able to live happily here together for the rest of our lives.'

"The temptation was too much for me. I wanted so badly to believe his pretty words, and so I promised Fausto I would

The Devil in Love

help him. I wept in her arms as I forced myself to urge her to return Fausto's love.

"'Why should I?'

"I repeated my brother's promises to her as though I believed them myself.

"Ursula didn't question me. She trusted me. She went through with it. She let Fausto court her. She let Fausto make love to her. She listened to all his lies and wild promises. She did it for my sake."

Amalia started to cry and couldn't go on. Ursula drew her close, a comforting arm around her shoulders. When Amalia's bitter tears were beginning to subside, Ursula took over where her friend had left off.

"It wasn't so horrible," she sighed. "It was just empty. Her brother is very attractive. He's easy on the eyes. He knows how to be tender. He's a superb lover. I'm sure there are many women who suffer from their lovers far more than I ever did. But when Fausto was on top of me, when Fausto was inside of me, I felt like a dead woman.

"That went on for two months.

"Then one afternoon Amalia was painting in the garden and needed a brush she had forgotten in her room. I ran up to the house to fetch it for her. There was no need to knock at her bedroom door, since I had just left her outside. Fausto was on his sister's bed, his bare behind pumping up and down on top of a young serving-woman. I backed out of the room, but not before he saw me.

The Devil in Love

"I returned to Amalia without the paintbrush. She laughed at me, and insisted she no longer needed it. She could see that something was wrong, and took my hand. I couldn't speak. She looked so happy there, beaming and full of love, in the midst of her work. I was too ashamed of what I had let him do to me. I said I had to get out of the sun, and went inside. Dearest, how I wish I had told you!"

Ursula grew quiet, remembering again the pain they had both managed to forget. "Can you tell the rest?" she asked Amalia, who nodded and pressed her hand.

"My brother must have dressed as soon as Ursula left," said Amalia. "And when Ursula retired to her room, he headed straight for the garden where I was painting. There he had the nerve to tell me that he had just surprised Ursula and the serving-woman in my bed together. I fainted. He must have carried me up to my room. When Ursula came in and tried to talk to me, I turned away and refused to speak. I was sure that I knew now why she had forgotten the paintbrush, why she'd gone indoors to get out of the sun. Every word she had spoken now sounded like a lie.

"Instead, I locked myself away from everyone and spent my sleepless nights and days painting a picture which covered half the wall, in which Ursula and the serving-woman lay life-size in each other's arms. All my hate and pain I poured into that painting. Every morning and evening Ursula came to see me, yet I always refused to open the door. Then, when the painting was finished, I left the door open

The Devil in Love

and concealed myself behind a curtain where I would be able to see her.

"She came that evening at the usual time. When she saw the painting, Ursula realized at once what Fausto had done. She cried out in distress. I mistook her cry for one of guilt. All my most horrible suspicions were confirmed. I tried to pull open the window. I was ready to end it all. Ursula caught me and dragged me back. I fought her, screaming at her, scratching her neck and shoulders. She had to shout the truth in my ears before I finally understood, and stopped struggling. Then I cried like a baby and wouldn't let go of her."

"And that," said Ursula, "was when we decided to move away together." She kissed Amalia lightly on the cheek. "If we had remained in the same house with her brother one more night, I don't think I could have kept my hands away from his lying throat. We packed up a few of our things, and fled without a word before dawn, venturing out into the hills and forests of the wilderness, as far away as we could get from Fausto, from Bolgaro, from men and their treacherous ways. Here we've built ourselves a new life. For five years now, we've been able to enjoy each other's love untroubled."

The three of them sat thoughtfully before the fire for a few moments longer. Then the two women bid Noraldo goodnight and retired to the bed in the corner, leaving the large, amiable fellow to read a few more pages of his book by the

The Devil in Love

firelight until it had burned too low for anything but sleep. His book became a pillow.

"Now I mustn't so much as stir," he thought to himself, quietly trying to find a comfortable position on the floor before the hearth. "I mustn't snore or grind my teeth, or talk in my sleep. I mustn't let my hand wander down between my legs. I mustn't…"

He was asleep.

The next morning, at the crack of dawn, Noraldo got up and quietly pulled on his boots. He was ready to leave, book under his arm, bag over his shoulder, before either of the two women had stirred in bed. From the doorway he said politely, "Thanks again, and may your happiness here continue undisturbed."

"Tell no man about us," cautioned Ursula.

"And no reading while you're walking," added Amalia.

As Noraldo trudged off into the trees, Amalia snuggled up next to Ursula in bed and said, "Now, aren't you glad we trusted him? No harm done at all."

Chapter 4
Death Comes to Bolgaro

After wandering back through the trees, Noraldo found the old forest road again and continued on his way south, until he came within sight of the Lost Lake. Long before he actually saw the three ancient towers of Bolgaro peering over the treetops, however, he heard all the bells of the city tolling mournfully. The hollow clanging sound echoed out across the still, gray waters. Black banners were draped over the walls above the gates. The armed guards standing by the open doors were dressed in black. So were the merchants leaving the city for the northern markets.

Once inside the gates, Noraldo went up to a food stall in the market-place. The woman cooking wore a black apron and looked unhappy, indeed, as she poked and turned the sizzling, splattering hunks of dough.

"Has something terrible happened?" he asked.

"You mean you don't know?" groaned the vendor, wiping the sweat from her forehead with the back of her greasy hand. She turned over the last two pieces of frying bread.

"I only just now arrived in the city," Noraldo explained.

The Devil in Love

"Well, you've arrived in a city without a King," said the woman, sniffling. "Some of these are done. Are you buying? There's a line forming behind you."

"Y-yes," stammered Noraldo, feeling around for his money. "Two, please. Do you mean the King is – dead?"

"Choked to death last night," she said, taking his coins. "Of all the horrible luck!"

"Murdered?" gasped Noraldo.

"No, of course not," she said, brushing away a tear that was sliding down her cheek. "Dinner. You know how he loved to eat. I've heard two different stories – who knows? A wishbone, an olive pit – what difference does it make?" Another tear squeezed out, which she wiped away. "Next, please."

The man behind Noraldo pushed him to one side. "Give me half a dozen," he growled. "Haven't got all day."

"But – but the King had no son," stammered Noraldo. "Who will be King?"

"That's a good question," snarled the man.

"Both of the King's brothers are dead, too," said the woman bleakly. The new dough patties she plopped into the oil began hissing and crackling furiously. "The crown falls next to the King's cousin – and that cousin just died yesterday of a lingering illness – so it goes to his cousin's son. Can you believe it? A spoiled brat of a boy who knows nothing about governing a kingdom. Nineteen years old, and

The Devil in Love

can't think about anything except poking himself into every pretty woman he sees!"

"Keep your treasonous comments to yourself!" barked the following man in line.

"Get your fried bread somewhere else!" snapped the woman. "Next, please."

Blowing on the hot bread as he hurried on his way, making sure he got no grease-stains on his precious book, Noraldo hurried down one narrow, cobbled street after another, quickly eating as he went, until he arrived at his uncle's magnificent house.

The servant who opened the door had red, swollen eyes and wet cheeks.

"Good day," said Noraldo. "Uncle Piero asked me to bring him this..."

"Everyone has already left for the funeral," said the servant.

"The King's?"

"No, Master Piero's funeral. I'm the only one left in the whole house."

"My uncle is dead, too?" cried Noraldo.

"Yesterday."

"Then I'm too late!" he groaned. "Which way is the cemetery?"

He ran all the way. The service had already begun. He joined the gathering of solemn people dressed in black, mumbling their prayers among the white tombs. He watched

The Devil in Love

as his uncle's coffin, wet with holy water, was lowered into the grave.

His weeping aunt gave a cry and sank forward, as though she were going to follow her husband into the pit. She was supported by her elegant, handsome son, whom Noraldo recognized as his cousin Ulisso, grown seven years older since the last time he'd seen him. From an awkward boy in the first flush of adolescence, Ulisso had become a poised, confident young member of the better families, with the broad shoulders of a man, classical features, proud, aloof eyes. He whispered a few words in the ear of his distraught mother. Though her face could not be seen beneath a cascade of black veils, she seemed to regain control of herself, kissing Ulisso on the cheek. He supported her with his arm intimately around her waist.

When the funeral service was over and some of the crowd had thinned, Noraldo humbly approached his aunt and cousin, who were standing beneath a black pavilion. In a speech of a few lines which he had prepared during the burial, he extended his sympathies and those of his father and brothers, apologizing for arriving too late with the book.

"What book?" said his aunt's voice from under the black veils.

"You mean you don't know?" said Noraldo, somewhat surprised. "My father received a letter from Uncle Piero. He wanted to read this old story from his childhood again."

The Devil in Love

"He became quite unstable near the end," said the voice from beneath the black veils. "He said many things that didn't make sense. I'm sorry if it put you to any trouble. Why don't you come back to the house with us, and have a bite to eat?" As though the thought of his declining was inconceivable, she took his arm and began steering Noraldo out of the cemetery.

"You'll have to excuse all the confusion at home," apologized Ulisso on the other side of him, falling into pace with his mother's stride. He already spoke with the authority of a young master of the household. "Everything's in an uproar, as you can well imagine."

"Of course," said Noraldo. Passing through the wrought-iron gates, they set off down the street.

"My mother has already found someone to rent the house, of course, but it will take us a while to gather our things together," said Ulisso. "We expect to be moving into the castle in just a few days."

With a sudden shock, as though he had cracked through an ice-covered lake into the freezing water below, Noraldo realized that Ulisso – his own cousin! – was the nineteen-year-old youth who had become the new King of Bolgaro.

Ulisso enjoyed watching the impact of his announcement on his cousin's face. Noraldo dropped to one knee and bowed his head. "Your Majesty."

His cousin promptly helped him back onto his feet again. "Not quite yet," he said, giving his poor relation a

The Devil in Love

condescending smile. "I won't become King all at once. I have to wait for my coronation. Until then, I'll be Prince Ulisso, but just cousin Ulisso to you. All the big civic decisions will be left to a committee of elders, who'll govern Bolgaro while I'm training to take over." He gave Noraldo a lingering look that filled him with confusion. "We must have a long talk after supper, cousin. Perhaps I'll be able to interest you in some position or other…"

Noraldo could not have been more surprised.

They reached his uncle's house, and he was shown to a guest-room where a bath was heated for him. Supper was an elaborate banquet down the length of a table as long as the hall. There were dozens of other guests, all of them better dressed than Noraldo. He was seated so far down at the other end of the table that he could scarcely see his cousin, much less speak with him. The several times after supper, however, when other people's conversations drew the cousins close enough together to talk, Ulisso almost appeared not to remember him.

Noraldo was ready to believe that he had been imagining things when, just before he excused himself to retire to his room, Prince Ulisso stepped up behind him and whispered so that only he could hear, "I'll knock at your door in about an hour, and we'll continue our conversation, just the two of us."

The Devil in Love

Chapter 5
Noraldo's Mistake

That night Noraldo lay on his bed staring at the ceiling, unable to sleep. There was no knock at the door. He let his hand wander down between his legs. An hour passed, and then two. His eyes closed. He awakened with a jolt sometime much later, to find a hot, heavy shadow seated beside him on the bed, smelling of wine.

"I feel like talking," slurred the voice of Prince Ulisso in the darkness. His hand groped around beneath the covers. "Are you asleep?"

Noraldo let him feel around for a while, and then laughed. "Are you going to keep that bottle all to yourself?" he joked good-naturedly. He reached out in the dark.

"That's not the bottle, and you know it," said Ulisso, brushing his cousin's hand away. "Oh, for a beautiful woman tonight!" he sighed, stretching out on the bed beside Noraldo. "Nothing like a woman! But it's really too late to go waking one up. I know what let's do. Let's tell each other about our conquests. Our best stories, with all the details."

Midway through Prince Ulisso's third lurid account, this one about two sisters, with Noraldo's excitement making a veritable tent of the blanket, the Prince stopped abruptly in mid-sentence. "But I'm tired of my own stories," he complained. "I've heard them all before. It's your turn."

Noraldo had worried about what he would say when the time came. The truth was, as far as women were concerned, he was still as innocent as a nine-year-old boy, and knew about as much on the subject. He groped desperately for some fragment of the truth which he could alter and distort into a tale to amuse and arouse the drunken Prince beside him.

"The reason I was late to your father's funeral," said Noraldo, "was because I met two lovely women living all by themselves in the forest. I guess I don't have to tell you what happened."

"Yes, you do," said Prince Ulisso, rolling half on top of him. "Tell me every detail. Don't leave a single thing out." Ulisso's thigh burrowed down between Noraldo's legs. "Go on – what happened?" There could be no doubt left in the Prince's mind as to how Noraldo felt about the situation.

Noraldo nearly wept with anxiety. He was trapped between his own scarcely restrainable desire and fear of offending, perhaps angering, his cousin, not to mention the future King of Bolgaro. How drunk was Ulisso, anyway? What kind of story did he expect? If only Noraldo had something to tell! In desperation, he began transforming what had really happened, on the spot, into an erotic tale like the one he had just been reading in his uncle's book.

The Devil in Love

"Well, the older one only liked women, I could see that right away," he began, faltering. "She was proud and strong, and all for sending me on my way. Her name was Ursula. You should have seen the way she held her garden hoe! But before she could drive me off, the young pretty one said I could stay for dinner."

"Ah ha!" said Prince Ulisso, snuggling closer. "What was she like?"

"Her name was Amalia," said Noraldo. "She was – well, very pretty."

"I knew it!" said Prince Ulisso. "Go on."

"Every time her friend wasn't looking, I'd find Amalia watching me with those eyes. Then she started making a big fuss over a couple scratches I got in the woods. She said she had some lotions that would make them feel better, and told me to come inside the cottage with her, while her friend finished her work in the garden.

"I didn't mind leaving the grouchy one outside, believe me. You should see the inside of their cottage! It's covered with Amalia's paintings – incredible! Dozens of naked women, beautiful beyond your wildest dreams, making love to each other in every position you can imagine – all over the walls and ceiling, in a cottage out in the middle of nowhere. As far away from men as Ursula can keep her. For five years, Ursula hasn't let a single man spend one night under the same roof with her pretty friend.

"Well, no sooner was I in the door than Amalia got out her lotions and told me to take off my clothes, she'd see to those scratches of mine. To tell you the truth, those lotions of hers looked like mud and dried leaves to me, but I did what she said. She could hardly take her eyes off of me. Then she started rubbing that mud all over my body. Whatever was in that mud made my skin get all hot and filled me with passion. I don't have to tell you what all her attention did to me – she got me until I was – well, like I am right now!

"She whispered in my ear, 'Do you know how long it's been since I've had a man? I'm so crazy for that thing between your legs, I can hardly keep my hands off of you!'"

"Did she really say that?" asked the Prince, his breath hot against his cousin's cheek. Noraldo could feel that the Prince was in the same condition he was. "Come on. Tell the truth."

Noraldo's hands at last slid boldly up underneath the Prince's clothes, over Ulisso's tight young body. "Those were her exact words," he whispered.

Suddenly Prince Ulisso was no longer sprawling across him, but was standing by the bedside straightening his clothes. "It's almost dawn," he said. "I'm in the mood for a woman. I'm going to pay those two friends of yours a visit."

Noraldo's mouth fell open in horror. "You mustn't!"

"Oh, mustn't I?" laughed the Prince. Then the door of Noraldo's room was swinging open, and his cousin was no longer there.

Chapter 6
A Portrait of the Prince

Sunlight shafted down through the forest branches in golden beams. Two birds were hopping and fluttering about their nest, which was half-hidden in a natural bower of wild flowers. Sunbeams, branches, nest, birds, and flowers were all reproduced, as though alive, in Amalia's painting, which was itself bathed in warm, morning sunshine. She added another careful dab of color to the edge of a petal wet with dew, and then glanced up again at the real flower.

Out from behind those wild blossoms stepped another young man, far handsomer than Noraldo. He was dressed in fine and costly silk, edged with elaborate embroidery and gleaming gems. His face was like a perfect blossom in itself. He had laughing eyes and a smile that seemed to take delight in everything.

With chirps of distress, the two birds abandoned their nest and flapped away out of the arbor. The intruder laughed softly, and the rippling sound was deep and happy like the stream.

"Forgive me for disturbing you," he said, with a polite bow. "My name is Prince Ulisso. Please don't be alarmed. I mean no harm." He gazed into Amalia's lovely face, and

The Devil in Love

sighed. "Until this moment, I thought I was lost. Now I don't want to be anywhere else in the world."

He stepped up beside her, so that he could see her painting. "Beautiful!" he exclaimed in a voice of hushed wonder, brushing up against her. "I've never seen anything like it. You're very gifted."

Amalia blushed. "Thank you, Your Majesty," she said, with a modest nod.

"What kind of things do you paint?" asked the Prince.

"Everything," said Amalia. "Whatever I see, wherever I can find beauty. There's beauty all around us."

"Some places more than others," said the Prince. "There's certainly a lot of beauty right here in this forest." He looked deeply into her eyes.

Amalia blushed even redder. He touched her hot cheek. "Since I seem to have frightened away the birds you were painting, perhaps I can offer myself as a substitute? I'd love an excuse to spend the morning with you."

"It would be a privilege, Your Majesty," said Amalia, her eyes brightening. "The light at this hour is perfect. I've never painted a handsome young Prince before."

"I am honored," said Prince Ulisso. "Where shall I stand?"

"There, by the tree," said Amalia. "It will take me just a moment to get ready."

The Prince stepped over to where she had pointed. Then, while Amalia readied another canvas and mixed a couple of

The Devil in Love

new colors, he quickly slipped out of his riding outfit, dropping his royal garments in the grass. When she looked up, she gave a soft gasp.

"I simply assumed," he smiled, "that you meant without clothes."

It was unexpected. At first she was dismayed, not only as a woman but as an artist, for his garments had been of the finest craftsmanship and quite breathtaking. Ulisso's body, however, proved to be of equal interest, with skin like creamy satin, firm as wood and smooth as polished stone, full of the eager health of Ulisso's nineteen years.

As Amalia painted, the Prince's manhood grew.

She painted him exactly as he was, radiant with animal energy, his eyes hot with desire, his member upthrust and urgent. Finally he was beside himself with frustration. Ulisso lunged for her. He took Amalia into his arms, covered her face and breasts with insatiable kisses.

"Stop it – what are you doing?" she protested, struggling. His ardor terrified her. His arms were like thick, smooth ropes around her. That thing was poking up against her in no uncertain terms.

"Don't act like you don't want it as much as I do," he murmured. "I can't live another minute without satisfying my desire for you."

Amalia pulled away from him, scrambling off through the wild grass in the direction of the cottage. "Ursu--!" she began. The breath was knocked out of her as he caught her.

The Devil in Love

Covering her mouth and throat with insistent kisses, he dragged her toward where he had tied his horse. When she tried to call again, he clapped his hand tightly over her mouth.

In a moment he had heaved Amalia up onto the saddle and clambered up behind her. Then Ulisso was riding away with her, leaving half his clothes and her unfinished painting fallen in the grass.

Chapter 7
The Stolen Book

After the Prince's abrupt departure, for the few hours left of the night, Noraldo tossed and turned miserably, unable to sleep. No matter how hard he tried to justify his behavior, he felt like a fool, and guilty for betraying the secret of the two women in the forest. Finally, just as the birds began chirping at the first light of dawn, Noraldo fell into a restless, exhausted slumber, tormented by dreams.

Bright sunlight woke him. He had slept later than he intended. His uncle's book lay beside the bed, where he had laid it last night after reading. How he hated to leave that book behind when he left today! He had hoped to read a last chapter before departing, and now there would be no time.

Abruptly, impulsively, Noraldo committed his second big mistake. He decided to take the book with him. It was too late for Uncle Piero to enjoy it, his aunt would never miss the book, and Ulisso didn't like to read. Besides, it would serve Ulisso right for breaking his trust. Noraldo stroked the book's cover lovingly, not daring to open it for fear of being unable to stop. Then he threw back the covers with resolution, quickly dressed, packed his travelling bag, and began scheming how to get the book out of his uncle's house undetected.

The Devil in Love

He tried putting the book in his travelling bag. No matter how he rearranged the other contents, the book's corners made projections on the outside of the bag which betrayed its presence. He pulled it out again. Where could he hide it?

Frowning in concentration, Noraldo was startled out of his plotting by a sudden volley of shouts and laughter among the guards on the battlement below his window. There was a cry to open the gates, followed by the clatter of hoof beats in the courtyard. Clutching the book, Noraldo rushed to the window. There, on horseback, was Prince Ulisso half-undressed with Amalia held prisoner on the saddle in front of him. Noraldo rubbed his eyes. He tried to wake up. He prayed it was a nightmare. Pinching himself only proved that his fears were true.

"No, no, no!" he groaned in horror. "Tell me it's not true! It's all my fault!" How could Ulisso indulge himself so shamelessly? The servants were agog.

"Back to work, all of you!" commanded the half-naked Prince. His servants dashed out of sight. Ulisso swung Amalia to the ground, and dismounted. She struggled to get away from him, but the Prince had no intention of letting her go.

Noraldo didn't linger in the window long enough to see more. No time to invent some scheme. He wrapped his cloak around the book, piled his travelling bag on top of it, grabbed his hat and bolted out the bedroom door.

The Devil in Love

Down the staircase he lunged, two stairs at a time. For all his efforts, he was still several stairs from the bottom when Ulisso bounded through the archway before him, dragging Amalia after him.

"Noraldo!" she cried in betrayal. "What are you doing here?"

"Thanks for your help, cousin!" called Ulisso with a laugh, as he hurried Amalia past him up the stairs.

"Your help--?" gasped Amalia.

"Wait, listen to me!" Noraldo shouted after them. "Amalia, it's not what you think. Let me explain..."

"Some other time," said Ulisso. "Right now she's busy."

Moments later, a door slammed upstairs, a lock clicked.

It was a long walk back to Valbrosa.

Noraldo returned to work at the shoeshop with his father and brothers. He said the book was a gift from his cousin, in remembrance. He was never the same. He kept the book hidden under his bed, so that his father and brothers would never be tempted to read it, or take it away from him. Noraldo read a chapter every night. When he woke up in the mornings now he always forgot his dreams, because he couldn't bear to remember them.

Chapter 8
"Do You Know This Man?"

By late afternoon, Amalia had still not returned home from painting in the forest. Ursula began to worry. At the first sign of approaching darkness, she knew she'd waited long enough. She dropped her hoe right where she was in the garden. Leaving her baskets scattered behind, forgotten amid orderly rows of beets and romaine, she abandoned any attempt to restrain her dreads and strode right into the forest calling her friend's name. It wasn't long before she broke into a run, searching, weaving through the trees shouting that treasured name in a patternless zigzag of fear.

By moonlight she found the arbor of wild flowers. She picked up the familiar brushes and paints and began to weep. To find them scattered there could only mean some unexpected mishap. Then she found a man's scattered clothing beneath the tree and the half-finished portrait in a style she recognized only too well, and carried them back to the cottage. There, by the roaring fire, she stared at Amalia's last portrait, a naked young man, stiff with eagerness. She memorized his features. She examined every stitch of his clothing. She forgot to eat that night. She didn't even consider sleeping.

The Devil in Love

The next morning, Ursula locked the door of the cottage behind her, and gave her garden one last, good watering. Then she set out in search of the one woman she had ever loved and the young man in the painting responsible for her disappearance.

Reaching the old forest road, she turned to the south and set out bravely for Bolgaro. Though she was afraid of the city, since she hadn't seen it or set foot there for five years, she was determined to find Amalia. She never hesitated once. Under one arm, in a velvet sack, she carried her friend's last painting, while in the bundle slung over her shoulder were folded the costly garments left behind by Amalia's abductor.

She had not gone far when she came upon a portly Bolgaro merchant riding toward her down the road, followed by seven mules heavily laden with rolls of the finest cloth. Behind the mules rode two ruthless-looking men with swords, keeping a sharp lookout on all sides for robbers hiding in the forest. They were heading north toward the markets of Valbrosa. Their swords rose as Ursula stepped before them.

She withdrew Amalia's painting from the velvet sack, and held it up before the merchant's astonished eyes. "This man abducted an innocent woman," she announced to the merchant and his two armed protectors. "Do any of you recognize him?"

All three of them gasped in amazement at that portrait of their young Prince not wearing a thread. Of course, they

The Devil in Love

recognized him. Didn't Ulisso always buy their most expensive merchandise?

"Turn around and go home, good woman," said the portly merchant. "There's nothing you can do about it now. Besides, the urge to carry off a woman is in a man's nature. You're just asking for more of the same trouble, wandering around in the forest all by yourself, displaying a picture like that. She probably encouraged him, anyway."

The two men with swords leered down at her.

Ursula gritted her teeth. "This woman did not want to be carried off, I assure you," she said. "Do you know this man? Tell me where I can find him."

"I've never seen him before in my life," said the prudent merchant, wising choosing to not become involved. The two swordsmen mumbled the same words. They whipped their mules and travelled past her, leaving Ursula in a cloud of dust.

She groaned, and trudged on down the road. Beyond a hill and around a bend, she came upon two bald old apothecaries kneeling in the weeds, harvesting all kinds of mysterious seeds and herbs, which they popped at once into little boxes, pouches and vials.

"Excuse me," said Ursula, removing the painting from its velvet sack, "but do either of you recognize this man? He has cruelly abducted an innocent woman."

The two apothecaries stared wide-eyed at the painting. They forgot all about mushrooms, roots, and healing teas. Of

The Devil in Love

course, they recognized him. No one bought more of their concoctions than Prince Ulisso. He was always ordering love potions, bath oils, and erotic creams in abundance, powders for headaches and hangovers, as well as a discreet deadly poison now and then.

"Abandon your search," sighed one old apothecary, shaking his bald head.

"We've never seen him before," said the other. They both went back to hunting through the weeds. Ursula wept a few tears, and trudged on.

She had not gone much farther when, off to one side of the road, Ursula saw a young hermit wearing only a loincloth, kneeling before a small cave on the side of the hill. His head was shaved. He was so skinny that his ribs showed, and was holding his bony arms up toward heaven in prayer. She climbed up the hillside.

"An innocent young woman has been abducted," she told him. "Forgive me for interrupting you, but this is a portrait of the culprit." She showed him the painting. "Do you know this man?"

The hermit smiled sadly. He slowly lowered his arms. "Yes, indeed, I recognize him," he said, shaking his head. "Only too well. His name is Lust. His name is Desire for Worldly Pleasure. He lives inside all men. Though we fight against his temptations, men don't always win. No, sometimes the Devil wins. Sometimes the Devil takes over completely. When that happens, there's only one thing to do."

The Devil in Love

Suddenly the young hermit leaped to his feet and tore aside his loincloth. His member was quivering stiff. "The Devil has got to be put into Hell!" he cried wildly. "And that's where I'm going to put him right now!"

With that, the hermit leaped on Ursula, pulled up her dress, and would have forced his bursting manhood down inside her then and there, if he hadn't been startled by the sound of horses riding toward them. With a curse, the hermit snatched up his loincloth and dashed off into the trees.

Scrambling to her feet and grabbing her belongings, Ursula ran down the hillside toward the sound of approaching horses on the road. Three young guardsmen rode into sight, on their way to Valbrosa on leave. They were laughing as they passed a wineskin back and forth. At the sight of Ursula running out in front of them, they reined their horses abruptly and then walked their mounts up close to her without dismounting, so that they surrounded her on all sides.

"Well, what do we have here?" said one, with a wry grin.

"One of the friendly local girls," said his companion, exchanging a wink with him.

Ursula was dirty, disarranged, and trembling. She was also afraid. Nevertheless, she bravely held up the painting before them. "This man abducted an innocent woman," she said. "Do you recognize him?"

The three guards roared with laughter.

"Of course we recognize him," said the first one.

The Devil in Love

"Though we don't often see him in that condition," added the second.

"Ought to recognize him," said the third one, with a belch. "He pays for our meals"

"Tell me his name," cried Ursula. "Where can I find him?"

They laughed again, as though she had said something uproariously witty. Then the middle one jumped down from his horse, walked up to Ursula with a big grin on his face, and looked very closely at her painting. "Tell you what," he said, his breath hot with wine, "I'll answer your question, if you'll answer one of mine."

"Yes, of course," said Ursula, "Quickly, ask whatever you wish."

Before she realized what he was doing, the young guard had pulled aside his clothes to reveal an upthrust, cruel-looking manhood. "Whose is bigger, sweetheart, his or mine?"

Ursula fled.

They pursued her off the road and into the trees, hounding her with obscene suggestions and cat-calls, two of them on horseback, the one who had exposed himself on foot. She clutched the painting as she ran, trying not to hear their shouts.

"Whore! You and your painting!" yelled the belligerent one on foot. "We know what you want – you want exactly what you painted, and that's what I've got for you!"

The Devil in Love

Ursula fought her way through the brambles, choosing tight, twisted paths. Soon the two horsemen were far behind, cursing, their horses unable to follow her. After a while, the guard on foot gave up, too, shouting after her that they'd catch her sooner or later, and show her what was what.

Sobbing, her dress torn, hair disheveled, arms and legs bleeding from scratches, Ursula staggered on deeper and deeper into the trees, leaving the road far behind her, putting as much distance as possible between herself and those fiends pursuing her. Though she escaped them, it was only into a different danger.

Collapsing at last, gasping for breath, she found that she was hopelessly lost.

Chapter 9
The Devil Laughs

The young Prince moved into the ancient castle of Bolgaro soon after his father's funeral, taking Amalia with him and quickly hiding her away as his prisoner. Somehow he managed to whisk her under the very nose of his mother, undetected.

His mother was already getting on his nerves. She was giving too many orders, assuming too much. It didn't take her long to wonder why her son kept disappearing, and to have him followed one night. The next morning she and her son had a loud and prolonged disagreement, after which the woman became suddenly and mysteriously ill. Ulisso's mother was promptly moved to a chamber in a far wing of the castle, where she was seldom heard from again.

She had discovered Amalia locked secretly away in a bedroom at the top of the north tower. Amalia's presence there was known only to the pageboy who brought her meals and firewood. Though the servants talked for days of nothing else than the half-undressed Prince carrying that unknown girl on horseback into the courtyard, they all assumed that the young woman had come and gone, like so many others in the castle's long history. Since Amalia had not been in Bolgaro for five years, no one realized she was missing. No one even suspected there was a prisoner in the tower. As Ulisso's secret captive, she was at his mercy.

Mercy was not one of Ulisso's outstanding traits. Although not cruel, he was used to having his own way, and did not have enough imagination to sympathize with people less fortunate than himself. Twice each day, in the morning and in the evening, the Prince climbed the stairway to her chamber and had his way with her. When she struggled, he called in his servants. Submitting to his advances was quicker and easier on both of them. Amalia came to know the sound of his footfalls on the stairs.

Her world shrank to the size of that room. Empty hours stretched out for twice their usual length. Finally, frantic with boredom, Amalia poked bits of charcoal out of the fireplace, using them to slowly cover the walls of her prison with drawings of Ursula, Prince Ulisso didn't say anything. Why should he mind, when her drawings seemed to leave her in a more compliant humor? Every day she added more, lovingly culled from her memories. The rest of the time, when she wasn't in bed, she wept by the window.

Day followed day. Amalia lost weight. Morning and evening, Ulisso climbed on top of her. With all the Prince's power and good looks, Amalia was the only woman who resisted him, and for that reason he desired her more than anyone. Soon her body had no secrets from him. She wept and drew, wept and drew. Then one sunlit morning, everything changed.

The Devil in Love

The Devil heard her weeping.

He had been strolling through the narrow streets of Bolgaro, looking unbearably attractive and filling everyone who looked at him with the agonies of lust, when his sharp ears perceived, over the crude noises of commerce, the faint, unmistakable sound of human misery. That sound is like music to the Devil's ears. Always on the watch for opportunities, he set out at once to investigate.

Amalia's grief attracted him like a magnet. In no time at all, the Devil was standing beneath the tower, looking up at her window. There she was, her face buried in her arms. His sharp eyes could make out streak-marks on the side of the tower where, for days on end, her tears had been falling to the ground.

"Such a vast capacity for grief!" thought the Devil with a cunning smile. "So many bitter tears shouldn't go to waste. Surely they could be put to use." He was in the mood for some mischief. Things had been far too quiet lately. "Too bad a plant isn't growing here," he thought, "to enjoy such an inexhaustible source of moisture." In a flash, he knew exactly what he was going to do, and burst into laughter.

Leathery black wings, like those of an enormous bat, ripped out of his tunic and surged up into the air out of the Devil's muscular back. People screamed on all sides and backed away from him. With a bound, the handsome trickster launched himself into the sky, soaring up above Bolgaro until he was moving too rapidly to be seen.

The Devil in Love

A dry rumbling like thunder moved north across the land. The clouds turned dark, massing together into an ominous, unnatural storm. That snarling knot of lightning and hissing rain carried the Devil from one end of the land to the other. Then, like an eagle, he dropped out of the sky, plummeting earthward. With a swoop, he dived down into a tunnel beneath the far, northern mountains. When he came to his feet again, the Devil stood in the secret underground gardens of Agatuzza the witch.

Even the Devil entered those gardens with caution.

Agatuzza was no one to insult or annoy. She had been there as long as the Devil himself, nurturing the land, guarding against the excesses of humankind, fostering the wildlife and preserving the balance. No one was old enough to remember if she had ever been young. But the old crone was far from weak or feeble. Her magic could shake mountains. Her anger could cause rivers to forge new beds, and the Devil never challenged her directly, because he had witnessed raging floods and forest fires when careless fools had made her angry, and he was far too smart for that. No one was there now, or the Devil would not have been intruding. He was certainly not afraid of the old hag, but Agatuzza was much too powerful to arouse unnecessarily, and the old witch would never have allowed the Devil to do what he was about to do.

All around him were the glowing, mysterious plants from which she derived her powers. They hung from the dripping ceiling and clung to the rocky sides of the cavern, all shapes and sizes, their leaves emitting a pale, pulsing light. The Devil inspected them carefully, one by one, until he found exactly the shrubs he was looking for, plucked off a shoot from three different plants, and rolled their stems together between his hot fingertips until with a sizzling sound their three stems grew into one, an eager, hungry vine with leaves like claws and thorns like needles and a single, living root which coiled affectionately around the Devil's wrist like a rat-tail.

"Dragonweed," he said, holding it up before his eyes. He blew on the young rootling, and the leaves rustled, growing larger. New thorns popped out along the stems, points gleaming wickedly.

The Devil's black wings beat the air. Before Agatuzza could return and find him trespassing, he flew up out of her secret cavern and back to Bolgaro, where he planted the dragonweed in the earth just below Amalia's window

Early the next morning, as the first light entered her tower prison, Amalia found several bits of charcoal in the fireplace, as usual, went to a bare patch on the wall, and began drawing another picture of Ursula. Then, when her miserable longing for her cherished friend overcame her, she sank down by the window, buried her head in her arms on the windowsill, and wept.

Down the tower wall ran her tears, and into the earth. They were at once sucked up by the hungry roots of the dragonweed, which began to branch out in all directions underground, every new rootling waiting eagerly for more.

They were not long in waiting. After the Prince arrived on his morning visit, undressed and threw himself on top of her, Amalia went back to the window and wept some more. That afternoon her grief again overcame her, and when Ulisso left that evening, she inadvertently watered the dragonweed again.

That night she was haunted by dreams of Ursula. The next morning she wept so broken-heartedly that she failed to even glance down from her window. All she could see was her own misery. All she could think about was the happiness she no longer possessed. Amalia didn't notice what was growing below her, what was creeping up and around the tower, stone by stone. By noon there was a briar of dragonweed eight feet tall wrapped around one side of the tower and quickly swallowing the other, reaching thorny claws every which way and steadily, rapidly growing.

Chapter 10
Dragonweed!

Shortly after midday, an old gardener noticed the briar, and returned with his sharpest shears and an ax, determined to remove it. Alarmed at how large it was, he shook his head and clucked his tongue, scandalized just to think of how long a weed that size must have gone unnoticed.

"Shameful!" he scolded. "These youngsters today just don't care anymore about doing a good job." In the back of his mind, he also thought, "These old eyes of mine must be getting weaker than I dreamed."

He set to work with his ax. The briar's branches were tougher than he expected. It took him five blows just to chop off the first branch, which should have needed only a single whack. "Am I getting weak, or are weeds getting stronger?" worried the old gardener bleakly. Another half-dozen blows were needed before a second branch fell to the ground. As it did, the old gardener noticed that the first had taken root.

"Oh no, you don't!" he exclaimed.

He promptly uprooted the branch, chopped it in two again where it lay on the ground, and went back to work on the briar. The next branch was the hardest of all to cut. When it finally thudded to the ground, the gardener was breaking into a sweat. Mopping his forehead with a handkerchief, he looked down bleakly at the three branches he had managed to hew away, and cried out in fear.

Three small plants were growing behind him out of the severed branches. Even now, the branch that had just fallen was already stirring, rustling, sending out roots.

The old gardener grabbed his ax and began wildly chopping. Every piece took root. Feelers began coiling up his ankles. The briar's branches swung down, reaching for him. Leaves rustled toward him, crawling around his legs. With a scream, the gardener tore loose the eager tendrils and backed away swinging his ax. Then he ran out of the courtyard, out of the castle gate, and all the way down the cobbled, twisting street to the local taverna, where he downed a bottle of wine before catching his breath.

By that time, the dragonweed completely surrounded the base of the tower, and had come to look something like a hedge.

An old man gathering firewood noticed it. An old woman searching for herbs looked twice. A young guard blinked and took another drink. Each of them quietly concluded that they must have failed to notice it before because nothing that large could have just popped up overnight. Nothing natural could grow that fast, and so the hedge must have always been there.

Twilight found the lower half of the tower completely engulfed by the plant, with tendrils already feeling their way over the courtyard and down into the city streets.

The Devil in Love

Prince Ulisso paid his evening visit to the tower. With his thoughts racing eagerly ahead of him, fired for unleashing his passion and eager to get a good night's sleep when he was done, he was swift and efficient in satisfying himself, assuming his submissive prisoner was sensibly growing to enjoy his muscles and prowess, and noticed nothing unusual rustling about in the shadows outside.

Amalia wept when he was gone.

All night long, while the castle slept, the dragonweed grew.

At first Amalia thought it was still night. She rolled over and tried to go back to sleep. Sleep was the best way to escape her terrible new life. Then she glimpsed several beams of light cutting through the gloom, much too large to be stars. She sat up in bed. The window was completely smothered in the leaves of a plant, which were blocking all but a few cracks of sunlight.

"But that's impossible," she thought. "I draw my pictures every day by the light of that window. No plant can grow that fast. My room is high in the tower, after all…"

She rushed to the window. It was a knotted mass of tendrils, branches, leaves and thorny stems. Amalia backed away from it. She screamed. The entire mass of greenery was moving, like a nest of snakes, crawling over the windowsill, climbing up the shutters, dropping down to the floor in leafy coils…

The Devil in Love

Prince Ulisso woke up earlier than usual that morning. After several unsuccessful attempts at rolling over and going back to sleep, he found himself stiffening into his morning condition and realized he was thinking about Amalia.

He pulled on a light morning robe and left his chamber. The earliest shift of servants were already at work, getting the fireplaces crackling and the ovens hot, all of them half-asleep yet. He climbed the stairs of the north tower. It seemed darker than usual, but his thoughts were elsewhere. He was wondering which positions he would take her in.

Ulisso opened the door. It was strangely dark – Amalia almost never closed the shutters. He could hear the familiar sound of her sobbing in the darkness, however, and approached the bed quietly, slipping toward her through the shadowy room like a phantom. He dropped his morning robe to the floor and bent down over the bed to take her helplessly into his arms.

A leafy arm wrapped around his throat.

He gasped and drew back. A thorn scratched across the back of his neck, drawing blood. Ulisso shouted.

Amalia leaped to her feet in terror from the corner of the floor where she'd been huddling. All around her the leafy crawlers had formed a circle, waiting for her tears. She screamed. The Prince managed to uncoil the creeper around his neck, and lunged for the door. He nearly fell. A vine had crawled out from under the bed and wrapped around his ankle.

"Guards!" cried Prince Ulisso. "Help!" He was shouting at the top of his lungs. The plant's hold on his ankle was too tight to uncoil. "What is this thing?" As his hands feverishly clawed at the weed, another tendril wrapped around his wrist. Ulisso whispered, and began shouting and swearing. He couldn't pry it loose. "Guards!" he howled. The weed around his wrist began tugging him in one direction, while the one gripping his ankle began dragging him in the other. "Get these things off me!"

Amalia was too terrified to take a single step toward that hideous plant. Trembling in horror, she watched the Prince thrashing and twisting on the floor, stretched out on a rack of thorns and leaves, straining in vain to pull free before the weeds tugged him in two.

Guards burst into the room. Though their eyes were wide with terror, they rushed past Amalia to the Prince's assistance.

"Cut me loose from these things!" cried Ulisso, who could hear the bones of his back beginning to pop. The guards hacked with their swords at the weeds' hold on his ankle and wrist. Their blades cut through, not a moment too soon.

Nearly weeping with relief, Prince Ulisso wasted no time in scrambling toward the door. "It's coming in through the window!" he shouted, snatching up his clothes off the floor.

The Devil in Love

"Close those shutters! We've got to keep those weeds outside. And don't let this woman get out of your sight."

With that, Prince Ulisso hurried down the tower stairs and into a living green nightmare which the citizens of Bolgaro would never forget.

Chapter 11
The Conquered City

Amalia wasn't the only one in Bolgaro that morning to wake up screaming. By that time, the dragonweed had multiplied into thousands of crawling, climbing, strangling plants that were growing so large that over a quarter of the city was infested. The citizens were terrified. There was no stopping it. The more you chopped it, the more it grew. Horses bolted at the sight of it. Tendrils of the dragonweed squeezed through fences, pried open shutters, lifted doors off their hinges, poked holes in roofs and ceilings, strangled chimneys, burrowed through walls, and broke apart the boards of the floor. It blocked alleys and swallowed houses.

Squads of guards from the castle marched through the city with flaming torches, trying to set the dragonweed on fire. Those leafy tentacles, however, wouldn't simply lay down and burn, like other plants. Instead they rolled over and burrowed in the earth, putting out the flames, smothering any blaze in a ready host of nearby leaves.

The Devil in Love

Alchemists and apothecaries were urgently summoned to the castle, where they were given unlimited funds to brew their deadliest poisons. Legions of guards carried those poisons throughout the city, pouring foul-smelling potions and fuming salts on that unstoppable weed. Any other plants nearby were invariably fried brown by those fatal compounds, but none of them affected the dragonweed in the slightest.

It only grew faster.

"How could Agatuzza do this to us?" cried the horrified citizens of Bolgaro, abandoning their homes to the encroaching thicket. "A curse on that witch! What kind of monstrosity has she concocted this time?" Driven into the streets by that moving jungle, mobs of citizens flocked into the square before the castle, clamoring for Prince Ulisso to do something fast about that infernal weed. Soon there were angry shouts.

"Bolt the castle gates," said the Prince, draining his third goblet of wine. His hands had finally stopped trembling from his ordeal. He glanced down from his balcony window at the growing crowd of homeless refugees in the square. He didn't have the wildest clue how to defeat the dragonweed, but he had no desire to deal with an angry mob at the same time. "If they begin to riot," he told his captain, "tell the archers to line the walls."

Prince Ulisso slumped down into his throne glumly. His forehead was beaded with sweat, his throat was like chalk.

The Devil in Love

"And bring me some more wine," he snapped at a pageboy. The boy fled.

"What in the world am I going to tell all those people?" the Prince thought to himself grimly. "What more can I possibly do against this weed?"

That was when Ursula pried her way through the weed-constricted gates of the city, still clutching her bag of the abductor's clothes and Amalia's last painting in its velvet sack. Her dress was in rags. There were burrs in her hair. She had wandered in the forest for days, living on nuts and roots, wild apples and berries, sleeping in trees. She had found nothing, not the slightest trace of her lost friend. Now, at last, her search had brought her to Bolgaro. Surely someone in the city would be able to identify the young man in the painting. Half-mad with grief, scarcely noticing the leafy creepers rustling over the cobbles beneath her feet, Ursula drifted like some scrap of human misery down the weed-choked alleyways.

The castle bells were tolling. Citizens of Bolgaro were pouring out of their houses, pushing through the congested streets toward the town square. No one would stop long enough to look at Ursula's painting or answer her desperate questions. "Let go of my sleeve!" cried one. "Get out of the way!" shouted another. "Can't you see what's happening? That weed has taken over the city!"

At every alley and corner, people were battling against those crawling, leafy tentacles. "Do you know this man?"

asked Ursula, holding up the painting. The frantic, puffing fellow she addressed was struggling to cut his wagon-wheels free, and swore at her. "Do you know this man?" she asked, but the woman was screaming for her lost child and pushed Ursula aside. "Do you know this man?" she asked, trying to show them the painting. They backed away when she approached, pointed at her, threatened her.

"Madwoman!" cried a couple of street urchins. They threw rocks at her.

The square in front of the castle was thronging with distraught townspeople. The royal heralds blew their trumpets on a balcony overlooking the crowd. The madwoman pressed forward. No one had to be asked twice to make way for Ursula. One look in her eyes was enough. She bumped her way in a daze up to the very front, staring intently into every face as she passed, searching.

Suddenly everyone around her began to roar. Ursula was confused, frightened. She turned around in circles, dismayed, then noticed that a crowned figure had stepped out onto the balcony above her. Some of the citizens were bravely cheering, but others were crying out in impatience and distress. The Prince held out his hands, and the square was hushed.

Ursula took one look at him and her body shuddered. Her arms stiffened at her sides. She stared like a dead woman. Her quest was over. The painting clattered at her feet.

The Devil in Love

"My good citizens," said the Prince. "I have considered every plan. The future of this good kingdom is at stake. If there is anyone within reach of my voice who knows how to rid us of this dreadful plant, I promise to give as a reward *anything* that is in my power to give."

Ursula's mouth opened, but no words came out. That was the only answer to the Prince's offer.

Chapter 12
Lightning Strikes

Stunned, unable to tell her left from her right, Ursula pushed her way blindly out of the thronging square. Her feet took her out of the city. She didn't watch where she was walking, or know where she was going, or care. Was there no goodness left at all among men, that brothers could prove so treacherous, hermits so debased, guards without conscience, rulers steeped in vice?

While Ursula wandered without hope or direction in the wilderness, her mind swirling with plots to murder the Prince, the sky grew dark as night though it was still afternoon. Ursula didn't notice. She didn't feel the first raindrops. She didn't hear the ominous rumble in the heavy clouds overhead. Then the storm drenched the land. Rain lashed her. The trees around her groaned and creaked, branches snapping, leaves torn whirling into the confusion.

The Devil in Love

Ursula saw a cave ahead. She clawed her way up a bank of muddy rocks, entered the cave in great fear, and then wept with relief to find that her shelter did not have a previous tenant.

Trapped in that cave by the raging storm, Ursula lost all track of time. She paced back and forth like a caged animal, hugging herself to keep warm, talking to the cave walls. Finally her clothes stopped dripping. Though not yet warm, she was at least beginning to dry out, when there was a flash of lightning outside the cave. In the moment's blaze, Ursula saw an old woman making her way through the deluge, struggling to remain on her feet in the throes of the wind. Ursula shouted to her and waved, trying to attract her attention, but the old woman apparently couldn't hear her above the roar of the rain. What was more, the skinny creature was wildly waving her gaunt arms about in the blast.

"Go ahead and blow!" she screeched. "See if I care! I'll say it again – you're a thief! You heard me – and I'm calling you a liar, too – it's time somebody did. It was you, admit it. Who else would maim my lovely plants? Who else would twist them into such a horrible weed? Don't let me ever catch you again in my secret garden, I don't care *who* you are. Do you hear me?"

In answer, a sky-splitting crack of lightning ripped jagged out of the darkness. An ancient forest giant fell over with a crash. From under it came a screech – one of the branches had come down on top of the old woman, knocking her flat.

Ursula cried out in horror. Though she knew there was nothing she would be able to do, she ran out into the downpour and was at once soaked to the skin. She could detect feeble movement up ahead, where the old woman's thin, frail limbs were still kicking weakly under the fallen tree. Ursula fell to her knees beside the mud-splattered gray head, anxiously drawing aside the wild gray hair in an attempt to find the face.

"Help me, help me!" groaned the old woman. "This horrible branch is crushing me. Both my arms are pinned. Get it off me!"

Ursula sobbed, "I'm strong but it's too heavy. It would take a giant to lift that branch."

"Nonsense!" complained the old woman. "You could lift this tree off me all by yourself, if you'd just set your mind to it. Please, please, lift up this tree!"

Ursula knew well and good that she would never be able to lift such a weight, but the old woman pleaded with her so piteously that Ursula agreed to try. She took hold of the branch with both hands, took a deep breath, and heaved upward with all her might.

The tree lifted. The old woman crawled free.

Then with a thundering crash the tree dropped down again to the earth. Ursula stepped back, amazed, gasping for breath. No sooner was the old woman out from under the pinning branch than she scrambled up onto her feet and dusted herself off. Strangely enough, once she'd had a moment to attend to herself, she appeared to have suffered only the slightest injuries.

"You're – you're scarcely hurt at all," stammered Ursula in wonder and fear. Lightning flashed. She and the old woman stood staring at each other in the rain. The eyes of the old woman glowed yellow-green, and for the first time Ursula began to suspect that she wasn't exactly human.

"Thanks to you, my good daughter," she said with a bow. "Thanks entirely to you, I have come to no harm." Scowling down at the blasted tree, she added, "No thanks to him! I suppose I deserved it. I shouldn't have shouted at him. He doesn't often get the better of my temper, but this time he just pushed me too far. I refuse to let him bully me, simply refuse. The problem is that nobody else will stand up to him. Easy to see why! Disagreeing with the Devil doesn't pay. He can get mean. He caught me off-guard, you see, pinned my arms so I couldn't do my magic. I would have been in a sorry state if you hadn't lifted that thing off me. Who knows how long I might have been pinned there!" The old woman clasped Ursula's hand gratefully. "I must do something for you in return, I simply must. I owe you such a great deal."

Ursula smiled sadly. "I'm afraid there's nothing much a dear old woman like you can do for me. I'm sure you're strong, but not strong enough to take on a Prince and an entire kingdom."

The Devil in Love

"Is that all?" said the old woman with a smile. "My dear, it's no small thing, I assure you, to have Agatuzza, the Witch of the Wild, in your debt."

"Ancient mother!" cried Ursula, when she realized who she had saved. She threw herself at the old woman's feet, trembling.

"Come now, get back up on your feet," chuckled Agatuzza. "For helping me today, I am in your service. You needn't tremble. Please give me an opportunity to repay you."

Ursula didn't have to think about it long. "Yes," she said. "Yes, there is something you can do for me. Show me how to destroy the plant which is swallowing our kingdom. That one secret is all I need to win back the woman I love. The rest I can do myself."

"Why, my dear," laughed Agatuzza, "your attitude touches my heart, and taking care of that dragonweed will be a pleasure, I assure you, and easy enough, too, since it was made out of my own magic plants. But I was going to do that, anyway. You shall have to come up with a better wish than that, if I am ever to repay you."

"When I have destroyed this dragonweed," said Ursula, "I shall win back from the Prince the one thing worth possessing. What more do I need?"

"Think about it," said the witch. "There's no rush. Surely you'll be able to dream up something. And about that dragonweed – wait until tomorrow morning, when you stand before Prince Ulisso himself, and he gives you his word. Remember, you have only to say my name to summon me."

Reaching into her baggy pocket, the old witch fished around and then pulled out a smooth, gray stone which she gave to Ursula. It was the size of her palm, unusually light, and radiated a mysterious warmth which seemed to flow through her whole, drenched body.

"Take it," said Agatuzza. "Just a little something to keep you warm and dry in that cave tonight. Get some rest, and think up a good wish. Believe me, my dear, aside from raising the dead, as long as my arms are free I can do just about anything."

With a wild laugh, Agatuzza bounded away into the downpour, disappearing into the trees.

CHAPTER 13
"My Price Is Amalia!"

That night not one citizen in all of Bolgaro slept in peace. All through the dark hours, from one end of the city to the other, screams rang out as the dragonweed continued relentlessly to engulf everything in sight. People woke up to find their beds being slowly dragged across the room by leafy branches, or to find tendrils creeping over their pillows, vines looping around their wrists. Who could sleep, while all around them they could hear the scratching and rustling of those tireless creepers, climbing up the walls?

By morning, the streets were choked, the windows plugged, the doorways blocked by masses of leaves and knotting vines. Many found themselves imprisoned in their own houses. On every side there were cries of terror and outrage. Climbing up the city walls, the dragonweed now all but covered dozens of rooftops, and the towers that rose above the walls were also turning moss green with the leafy infestation. Ursula emerged from the forest to stare in wonder at Bolgaro's transformation.

A fat, green root had forced its way between the two doors of the gate, bending the doors open, so that she had no trouble re-entering the city. Being careful to avoid as many of the dragonweed's sharp thorns as she could, Ursula began

The Devil in Love

slowly picking her way through that restless jungle in the direction of Prince Ulisso's castle.

In some places, the lower branches had become as thick as tree-trunks, blocking the narrow streets. Ursula had to climb over them, crawl around them, squeeze through sideways, and sometimes clamber from branch to branch. Even then, some streets were impassable. She could hear people shouting and banging inside some of the houses, trying to get out. The marketplace had become a weed-infested wilderness, with some stalls literally lifted clear of the ground and now hanging lop-sided, suspended in the air along with barrels, crates, tubs, and several wagons.

At last she reached the castle.

Going up to one of the terrified guards on duty, Ursula said, "Tell the Prince that I know how to defeat the dragonweed."

For a moment the guard stared at her haggard face, her weather-beaten body, scratched and torn clothes, and determined, otherworldly eyes. She looked like a madwoman, a laughingstock, and yet her eyes blazed with urgent intelligence. He dared not believe her. He left his post and ran into the castle. A moment later, he returned and guided Ursula into the presence of Prince Ulisso.

The audience chamber was in an uproar. The lords and barons were all talking at once, louder than usual because they were frightened, masking their fear as anger, and becoming angrier and angrier, urging one desperate solution after another.

"Evacuate the city!" cried one lord.

"Are you mad? Leave our homes?" cried another. "Never!"

"Stay and fight like men!"

"Set it on fire!"

"Cut it in pieces!"

"Use acid!"

"Use poison!"

Prince Ulisso's handsome face was gray with worry. Long gone was the twinkle of confidence in his eye. He was slumped in his throne, brooding, hair uncombed, his forehead lined with scowling. He didn't appear to be listening to a word that his lords and barons said. One of his fists continued to pound uselessly, repeatedly, on the arm of his throne, as though he could hammer the solution out of the armrest.

He was expecting only nonsense from the madwoman at the door. The moment she stood before him, however, his eyes opened wider and he sat up straighter. Ulisso recognized at once the face which had been reproduced in charcoal hundreds of times over the walls of Amalia's tower chamber. "So this is the other woman Noraldo met in the forest," mused the Prince. In her present condition, Ursula was certainly not as lovely as Amalia had depicted her.

"Your Majesty," said the madwoman, "I have come in response to the offer you made yesterday."

The Devil in Love

"So I am told," said Prince Ulisso. "My guard says you claim to be able to get rid of this accursed plant." A bitter smile touched the corners of his mouth as he spoke, while he secretly wondered if she were really as mad as she looked. "Is this true?'"

"Yes," said the ragged, disheveled woman before him. "I can destroy the dragonweed."

"And just how do you propose to do this?"

"Agatuzza, the Witch of the Wild, has promised to come the moment I summon her," announced Ursula, in a voice which rang from one end of the hall to the other. "At my bidding, she will put an end to this troublesome plant."

The audience chamber rumbled with excitement as the lords and barons crowded closer.

"But Agatuzza is the one who unleashed this weed upon us," objected the Prince, trying to sound like he knew what he was talking about. Several angry barons echoed him in agreement.

"No, Your Majesty," said Ursula. "The dragonweed is not of this world. It is the Devil's work, created out of shoots he stole from Agatuzza's secret garden."

"If this is true," said Prince Ulisso warily, "then you must summon Agatuzza at once."

"You have not yet asked my price," said Ursula, standing her ground. "You have offered anything."

The Prince was not a fool. He recognized her. He knew who she was. He knew what she wanted. He could see where

The Devil in Love

this was leading, but he was helpless to stop it. His kingdom was in dire straits. He dared not refuse her terms. If he tried, the council of elders was sure to intervene. "Anything is the offer," he said. "Name your price."

"My price is Amalia."

Ursula stepped forward. She laid the sack containing the painting and the sack containing his clothes at Prince Ulisso's feet. "You will recognize this portrait. You will recognize these clothes. I know what happened in the forest. Promise to give her back to me, and I'll get rid of the dragonweed."

The Prince tried to smile, but it was a grimace of bared teeth. "Very well," he said curtly. "Destroy the dragonweed, and I'll let her go."

Ursula turned away from the throne and walked out of the audience chamber without another word. Down the central hallway of the castle she walked, followed by an excited buzzing of voices, a rumble of eagerness mixed with skeptical whispers and hoots of derision, as lords and barons followed after the madwoman out the doors of the palace into the weed-strangled royal gardens.

The Devil in Love

CHAPTER 14
The Witch's Hoe

All around her stirred the many roots and tendrils, vines and leaves and creepers of the dragonweed, slowly crawling and climbing in all directions. Ursula stood in the midst of them, while from the windows and balconies of the castle all the lords and barons watched in suspense. As leafy tendrils began coiling around her ankles and creeping up her legs, Ursula lifted her arms in supplication.

"Agatuzza!" she cried out. "Mighty Witch of the Wild, come as you promised. Destroy the dragonweed which infests this kingdom."

Lightning flashed over the gardens, and the old woman suddenly stood before her. Lords and barons shouted in alarm. Maids and cooks screamed and backed away from the windows and doorways where they had been watching. A wind swept over the gardens from the lake. Agatuzza's ragged, green dress flapped wildly about her boney body. Her streaming gray hair blew about her eyes. Over her shoulder, the old witch carried a gardening hoe, the edge of which had been honed and filed till it was sharp as a razor.

"Here I am, my dear," said Agatuzza, "just as I said I would be." The old witch completely ignored Prince Ulisso and all the gawking lords and barons peering down at her, as

The Devil in Love

though they weren't important enough for her to acknowledge. Her only concern seemed to be leaning over and helping Ursula pull herself free of the eagerly-coiling creepers. More and more onlookers surged around the outskirts of the weed-choked gardens as word rapidly spread through the castle.

"Agatuzza is here! Agatuzza!"

Ignoring the hubbub all around them, taking Ursula by the hand, as though they were the only two people there, the old witch said, "We should be on our way to the tower now, my dear. There, I believe, we will find the dragonweed's source of nourishment, as well as the mother dragonweed's heart."

Between them and the tower stretched a tangled, rustling thicket of leafy branches. The branches were slowly interweaving, knotting together, blocking their way. Beneath the leaves winked sharp, black thorns.

Agatuzza strode up to that uncrossable briar. Her hoe swung up into the air, and then came down with a swoosh and hiss, first on the right, then on the left. Wherever the sharp edge of the hoe struck the dragonweed, it cleaved right through the plant. Left and right, Agatuzza swung her hoe, so that severed pieces of the weed were flung hurtling away to either side. Wherever they fell, however, they quickly re-rooted.

Chopping a path through that thorny tangle, the old witch began making her way across the jungle that had once been the castle gardens. Ursula followed right behind her down the narrow path of sliced branches and roots, all of which were promptly growing together again behind them. Slicing and hacking, Agatuzza led Ursula slowly but surely across the gardens to the weed-smothered courtyard below the weed-strangled tower.

There Agatuzza's hoe at last came to rest beside her. The old witch leaned upon it while she caught her breath. The two of them had stopped at the tower's base. Ursula's eyes could look nowhere else but up, toward the edges of a window mostly concealed by leaves.

"Amalia," she whispered.

As though in answer, there was a cry from above, and the sound of boards being torn and ripped away. "Ursula!" cried a familiar voice. A white hand thrust itself out for a moment through the vines, and then was gone.

Ursula felt as though she had been stabbed through the heart. She flung herself against the door of the tower, as though her rage would be enough to rip open the lock. She pounded on it furiously with her fists, shouting the name of her imprisoned friend.

Then a shadow seemed to loom over her, darkening the door. Ursula turned around. Having completely swallowed up the trail out through the gardens, the dragonweed was crawling nearer. Its mighty thorn-encrusted branches were now rising up all around Ursula and the witch, sinisterly reaching out for them while blocking out the sky.

The Devil in Love

"This is it," said Agatuzza, wiping the palms of her hands on her dress and getting a good grip on her hoe. "Stand back, my dear."

Agatuzza's hoe whacked down into the thick trunk of the dragonweed, right at the foot of the tower where the Devil first planted the stolen rootling. The razored edge of her hoe sliced halfway through at one blow. A high-pitched whine rang through the air like a faraway scream, as a white geyser spurted out of the cloven trunk. Agatuzza was drenched.

A reawakened, angry life seemed to pulse through all the branches and creepers around her. Thorny tendrils leaped out at her, wrapping around her ankles, sinking their little black spikes into her skin like teeth. She lifted her hoe again, gripped in both hands, and delivered another blow even stronger than the first. The trunk was sliced in two. There was an earthshaking rumble, as though the tower were about to collapse. The ground shifted underfoot. There were cries of fear on all sides.

Before the old witch could raise her hoe one more time, a leafy arm of the dragonweed wrapped around her chest like a python and heaved her up off her feet, sinking its thorns into her chest. Both of her skinny arms were pinned to her sides. Her legs were kicking. The hoe fell clattering to the courtyard below.

"Ursula!" cried the old witch. "My hoe! I can't – my arms – it's up to you!"

The Devil in Love

With a gasp, Ursula ran for the fallen hoe, while Agatuzza was lifted higher and higher into the air. Creeping vines got to the hoe first. They dragged it toward the shores of the lake. A branch of the dragonweed tripped Ursula, sending her falling into the thorns. She scrambled to her feet. One of her bleeding hands grabbed the handle of the hoe. With a savage cry, she wrenched it away from the tendrils that were dragging it, chopped just as she had seen the old witch do, fighting her way back to the base of the tower.

"Hurry!" cried Agatuzza, wrapped and bound in creepers until she was almost invisible in a leafy cocoon. "The dragonweed's heart – right where I was chopping – into the stump – one more blow, dear, one more mighty blow should do it..."

Ursula slashed down into the stump with the old witch's hoe. A white fountain erupted out of the gash, with a high-pitched shriek. Ursula dropped the hoe and covered both of her ears with her hands. The bubbling white sap of the dragonweed's heart made a puddle at her feet.

All the branches and long green stems of the weed, from one end of Bolgaro to the other, shuddered. For a moment it almost seemed as though a ferocious wind were lashing all the leaves and tendrils, except that there was no wind. There was only a blaze of sun, beating down on a kingdom engulfed in heaving leaves. One last, convulsive tremor, and the dragonweed was still. Throughout the kingdom, every branch dropped from the wall it was clinging to, every tendril released its grip on houses, trees, wagons. Every creeper went limp. Every leaf wilted. Every root stopped burrowing. Every thorn began to shrivel. Every briar of dragonweed across the kingdom stopped growing, sagged, and collapsed with a groan.

Agatuzza thudded to the ground not far away, and at once began struggling to free herself from the thorny branches around her waist and legs. Ursula rushed to help her, but by the time she got there, the witch had already wriggled free, scrambled to her feet, and was dusting herself off. Together they looked around them on all sides, at the vast, serpentine ruins of that Devil-sent weed.

A few cheers rippled through the sunlight. Then more cheers. Then an uproar.

"Very well done, my dear," said the Witch of the Wild. "This weed won't be causing any more problems, I assure you."

"I couldn't have done it without your hoe," said Ursula, picking it up and handing it back to her.

"True," said Agatuzza, with a shrug and a cackle. "At any rate, your half of the bargain has now been fulfilled. I'm going home for a nap, and it's time for you to go and collect your reward."

Shouldering her hoe once again, Agatuzza gave a sweeping, comical bow toward her crowd of onlookers, and winked at Ursula. Then there was a jagged flash of lightning and the witch was gone.

The Devil in Love

Ursula walked over to where Prince Ulisso was nudging a dead limb of the dragonweed with one foot.

"I have come for my payment," said Ursula.

"Yes, of course," said Prince Ulisso. He smiled, and bowed courteously, while the lords and barons, pageboys and cooks, maids and stable-hands who had witnessed the ordeal cried out happily, shouting their gratitude.

"On behalf of all Bolgaro," said the Prince, "I thank you for ridding us of that infernal weed. And now, since I promised to let Amalia go, I shall keep my promise. A slight change, however, has occurred since we spoke. While you and Agatuzza were kindly ridding us of the dragonweed, I've been up in the tower having a long talk with Amalia. I'm afraid there's been an unexpected development. I appear to have promised you something which was not mine to give."

"What do you mean?" whispered Ursula, as her heart turned cold with dread.

"Perhaps Amalia ought to tell you herself," smiled Prince Ulisso.

He tugged open the tower door. Amalia was standing there, staring, remote, more like a statue than a breathing woman. Her face was pale. Her hands were trembling. Ursula gasped. She would have thrown herself into Amalia's arms, but to her horror she saw that Amalia was wearing the crown of a princess, and that Amalia's eyes no longer welcomed her.

The Devil in Love

"It's true," said Amalia in a wavering voice. "I'm not coming back. Ulisso is everything any woman could ever want. I was just being silly. I didn't know my own mind." She took the Prince's hand. "But I know it now. I'm going to stay and rule Valbrosa by the side of the man I love."

Chapter 15
The Profligate's Vow

The dragonweed had been conquered.

That night the streets of Bolgaro were lined with bonfires. The houses echoed with laughter and music. Every window and doorway was brightly lit. Children were up far past their bedtimes, and no one noticed or cared.

All day long the overjoyed citizens had been chopping down the leafy creepers and crawlers which covered their city. Houses were unburied from beneath the lifeless vines. Trapped families were set free. Streets were cleared of blockage. The dead branches and trunks were heaped in gigantic mounds in the middle of every street corner. At twilight, torches transformed those mounds into flaming pyres. All that remained of the dragonweed infestation was consigned to the flames. The squeals of children rang out over the roar of the bonfires, as dancing black silhouettes leaped around the blaze.

The Devil in Love

Two long days of fear now erupted into frolic. Fiddles began to whir, accordions to wheeze and bellow. In every house of Bolgaro there was merry-making and rejoicing.

Though there was usually some kind of party in progress, anyway, at Fausto's house, that night it was intensified by the general festivity of the liberated city. The revelers at Fausto's party were undeniably more abandoned, of course, since they were far more practiced in drunken exuberance. Those who had copiously toasted their doom in the grip of the dragonweed now drank to the conquest of their enemy with even greater enthusiasm and lack of restraint.

Midnight had long passed. There were fewer guests. People were beginning to leave, as wine and the day's exhausting strain made them ready for their beds. As far as Fausto was concerned, however, the party was far from over. His flushed cheeks were still hot with life. Shadows deepened the sockets around his handsome brown eyes, which gleamed out of those pits with a haunted glow, restless, unsatisfied. His parted, sensual lips were wet with wine. A goblet hovered before his mouth, momentarily forgotten but nearby and ready to attempt to slake his perpetual thirst.

The intense fear he had experienced during the dragonweed's siege of the city had left Fausto's face looking haggard, older. The plant had engulfed the entire house. He had responded to the situation by retreating to the wine-cellar, locking himself inside, and drinking himself unconscious. That was where the servants found him after the dragonweed had been slain. His first words when they revived him and told him the good news were, "Tell Sergio to invite everybody we know. There's going to be a party."

Fausto tipped back his head and drained his goblet.

Reduced to silhouettes, the remaining guests teetered and wove about, laughing and sloshing their cups, stumbling into drunken embraces beneath a huge painting covering most of the back wall, in which Ursula and the serving-woman made love. That painting had been his sister's last mysterious gift to him. He had found it in her room, left behind on the night she and Ursula had disappeared. He had never seen Amalia again. She was nowhere in Bolgaro, of that he was certain. After five years, she was only a memory. Isabella, the serving-woman, had continued to amuse him for several more weeks after Amalia had fled, and then he had grown weary of her and fired her.

Fausto had long since sold most of Amalia's paintings to pay his debts, but not that last one. Even though he knew that the two women had never made love together, since Isabella had numbered among his own conquests Fausto found the painting particularly arousing. It never failed to have a stimulating influence on parties like the one he had thrown there tonight.

He grabbed a nearby wine-jug and up-ended it over his empty goblet. The jug was empty. He flung it crashing into a corner.

The Devil in Love

Isabella was standing in the doorway. At the very moment the jug smashed into fragments, she seemed to have stepped down from the painting. Fausto blinked, and for a moment thought he had drunk too much. What was she doing there? He had no desire to even see her. She was moving toward him now through the other guests. Fausto prepared himself for an unpleasant scene. Then Sergio's arm reached up from the bed, grabbing Isabella's hand, pulling her down into a sliding, nuzzling heap of limbs and wine-dampened bodies.

Fausto was glad to see her intercepted. He spilled his last few drops of wine across the backs of a couple thrashing about on the floor as he walked out onto the balcony overlooking the leaping flames.

Down in the street a dog was barking at one of the bonfires, and a last derelict accordion-player was weaving away home down an alley. Fausto's goblet slipped off the edge of the railing, clattering on the cobblestones below.

He had depleted his inheritance. He was hopelessly into debt. He managed to live by gambling and cards now, and when he lost, by selling the furniture, piece by piece. Soon there would be nothing left to sell, but Fausto tried not to look that far into the future. He tried to think only of the next lovely creature he intended to taste in bed. Who would it be? More than anything tonight, he longed to indulge all of his senses, to make himself blissfully numb with pleasure.

The Devil in Love

Though dawn could not be far away, he was still far from tired, still unsatisfied.

A hot, unsteady shape backed out of the party onto the balcony beside him, becoming his friend, Sergio. Weaving slightly, with a tilted grin, Sergio draped one arm around Fausto's neck and gestured back into the room toward Isabella.

"Very attractive," said Sergio. "Still looks a lot like your sister. Too bad she doesn't kiss as well."

Fausto was drunk. "How would you know?" he said. He flung Sergio's arm off his shoulder, and backed him up against the railing. "You're not good enough to talk about my sister," said Fausto in a tense even voice, "so shut up."

"Not good enough?" snapped Sergio, bridling. "Since when?"

"Since right now," said Fausto, one hand gripping the front of Sergio's shirt.

"You're drunk, Fausto," said his friend angrily through clenched teeth, straining to pull Fausto's hand away.

"Don't ever talk about Amalia like that again," said Fausto. "Compared to her, you belong in the gutter."

Sergio's temper flared. He was tired of Fausto ordering him around and insulting him, as though he were some kind of servant. "I'll say what I like. I don't take orders from you. Want to know the truth? Isabella says your sister has become the Prince's whore."

The Devil in Love

Fausto bent him back over the edge of the balcony, his hand sinking into Sergio's throat. "Take it back," he hissed.

"She – just – told – me," gasped Sergio. "She ought to know. She works at the castle."

The two of them twisted, shifting their weight, straining until the veins stood out on their temples. Then Sergio suddenly kneed him between the legs. Fausto buckled with a gasp. His grip loosened just long enough. Sergio was on top of him in a moment, pinning him to the balcony floor.

"Liar!" shouted Fausto hotly into his face. "She's been dead for five years."

"The Prince doesn't go to bed with dead women," said Sergio scornfully. "She can't be as dead as all that."

"The bitch is lying!"

"I'm telling the truth," said Isabella.

She stood above them, foremost among a small crowd of guests gathered watching the fight. Her clothes had been disarrayed. Her voice trembled with emotion. "He keeps her locked in a room in the tower. He takes his pleasure with her like a maid. Her friend Ursula was the one who slew the dragonweed. She came to rescue Amalia. But your sister has grown to like being Ulisso's whore. She was given a chance to escape, and she chose to stay."

A hush settled over the party. Sergio pushed away from him and rose to his feet. Fausto remained where he was.

"Go home, all of you," said Fausto. "The party is over."

The Devil in Love

Sergio turned away from him with a look of contempt, leaving him alone on the balcony. The dog in the street started barking again. The bonfires were dying. He saw Sergio and Isabella walking away into the night together between the charred and smoking remains of the dragonweed.

The bitter smoke rose up before Fausto's eyes.

He didn't see them sinking down behind the bushes, unable to restrain themselves. Sergio made believe that she was really Amalia. Isabella imagined that Fausto was embracing her. Sometime later, Isabella walked away down the street alone, a jug of wine swinging beside her, weeping.

Fausto was still out on the balcony as the first gray light of dawn set the birds to shrilling and chattering in the trees. His eyes were open, vacant. He didn't see anything. All that was left of him was a morbid ghost of the man he had been, brooding over the unrighted past.

"Nothing left," he thought bitterly. "Sister gone. Money gone. Friends gone. Now honor gone. The Prince's whore!" He gritted his teeth, smiling like a death's head. "Well, when you've got nothing left, you've got nothing to lose."

Fausto began making the last plans of his life. Full of self-pity and shame, his temples pulsing with a hangover, he vowed to neither eat nor sleep till he had avenged the lost honor of his sister by plunging his dagger up to the hilt in the body of Prince Ulisso.

Chapter 16
The Truth

"We'd love to have you stay for the wedding," said the Prince.

Ursula walked away from them. She walked out of the castle without looking back. She walked out of Bolgaro without saying a word. Her heart was cold inside her. The Amalia she had once loved no longer existed. She saw nothing around her. All she could feel was pain.

She walked along the shores of the Lost Lake. She fell to her knees in the wild grass. She wept until she lost consciousness. She had forgotten how to live without Amalia. Sleep brought her the only comfort she could hope for, a temporary respite from her unbearable existence.

When she awoke the next morning, her first thought was regret that she was still alive. She made her legs get up and carry her onward. It was the longest day of her life. She couldn't force herself to eat as much as a nut or a berry. As the long, long afternoon at last began to fade, Ursula knew that she was going to drown herself.

"Tonight my bed will be under the water," she resolved. "I don't ever want to wake up again." She climbed up a rocky escarpment over the lake. Birds screamed around her a last melancholy dirge. As she stood on a jagged ledge jutting out

The Devil in Love

over the water, she whispered bitterly, "If only I knew the truth!"

Lightning flashed on her left, and Agatuzza appeared on the precipice beside her. "The truth," said the old witch, "since you wish for it, is that Amalia lied. She married the Prince to save your life."

Ursula's face paled. She seemed about to faint. "She lied?" she whispered, "I don't understand. Please, go on."

"The Prince told her that if she left with you, he would have you killed," said the witch. "The only way Amalia could save your life was if she refused to return to you."

Ursula groaned with reawakened hope. "You mean – she was only pretending?" She would have collapsed then, had not Agatuzza caught her in arms that were surprisingly strong.

"At this very moment," continued the witch, "Amalia feels so wretched about lying to you that she no longer wishes to live. She is sitting up in her bedroom prison, weeping by the window. Ulisso came upstairs after supper for his evening visit, and now he's sound asleep. Little does he dream that he's forced himself upon her for the last time. While he sprawls there unsuspecting, Amalia has sent one of the pageboys to an apothecary for a vial of deadly poison. She's waiting for him to return right now. Unfortunately, that poison is not for the Prince."

"No!" cried Ursula in despair.

The Devil in Love

"She intends to drink that poison herself," said Agatuzza, "rather than let him share her bed one more time. The pageboy just left…"

Before Agatuzza could say another word, Ursula embraced the old witch in gratitude, then turned from the shores of the Lost Lake and raced back toward the castle in a frenzy. She screamed like a wounded bird, she tore her hair. No one knows how she got past the castle guards, whether she bribed them or dashed behind them, or forced her way in through a servant's entrance, or chambered through the crack in the far garden wall.

Back through the night-darkened wreckage of the dragonweed she made her way, to the foot of the tower where Amalia had called her name. Ursula raced all the way up the stairs. She flung open the door. Dozens of charcoal-drawn faces of Ursula looked back at her as she stood in the doorway. Stunned, she regarded that room full of mute witnesses testifying to Amalia's unwavering love.

But Amalia wasn't there.

"They've moved her to a different room!" she sobbed.

Down the dark hallways of the castle she ran, like a grief-stricken phantom, peering first on one side and then on the other as she searched frantically for Amalia's new prison. "I'll never find it in time!" she wailed. "I've got to find someone who can show me."

She seized the first person she saw, a terrified pageboy, seizing him by the throat of his shirt, so that his platter of

The Devil in Love

cheesecake and hot rice pie, intended for the Prince's midnight snack, splattered skidding across the floor. "Amalia's room," she hissed, slamming him up against the wall, knocking the breath out of him. "Where is it?"

"In – in the w-west tower," stammered the pageboy in fear, his face turning red from choking.

She dropped him and ran in the direction he'd pointed.

She found the west tower. She dashed across the courtyard. She lunged inside, bounding up the coiling stairs two at a time, every minute seeming like hours, her heart hammering wildly in her chest. At last she came to the third level and flung open the last door.

The room was very still, but not empty. There was a single motionless occupant. Ursula stood frozen in the doorway, staring down in horror at the crumpled form on the floor. The poison had done its work.

Ursula groaned and sank to her knees. Though one trembling hand reached out in the direction of the lifeless young woman, Ursula could not bring herself to approach one step closer to the cold, stiff imitation of her friend.

Her grief was succeeded by her rage. Before her swollen human heart burst in wretchedness, before she joined Amalia in death, Ursula decided she had one last thing to do.

"Agatuzza!" she whispered fervently.

Lightning flashed down the side of the tower.

Chapter 17
Ursula's Wish

The Witch of the Wild appeared before her at the top of the stairs, plainly disturbed by the sight of the dead young woman before her. "My dear," she began, "you poor thing…"

"Agatuzza, I'm ready to make my wish!" sobbed Ursula.

The old woman groaned. "I know what you're going to say, but my dear, there's been a misunderstanding…"

Ursula was at the end of her tether. "Did you not promise me the fulfillment of a wish?" she cried shrilly.

"Yes, of course, my dear," said the witch, attempting to calm her. "But I'm afraid that…"

"Then I am ready to call upon your honor to fulfill your word," said Ursula. "Surely you are not like the Prince, to promise one thing and do another?"

Agatuzza was stung, and replied sharply, "I have always kept my word, as I will with you. But my powers have limits and I cannot undo the past. I cannot defy the laws of the Afterworld. For anything else, *anything else*, you have but to make your wish known to me."

Ursula fought to stop trembling. "Then listen well," she said. "I call upon you, Agatuzza, to take under your personal care all the women in Prince Ulisso's kingdom – yes, every single one of them, from the oldest grandmother to the

The Devil in Love

youngest baby girl. I want you to lead us all away from here – far, far away, beyond the White Demon Mountains in the north, to a new land of peace and prosperity, a place *without men*. Ancient Mother! Let them not so much as remember us. Erase all memory of women from their minds, or else they will come searching. Don't leave behind a single clue that women ever existed. Take us where they will never find us, to a kingdom where we can live together in freedom."

The Witch of the Wild stared at Ursula in amazement. "Foolish girl, do you expect me to remake the world? Only the Devil can do that!"

"Grant my wish," said Ursula.

A strange twinkle of amusement sparkled in her eyes. "But, my dear," asked Agatuzza, "what in the world are we going to do with all these men?"

Ursula looked up at the thin, ancient woman. Her own young face was harrowed by grief, twisted with contempt. "As far as I'm concerned," said Ursula, "you can take all of Prince Ulisso's foul kingdom – no take this entire land, from the mountains in the North all the way to Hell itself – and you can give it, and every damned man left in it, to the Devil."

An appalled hush froze the world all around them, as though there were no air left in the tower to breathe.

"Your wish is granted," said Agatuzza, wearily summoning up the vast reserves of her power. Her words rang hollowly up and down the tower staircase. "Tonight at midnight, all the women will leave this land. I will lead you all into a new kingdom, beyond the mountain wall. There we will live in peace." Agatuzza cackled and rubbed her leathery old palms together. "This ought to be quite enjoyable. Change can be so refreshing. We'll start all over again without those bastards. Now, what I was trying to tell you…"

A pattering slowly grew louder. Someone was hurrying up the stairs.

"That poor pageboy," said the witch. "You scared him so badly, he forgot his own name. Force isn't always the best means of getting information out of people, my dear, and this is a perfect example."

The footsteps came more rapidly.

"I don't understand," said Ursula.

Agatuzza walked over to stand above the crumpled heap in the middle of the room. "She's been dead since yesterday."

"Yesterday?" said Ursula, in a blank, chill voice. The footsteps rounded the second landing, and raced up the last flight of stairs. "But I thought you said…"

"No one ever comes up here, or they would have found her. She had a drinking problem, poor thing."

"*What?*" Ursula's mind had been spinning, and now it abruptly knotted. "Amalia never drank in her life."

"Who's talking about Amalia?" said the witch. "I'm talking about Isabella – this poor dead woman here. Spilled her wine, slipped in it, broke her neck. I'm afraid the pageboy was so frightened he told you the wrong tower…"

Then a familiar voice in the doorway said, "Ursula."

Chapter 18
Shadows in the Castle

Agatuzza had to pull them apart. Otherwise, they would have clung to each other there in the wrong tower for days, locked in each other's disbelieving arms, kissing lips they had thought never to kiss again.

"How did you know I was up here?" asked Ursula, pulling her mouth away from Amalia's just long enough to speak.

"This good woman told me," said Amalia, gesturing toward the Witch of the Wild.

"I asked the pageboy cleaning up cheesecake all over the floor," said Agatuzza. "All right now, my dears, that's enough for now. After all, there's a dead woman in the room. You'll have plenty of time for that kind of thing on the other side of the mountain wall. Your wish, Ursula, is about to come true. We should be getting out of this tower." She turned to Amalia. "Is the Prince still in bed?"

"Sound asleep," said Amalia. "I left him just a few moments ago."

"Follow me," said Agatuzza, hurrying down the tower stairs. Ursula and Amalia were right behind her. Across the dark courtyard they ran, the witch for all her age eagerly leaping ahead of them, into the south tower and up the staircase, around and around and up.

The Devil in Love

Amalia opened the door.

Prince Ulisso lay across the bed, his mouth fallen open in sleep, an arm dangling over the side.

"Let me smother him in his own pillows," said Ursula.

"Leave him to his dreams," said the old witch. "The Devil will soon take care of him for us, and every man from the northern mountains to the shores of Hell. When they wake up, there won't be a woman left. We'll see how they like a steady diet of their own company. The Devil will keep them busy, I promise you." She cackled in anticipation. "Hurry now, Amalia, gather up whatever you need. We have a long journey ahead."

Soon the three of them were quietly closing the door on the slumbering Prince.

"But I can hardly understand any of this," complained Amalia. She turned to face the witch. "Where are we going? What do you mean about a wish coming true? And who *are* you? Ursula, you haven't introduced me to our rescuer yet."

Before Ursula could apologize, Agatuzza chuckled and said, "Ah, but I know who *you* are, my dear. Often I've stood right behind you, looking over your shoulder in the forest, while you painted your lovely pictures of all my children."

"I don't know what you're talking about," said Amalia, clearly more confused than ever.

"Forgive me," said Ursula. "We are being aided by no one less than the Witch of the Wild herself."

The Devil in Love

"Agatuzza?" gasped Amalia, taken aback, with a tremor in her voice. "Is it possible? Where is she taking us?"

"I'll explain as we go," said Ursula, "We're going away. Beyond the mountain wall. All of us."

Agatuzza led the way back down the stairs. Ursula and Amalia hurried down the coiling staircase after her. At the bottom of the tower they paused briefly in the doorway until the guard walked past. Then they rushed into the shadows of a corridor which led through the servants' quarters and out of the castle, toward the northern gates of the city.

They failed to notice one living shadow flattened back against a doorway, not breathing until they were past.

When he could no longer hear their footfalls, Fausto emerged from the darkness. The sight of his sister and Ursula had caused the blood to begin roaring in his temples. His lips were dry, his hands wet and cold. His forehead was beaded with sweat. How he longed to follow them! But they were separated from him now by his own lost honor, by a depleted inheritance, and a vow which demanded blood.

He slipped away in the opposite direction, heart beating fast, a dagger strapped to his side, beneath his shirt. He had been to several parties at the castle, and had a good enough idea how to find his way through it. When he encountered a sleepy pageboy in one of the back halls, Fausto said that he had been summoned to report to His Majesty at once, and the boy readily pointed out where Prince Ulisso was to be found

The Devil in Love

– in the luxurious suite of rooms climbing up the southern tower.

At the end of the hallway, Fausto had to wait for the guard to pass. It took so long Fausto wondered if he would have to kill him first to kill the Prince. His fingers were slipping under his shirt toward the sheath of his dagger when the guard moved on. Fausto darted up the staircase, an angel of death intent on the conclusion of his grim mission.

Quick as a cold wind, he bounded up the stairs toward the top of the tower, just as the pageboy had instructed him. Then he opened the last door, and stopped dead in his tracks.

By the light of a cresset outside in the hall, a half-drawn charcoal face of Ursula almost as big as the wall itself looked back at him. No one else but Amalia could have drawn that face on the wall. There before him, being watched by those charcoal eyes, sprawling across the bed in the middle of the room, lay his sister's abductor. Fausto's hand edged beneath the cold silk of his shirt, slipping the dagger out of its sheath.

For a moment only, he hovered over the side of the bed, uncertain whether to plunge it into Ulisso's proud belly, his merciless heart, or his lying throat. At the same moment, as he loomed over the sleeping Prince, on a silent hilltop overlooking the castle and the lake, Agatuzza raised her old arms high into the night sky.

CHAPTER 19
Bells at Midnight

A dull roaring filled the darkness. Dogs looked up and whined in the back alleys of Bolgaro. Horses nickered uneasily in their stables. A mysterious turbulence seemed to be disturbing the night sky, lashing and roiling the clouds, scattering them into fragments. Birds huddled low in their nests, burying their heads under their wings. Then the wind came, rushing out of nowhere. It swept through the grass of the hillside as though intent on ripping it out by the root. Over the city walls, over the rooftops, it howled.

One by one, in that strange, enchanted wind, every one of the bells throughout the city, throughout the kingdom, throughout the land, began to ring. Tolling, bonging, gonging and clanging, without anyone touching them or pulling on their ropes, every bell began to swing and join its voice to a swelling sound which echoed through the sky from one end of the land to the other.

Fausto swayed dizzily. The dagger slipped out of his hand and clattered to the floor, where it spun under the bed. Fausto's eyes sank heavily shut. His knees collapsed. He dropped like a dead man onto the bed, across the body of his intended victim.

The Devil in Love

Every man who heard that sound at once went limp. Instead of being jolted into alarm, they dropped at once into a deep sleep. Every tension drained out of them, every muscle went slack, their legs folded beneath them. Fortunately, since it was midnight, most of them were already in their beds. Those in the *tavernas* slumped over their tables. Some thudded off their benches onto the straw-covered floor. The few men on horseback that night took flying tumbles.

The sound of that mysterious ringing had a very different effect, however, on the women who heard it. They awoke at once to that jangling clamor, but none of them experienced fear or any enchanted drowsiness. Instead, in a calm and orderly frame of mind, every woman began packing up her few most precious belongings, knowing in her heart that her life there among men was irrevocably over, and that a great journey toward a new life lay ahead.

There was no resisting Agatuzza's call. One by one, wives rose up from the arms of their husbands, young women from the hot embraces of the eager young boyfriends. Little girls kissed their sleepy little brothers goodbye. The men moaned and tossed about in bewilderment, thinking they must be dreaming. They rolled over in bed and went back to sleep.

Throughout Bolgaro, the doors began quietly opening and closing, as women and their daughters stepped out into the narrow streets. All of them seemed to know instinctively which way to go. Soon the streets were crowded with a silent

The Devil in Love

army. Women of all ages, with their bundled belongings, began converging on the northern gates of the city. An advance contingent stepped over the sleeping guards in the gatehouse. Soon the gates were groaning open as they let themselves out of Bolgaro, heading north on the old forest road which led to Valbrosa.

When the army of women emigrants arrived there, they found the streets of Valbrosa were also thronging with women leaving their city. They, too, headed north toward the mountains. Far to the northeast, the women of Antichi were already starting out along the banks of the Saluzzo, as they followed it down through the pass. They were joined by the women of Torello. From out of the forest came women from kingdoms so far away or inaccessible that their names were legends – women from Strozzi beyond the marshes, women from the high mountain city of Oppola. From villages and far, scattered farms and vineyards, from every kingdom and cottage between Hell and the White Demon Mountains, came all the women of the land in answer to Agatuzza's summons.

Throughout the night they trekked from their various cities up into the northern hills, leaving all their menfolk asleep behind them.

Ursula and Amalia were no more than two women in the midst of them, swept up in the currents of that angry wish come true. With so much to say to each other, sometimes they both talked at the same time, pressing each other with urgent questions, and at other times, choked with emotion, they both became tongue-tied and were able to say nothing at all, simply clasping each other's hand as they walked along, in a grip that would never again allow itself to be broken.

At last that torrential river of women reached the mountain wall, and the high craggy ledge where Agatuzza stood waiting for them. Ursula and Amalia led the way up a narrow, winding path. The lower slopes of the mountain wall were covered with women. The Witch of the Wild stood before them, with jagged windswept peaks on either side.

Facing the rock cliff above them, Agatuzza raised her skinny arms, and cried, "Open, mother! Show us a better land."

The earth trembled. A crack zigzagged down the rock. The sides of the crack groaned apart. The mountain wall slowly torn open with a horrible wrenching sound, revealing through the jagged doorway a land of gentle hillsides and flower-filled glens, with sun-dappled trees bending over clear, shallow streams, their branches heavy with juicy, ripening fruit. The women's hearts with filled with a quiet elation and hope.

Hand in hand, Ursula and Amalia stepped up to one side of the rocky doorway. They beamed with joy as they watched all those women taking their sisters and daughters by the hand, walking down through the rocky passageway into the new kingdom.

"We'll be happy here," said Ursula, squeezing Amalia's hand. "The way we were in our cottage in the forest."

The Devil in Love

A shadow crept over the land.

The earth began to rumble. Footsteps shook the ground, heavy enough to be a mountain walking. The vast army of women began to stir in alarm, their heads turning this way and that, murmuring, questioning. Dark clouds thickened and clogged the sky. Then the darkness parted, and the Devil stepped forward out of the noisy storm clouds in which he so often enjoyed traveling, smiling broadly, unbearably good-looking. There were screams.

"Did I understand you correctly?" grinned the Devil. "You're conceding to me all of the land between here and Hell?"

"And welcome to it," cackled the Witch of the Wild. "We've had enough of men to last an eternity. We're leaving. It won't matter to us what you do with it."

"But what about all the men you're leaving behind?" he asked.

"All yours," said Agatuzza. "Prince Ulisso, Fausto, and all the other scoundrels – yours to torture as much as you like. Men aren't worth the trouble. They're born with mischief in their souls. Go ahead, play with their lives, trick them, trap them. Do your worst – they deserve it. And for love, since they've always treated women so poorly, let them turn to each other now and see how they like getting it back again."

Agatuzza stepped backward through the door in the mountain wall, and then raised her skinny arms. The jagged cliffs on either side of her began to tremble and slide toward each other.

"Come, my daughters," she said, reaching out a hand toward Ursula and Amalia. "The time has come for us to leave."

The two women stepped through the closing doorway.

For a moment, Ursula turned and looked back through the closing rock doors at the hills and forests she was leaving forever. There stood the Devil, hands on his hips, sunlight streaming down his broad shoulders, looking out over his new kingdom. She hoped someone would find and take care of her vegetable garden.

Then Amalia's hand tugged on hers, drawing her away from the past. Turning her back on the closing door, with Amalia safe by her side at last, Ursula followed the Witch of the Wild down into the new land.

The mountain wall came together with a resounding, rock-grinding roar. There was no longer a doorway. Even the footprints of that departing army had vanished from the dust.

Chapter 20
The Devil's Land

Fausto's eyes snapped open. He blinked. He could not make sense of what he saw. He lay in a gilded bedroom which was not familiar, on top of a handsome young man without any clothes who looked impossibly like Prince Ulisso.

For a flickering moment he thought, "Where's my knife?" He felt a flash of panic. It faded quickly, however, to be replaced by a question, "What knife?" What in the world would he have wanted with a knife in what appeared to be the Prince's bedroom? What, for that matter, was he doing in bed with the Prince?

One of Ulisso's well-shaped thighs was nestled warmly between his own. Ulisso's arms were wrapped around him fondly. One of his hands had burrowed up under Fausto's silk shirt. The other was snug and warm down between Fausto's legs. Prince Ulisso stirred in his sleep, moaning contentedly. He rubbed up closer against whoever happened to be in his bed at the moment, getting his usual morning erection, kissing his bed partner tenderly on the lips.

Then the Prince's eyes blinked open. He looked blankly down into Fausto's handsome face, slightly bewildered, trying to remember his guest's name. Had he ever learned it?

The Devil in Love

"Must have been some party," murmured Ulisso. For one fleeting moment, gazing around him at the blank walls of the room, the Prince felt vaguely as though something were missing. Had there been a third party in bed with them? Then his knee touched Fausto's cold belt buckle.

"Why are your clothes on?" asked the Prince. "I hope you don't think you're leaving."

Fausto didn't put up much of a struggle. It was easy to see why, especially when he undressed. Ulisso had him out of his clothes in no time.

"It's always like this in the morning," said Fausto, with a blush. "I see you have the same condition." There was no concealing their mutual interest. The Prince didn't wait to ask permission. Soon they were both occupied pleasuring each other with a dedication each of them generally reserved only for himself.

Afterward, both of them were ravenous.

"I feel like I haven't eaten for days," complained Ulisso. "Sleeping with you has given me an incredible appetite. By the way – I don't believe we've met."

"Fausto, at your service," said his attractive guest. "I don't have to ask who you are, Your Majesty."

"Have we met before?"

"I would remember, Your Majesty."

"For some reason you look familiar," said the Prince, "like someone I used to know. Do you have a brother?"

The Devil in Love

Fausto hesitated. "No," he said uncertainly, adding, "I don't think so."

The Prince shrugged. "Never mind." He reached for the bell on the wall. When the pageboy arrived, he ordered stuffed game-hens and cannelloni.

They made love until the food came.

By that time, the Devil was there watching them, standing as tall as the southern tower itself, his grinning face filling the window. Neither of them noticed. They were sitting naked on the bed together, their lips and cheeks already red with tomato sauce, attacking the cannelloni like starved wolves.

"Two young men who thoroughly deserve each other," thought the Devil, pleased with himself and smiling wryly. "I think I'm going to become quite fond of these two. Just the kind of powerful men I can rely on to amuse me. Self-indulgent, ruthless, and good-looking."

Leaving Fausto and the Prince to themselves, the Devil drew away from the tower, found himself a comfortable place in the royal gardens, and stretched out among the flowers, kicking off his sandals, folding his hands together behind his head. Luckily there was no one awake yet to see him, for the sight of that tormenting body lounging idly in the early morning sunlight would have driven anyone into a frenzy.

The Devil quickly became lost in thought and began chuckling to himself – never a good sign for the human race. That perverse imagination of his was already whirling with a

The Devil in Love

host of plots and schemes for his new domain, subtle alterations and rearrangements, magic transformations, a cruel experiment or two, and disappearances of all kinds.

"That old witch was more powerful than I thought," he mused. "Well, good riddance! This new arrangement should prove to be quiet interesting. Men will be so much easier to tempt and fool without women around. And I won't be sorry to say goodbye to that old biddy, either. Well now, a land all to myself…"

A grin spread over the Devil's handsome face. "Here things are going to be different," he resolved. "Just the way I want them to be." He began dreaming up one new condition after another, and laughing to himself as he did. No sooner did he conceive of each new change, than the demons of his mind rushed laughing through the land to carry out his commands.

Over the mountains and rivers and forests they flew, swooping down to infest the half-dozen little fortress kingdoms huddling in the wilderness, sweeping away all the evidence and memory that things had ever been different. As soon as they had accomplished their mischief, they returned to the Devil's mind.

Thoroughly satisfied with his new kingdom, the Devil rose up from among the flowers, brushed a few petals off the backs of his legs, and soared up into the sky, where he drew a magic circle completely around the perimeters of his land, so that no one would ever be able to find it. Then, weary from

The Devil in Love

his creative endeavors, he summoned a thunderstorm and travelled home across the morning, to his flaming castle in Hell, where he settled down for a short nap.

Throughout his new domain, from the White Demons in the north to the Infernal Mountains in the south, all the men and boys were just yawning and stretching, getting ready to start another day. None of them noticed that the women were gone. None of them remembered that women had ever been there.

None of them realized that they were waking up that morning as the first inhabitants of the Devil's Land.

*

The Devil in Love

BOOK TWO
SPELLBOUND

CHAPTER 1
Late Knock at the Shoeshop

The old shoemaker grumbled to himself as he hustled about the shop, inspecting the day's work, finishing up the last odds and ends, getting the merchandise ready for tomorrow. Not quite as many shoes repaired as he would have liked, and he knew why. Petroccolo was far from pleased with the recent behavior of his third son. The boy's mind simply wasn't on his work anymore.

"Every time I turn around, he's got his nose in that damned book!" he complained to the half-finished shoes all around him, as he swept the scraps out from under the workbench. When he wasn't sitting at his stool in the shop making shoes with his two older brothers, Noraldo was almost certain to be found hidden away upstairs in the family lodgings, shoulders hunched over a candle, lost in his reading.

"And not a word of truth in the whole book!" groaned Petroccolo. The shoes listened to him in mute amazement, their tongues hanging out in disbelief. "All make-believe nonsense! Wasting his time. Why couldn't he have grown up sensible and practical like his brothers? Where did I go wrong?

Petroccolo knew well enough where he'd gone wrong. He'd sent his son to find that dusty old book of nonsense. If only his dying brother hadn't asked him to search for it. If only his third son had never laid eyes on it!

Noraldo hardly ever set foot outside their door anymore. As soon as he finished his work for the day, up the ladder he scrambled to the floor above, where his book was kept safely tucked away under the blankets of his bed. At meal times, instead of talking with his father and brothers, the book lay open in Noraldo's lap and the boy simply read and chewed. The only way to get him to stop reading at night, when the shoemaker and his brothers were ready to sleep, was the blow out his candle.

Petroccolo finished sweeping, and tossed the scraps and shavings out the door. The piazza outside had grown dark with evening. Shadows were hurrying homeward. Across the way, two torches were already crackling and sputtering outside the doorway of the neighborhood *taverna*, where

The Devil in Love

Noraldo's brothers had gone for a drink before bed. Petroccolo could hear an accordion inside beginning to wheeze out an old familiar tune. It was time to close the shoeshop.

Two long wooden shutters extended horizontally across the length of the shop front, the top one propped into an awning, the bottom one folded downward and serving as a display counter. The old shoemaker closed them both and was just sliding the bolt into place when there was a banging and rapping on the outside.

"Now, who can that be at this time of night?" grumbled Petroccolo. Expecting to find some customer outside with an urgent, last-minute request, he did his best to look exasperated as he re-opened the shop, so that he could charge a higher price. Instead of a customer, however, Petroccolo found himself looking at a smiling young man standing there, cap in hand, who looked vaguely familiar. The shoemaker blinked, squinted, and suddenly recognized the baker's son.

"Filandro!" he cried. "Are my eyes playing tricks? What are you doing back in Valbrosa?"

"I'm your neighbor again," laughed the youth.

"What? Across the piazza?" gasped Petroccolo.

"I've moved home," explained Filandro. "I'm going to be helping Father in the bakery again."

"I didn't even recognize you," cackled the shoemaker. "Come in, come in. What a pleasant surprise. How you've grown! Just look at you!"

The Devil in Love

No sooner had Filandro entered the shoeshop than the old shoemaker embraced him like a son, then held the boy at arm's length and regarded him with a beaming smile. Filandro was a year younger than his own Noraldo, lean and healthy, with fair skin and thick chestnut-colored hair. His face was long and slender, with shy eyes and a sensitive mouth over a strong, handsome jaw. He was at least four inches taller than Petroccolo remembered him, still flat as a board but with broader shoulders now and a little more weight.

He wasn't actually related, although he was like a brother. Technically Noraldo had two older brothers who acted more like uncles and a cousin, Ulisso, that he should have been closer to, and wasn't. His father, the shoemaker, was one of three brothers, the sons of a wealthy merchant. His Uncle Piero had married royalty, which was how his son, Ulisso, had become the young ruler of Bolgaro. His Uncle Pasquino had written down the invented fairytale of their childhood and then run away. Filandro was the closest thing Noraldo had to a brother and a cousin rolled into one. The baker's son had eaten as many of his meals growing up at the shoeshop as at home. The two boys had been almost inseparable.

Over the years, the shoemaker had watched them change from little boys into handsome young men, always standing up for each other, always coming to each other's support. Filandro had been the more energetic of the two, the more outgoing, but also more given over to moodiness and strange, unexplained sulking. He had always been more worldly and experienced than book-loving Noraldo, and for that reason less inclined to be open about his feelings. The two of them were always slipping off alone together, but Petroccolo could remember one New Year's party several years ago when his son and Filandro, transported by the wine out of their usual shyness, had blended their voices together in a drunken song, their arms around each other's shoulders.

"How long has it been?" asked the shoemaker. "Two years?"

"Almost three," said Filandro.

"Impossible!"

"Back when my brother first opened his shop in Torello, the Duke hadn't even taken over yet."

"Has it been that long?"

"Count Guilio was still living in the palace," said Filandro. "I remember how jealous the other bakers were when the Count began ordering his loaves from an outsider."

"And now Duke Federigo has joined us both into one kingdom," said Petroccolo proudly. "What a mighty and clever ruler we are blessed to have!"

"I only hope he had nothing to do with the Count's death," said Filandro skeptically. "There are plenty of rumors in Torello, I can assure you."

"Rubbish!" said the shoemaker. "Of course, he didn't. He didn't need to. The people of Torello *want* Federigo to

The Devil in Love

rule them. One of his own citizens poisoned the Count, believe me. And now, tell me – your brother's bakery? How is it doing?"

"Thriving," smiled Filandro, glad to change the subject. "That's why I'm home. My brother can bake rings around those bakers in Torello. He's hired a couple of apprentices now to take my place. Business is so good that it's all we can do to bake enough loaves every morning. Now that Father is laid up in bed, I've come back to help out with the baking at home."

"I haven't noticed your father around lately, now that you mention it," said Petroccolo. "Nothing serious, I hope."

"His back, again," said the baker's son. "But he seems to be better. Anyway, I don't mind coming home at all. I missed Valbrosa. How have things been with you?"

"Fine, fine," said Petroccolo. "Selling more shoes and boots than ever."

"And Noraldo? How's he?" Filandro couldn't conceal the eagerness in his voice. "I just got back a few hours ago, and I thought I'd surprise him."

"He's upstairs reading," said the shoemaker sadly. "Where did you think he'd be? Some things don't change, they just get worse."

"Reading, eh?" repeated Filandro. "As much as ever?"

"Twice as much." Petroccolo shook his head. "A more impractical boy I've never seen."

The Devil in Love

"But he's always loved books," said Filandro, defending his friend. "That's why he's so smart. He's been reading at the dinner table as long as I've known him."

"Yes, but this is worse. Now it's garbage that he's reading, ridiculous nonsense, fairytales, a complete waste of time. And that's all he ever does anymore. Ever since he came back from my brother's funeral in Bolgaro, he's been lost to the world. If only they hadn't given him that damned book! Yes, yes, go up and surprise him, by all means. Maybe seeing you again will bring him back to reality."

The Devil in Love

CHAPTER 2
Plans and Promises

The rungs of the ladder leading up to the next floor gave so many creaks and groans under Filandro's weight that he was surprised when he reached the top to find his friend still intently hunched over his book, reading. Noraldo hadn't heard a thing: not his friend's voice downstairs, nor the clatter of his feet ascending the ladder. He was staring into the book in fascination. The look in his eyes belonged to another world.

"I hope I'm not interrupting you," said Filandro.

Noraldo looked up with a jerk, startled out of the spell. His eyes widened. Then he and the friend of his childhood were embracing happily.

"You're back!" exclaimed Noraldo. "Am I dreaming?"

"To stay," laughed Filandro.

"Really?"

"Honest. I'm going to be helping Father at the bakery. Just like old times."

"You've got to be kidding. That's too good to be true!" He grabbed Filandro by the shoulders, joyfully shaking him as though to make sure he was solid flesh. "It's really you!"

They talked for an hour without stopping, their arms wrapped around each other's waists, ruffling each other's hair, getting used to the idea that they were really together again.

"Listen," said Filandro at last, "I promised my father I'd go into the forest the day after tomorrow and shoot a couple rabbits for supper. I won't be going far, just the other side of the river. Why don't you come with me? We've got so much to tell each other."

From the look in Noraldo's eyes, Filandro could tell that he had managed to interest his bookish friend.

"I don't enjoy hunting much, though," said Noraldo reluctantly. "Besides, you know I'm not a very good shot."

"I didn't think you were," laughed Filandro. "Leave the hunting to me. You can at least enjoy the fresh air and the scenery. It'll be good for you to get out of Valbrosa. Tell your father you want to spend the day hunting with me, and I'm sure he'll let you go. We'll bring him back a couple of fat rabbits for supper. I'll bake them into a rabbit pie that'll make his mouth water."

"You haven't forgotten the way to my father's heart," smiled Noraldo. "Why don't you ask him yourself tomorrow morning at breakfast? Be over here by dawn. Will you be up by then?"

"Up?" laughed Filandro, punching Noraldo playfully. "A baker gets up earlier than a shoemaker any day of the week. I'll have loaves already in the oven by the time the bell in the tower rings three!"

The Devil in Love

Breakfast was over. Noraldo's brothers had already gone back to their stools at the work-bench. The cat was licking the greasy plates clean in a pool of morning sunlight. Finally Filandro brought up the subject.

"Well, my good neighbor," he said politely to Petroccolo, "I agree with you completely that Noraldo spends too much time reading that book. He needs to get out of the house more, to see what real life is all about."

"My very words!" cried Petroccolo. "But do you think he'll listen to me?"

"Perhaps I can be of service to both you and your son," said Filandro. "Tomorrow morning I'm going hunting in the forest across the river for rabbits to make into pies. Let Noraldo come along with me, and I'll make a couple of extra pies for you and your sons."

"Rabbit pie!" exclaimed Petroccolo. "That sounds positively delicious. But if we have to depend on Noraldo shooting the rabbits, those pies will be nothing but empty crust. His aim with a bow and arrow is so bad that you might be in danger yourself just being near him."

"I promise to watch him carefully," laughed Filandro. "Do you think you can spare him from the shop?"

Petroccolo turned to his third son. "Would you like to go rabbit-hunting with Filandro?"

"Yes, indeed, Father," said Noraldo. "Very much."

The Devil in Love

"Will you promise me to keep your eyes open and do nothing foolish?" said the shoemaker. "Hunting can be dangerous for someone who doesn't know what he's doing."

"I'll keep my eyes open," promised Noraldo.

"Well, if it's something you want to do," said the shoemaker, "I won't stand in your way. As long as Filandro is with you, I know you'll be safe from danger. Whatever you do, don't go wandering off alone and get lost. Never let Filandro out of your sight."

Noraldo laughed. "Really, Father, I'm twenty years old. I'm not a child anymore."

The shoemaker shook his head sadly.

"Someone like you, my boy," said Petroccolo, "with your natural tendency to bungle things, can never be too careful."

Chapter 3
Into the Forest

The next morning, just as dawn was lighting the piazza, Filandro rode up in front of the shoeshop mounted on one of his father's horses and leading another one behind. Noraldo had been watching for him from the upstairs window, but had opened his book on the windowsill to read a few pages before Filandro arrived. He was now so lost in the story that even the clattering of hooves on cobblestones railed to rouse him.

"Have you changed your mind about going?" called Filandro from his horse.

Noraldo looked up with a start. "No, of course not," he said, jumping to his feet and closing the book. "I'll be right down." When he appeared in the street a moment later, however, the large book was tucked under his arm.

"You're not taking that with you?" groaned Filandro in disbelief.

"I thought I would," said Noraldo. "Just in case. Can't I pack it right back here on the saddle?"

Filandro started to protest, but in the end the book went with them.

Out through the gates of Valbrosa they rode, across the bridge over the Saluzzo, and into the forest. Soon the trees had closed around them, until no matter in which direction Noraldo looked, there were only trees and more trees.

Before long Filandro held up a hand for silence, and drew his horse to a stop. At the other end of the glade before them, something small and brown darted from one clump of wild grass into another and froze. An arrow seemed to glide out of Filandro's quiver, notching itself on his bowstring. Then a twang, the whirr of death, a thud, sudden kicking in the tall grass, silence.

With a laugh, Filandro rode across the glade and leaped down from the saddle. A moment later he had tugged his arrow out of the rabbit's body and dropped the bloody mound of fur into his hunting bag.

"There's one pie," he crowed. "Now for pie number two."

Before the sun was directly overhead, Filandro's whistling arrows had accounted for the contents of seven pies. The hunting sack on the back of his horse was wet with blood and heavy with little bodies. Whatever he aimed at was doomed from the moment he saw it. When he tired of rabbits, Filandro began shooting birds. They fell thrashing out of the sky to land at his feet.

"You've got enough now to keep you baking all the rest of the week," said Noraldo. Though he had fired half a dozen arrows himself, the denizens of the forest seemed to have some strange immunity to them, for his arrows struck only air. Noraldo felt that it was just as well. The sight of that

The Devil in Love

bulging, blood-stained bag on the back of Filandro's horse was having a strange effect on him. He was getting dizzy, there was a curious buzzing in his ears, and for some reason he was starting to get an erection.

"Are you about ready to stop and eat something?" asked Filandro. When Noraldo didn't answer, he turned around in the saddle. His friend's face was pale. "Noraldo, are you all right?"

"Just a headache," said Noraldo. "Yes, I think some food and a little wine would be perfect about now. I haven't ridden on a horse this long in years. I'd love to get down on some solid ground again."

They tied their horses to a tree on the edge of a sunlit glade. Across the clearing, a shallow creek rippled in the sun, gurgling over the polished rocks. Filandro unpacked meat pasties and a loaf of nut bread, as well as half a cheese and some of his uncle's wine. They spread a blanket in the sun. While Filandro got the food ready, Noraldo stretched his aching body on the blanket. He groaned with relief.

"Don't die until you've had a chance to taste this nut bread," said Filandro. "As soon as I finish slicing this cheese."

"Do I have time to read a chapter?"

"No," said Filandro firmly. "Sit up and have a drink of this."

The wine restored him, brought the color back to his cheeks. Some of the pasties had slices of sausage inside, some had bits of pepperoni. Filandro was in the best of spirits, overjoyed to be home again, with his best friend again, hunting again in the forest of his childhood. Soon he had Noraldo laughing and drinking freely.

They talked for hours. They relived the past, retold the tales of their old adventures, until the glade was haunted with the ghosts of memory, ringing with the laughter of the two little boys they used to be. They lay with their arms around each other, like the most intimate of brothers.

"I feel like I'm about twelve years old," chuckled Noraldo drunkenly.

"Me, too," said Filandro. His lips were close to Noraldo's ear. He half-whispered, "You feel like doing what we used to do?"

His words caused Noraldo's manhood to begin shifting and growing. "I wouldn't mind, actually," said Noraldo, attempting to sound disinterested. "If you want to."

Filandro's hand slid down past Noraldo's belt. "Feels to me like you're in the mood," he grinned.

"Take a look at your own," said Noraldo defensively.

"That's just its natural size."

"Sure. Well, mine gets big over nothing, sometimes."

"I'll bet," laughed Filandro.

They they both stopped clowning, stopped pretending, as desire flushed their cheeks and their hands began eagerly pulling off each other's clothes.

The Devil in Love

CHAPTER 4
The Black Stag

Abruptly Filandro stopped. His whole body tensed. "Don't move," he whispered. "Listen."

Noraldo heard it, too. The rustling and crackling of leaves. The snap of a brittle twig. Their eyes searched the trees. Filandro pointed. A leafy branch moved slightly, shuddered, and bent aside.

Into the clearing stepped a tall and majestic stag. From his mighty antlers to his hooves, the stag was pure black. The creature looked at them with eyes that were almost human, pawed the ground with one hoof, and then stepped out of sight into the shadows of approaching dusk.

For a moment the sight took their breath away. Then Filandro leaped to his feet, and began scrambling into his clothes. "Come on, quick!" he whispered to Noraldo. "Get dressed. This is the chance of a lifetime." He pulled on his tunic over his head. Seizing his bow and arrows, he began loping quietly across the glade.

"But, Filandro," objected his naked friend. "It's getting dark. We should be starting for home."

"Let me try one shot at him, or I'll kick myself for the rest of my life," Filandro whispered back to him. "You stay here then. You're not even dressed yet. Just one arrow, and I'll come right back."

With that, Filandro slipped away into the trees.

Noraldo found himself standing naked and alone in the forest glade. He hugged himself, shivering with the chill of approaching twilight, and began to hunt around for his clothes. He tried to remember which direction they had come from. "Valbrosa must be somewhere over that way," he thought, trying to feel more certain than he was. "I should pay better attention. When Filandro gets back, I've got to remember to ask him."

He brushed off his clothes, shaking off the burrs and twigs and bits of dead leaves. Noraldo had almost finished dressing, and was looking around for his belt, when he happened to glance up and found himself standing less than three feet away from the black stag, looking directly into the creature's eyes.

Filandro was nowhere in sight.

Those intelligent black eyes regarded him silently. Something in them beckoned him, urged him to follow. The stag went off a few steps into the trees, and then looked back to see if Noraldo was coming. Another glance into those eyes, and Noraldo could no longer resist. His feet followed after the stag of their own accord. He didn't even think about reaching for his bow and arrows, for he would never have been able to fire at such a creature. First one step, and then another. He left the safety of the glade behind. He only hoped that Filandro wouldn't mistake him for the stag, and send an arrow thudding into his chest.

Like a phantom, the stag bounded ahead of him. Whenever he had just about caught up with it, away it leaped into the trees, its every movement a perfect balance of muscle and grace. Noraldo never let it get out of sight. As soon as he came within touching distance, the black beast would toss its head and then bound away – but only a short distance, always turning back, always pawing the ground impatiently with its hoof, waiting just long enough, until Noraldo's outstretched arms could almost reach it, only to bolt away deeper into the forest. Noraldo became so intent on catching the stag that he didn't pay attention to where he was going. When the stag abruptly disappeared, he found himself gasping for breath in a completely unfamiliar part of the forest, without friend or horse.

That brought him to his senses.

Noraldo stood there alone amid the dark branches, and a shudder of fear went through his whole body. "What in the world am I doing?" he thought to himself desperately. "Have I gone mad?"

An invisible owl hooted at him out of the shadows.

"Filandro!" he shouted. "Filandro, I'm over here!"

Not even an echo answered him.

There was still a light burning in the shoeshop, though the piazza was black with night and the bell in the tower had long ago tolled midnight. No matter how slowly Filandro walked across the cobblestones toward that flickering light, he knew he would get there too soon. His head hung dejectedly. His shoulders slumped as though he had been whipped.

He had already returned the horses to their stable, and had stopped home at the bakery just long enough to reassure his own father, leaving there both his bulging game-bag and Noraldo's book. How lonely that book looked without his cousin clutching it! How Filandro wished there was something else that needed doing, so that he could postpone indefinitely the delivery of his unhappy news to Noraldo's waiting father.

Petroccolo opened the door before Filandro even had a chance to knock. "You're so late!" scolded the shoemaker. "Really, I…" His features suddenly fell slack with fear. "Where is he? Filandro, tell me what's happened!" Petroccolo practically dragged him into the shoeshop.

There the exhausted baker's son spilled out the whole story piece by piece without any preamble, half of it out of sequence, most of it incoherent with grief. Petroccolo listened in horror.

"Once I lost track of the stag," said Filandro, "I went back to where I'd left Noraldo. His horse and his book were there, but not him. I shouted his name, but he must not have heard me. I've been searching for him for hours. I came back just long enough to tell you and my father what happened.

The Devil in Love

I'm going back out into the forest first thing tomorrow morning. I won't stop searching until I find him."

"Noraldo!" wept the shoemaker. "My poor boy!" He sank down onto his stool at the work-bench, and covered his face with his hands. "He'll never survive the night."

Chapter 5
The Mysterious Palace

Noraldo was crying as he felt his way through the darkness. There was no one in the forest to see him, and even if there had been, it was too dark to see anything anyway. The tears ran openly down his face as he slowly made his way from tree to tree. Why bother to hold them back? He'd never been more afraid in his life.

There was a sudden, sharp pain in his knee. His legs were knocked out from under him. He fell sprawling amid the roots and dead leaves. His heart hammered wildly. He dared not move. Then he saw from the ground what he hadn't noticed standing up – the thick root of a fallen tree projecting across his path. Noraldo picked himself up, brushed off his clothes. He sat on the dead tree-trunk. He cried a little more.

He was wiping his eyes on his sleeve when what he had taken as a low star in the night sky flickered strangely, and he realized it was not a star at all. Noraldo rose slowly to his feet. The light came from far off, and appeared to be some kind of house on fire up in the hills.

Noraldo at once began making his way toward the light. There, at least, he was sure to find other men, and directions on how to find his way out of the forest.

The closer he got, however, the less certain he was that the dwelling was actually burning. The light was unusually bright and seemed to surround the house in a kind of nimbus, shimmering unsteadily, almost as though the walls were studded with gems. This enchanted glow seemed to emanate from the very walls themselves.

Rays of light sifted toward him through the branches. He stepped into the blazing clearing. Noraldo's feet stopped. There could be no denying what he saw, and yet it was impossible. The most beautiful, breathtakingly elaborate palace he had ever seen or dreamed of stood before him, utterly alone in the midst of the wilderness, far from any other human habitation, gleaming with some kind of hovering, magical aura, a radiance like moonlight.

The two front doors of that elegant palace hung open. There wasn't a single guard in sight, or any sign of human life. The palace almost seemed to float there, not constructed of solid rock but of spells and mist.

Slowly, fearfully, Noraldo approached the palace, peering around him on all sides, listening for the faintest noise. He walked up to the vast marble staircase which mounted toward the columns of the entranceway. The stairs glowed. He hesitantly set one foot down on the lowest stair, and then quickly drew it back. But there was no pain, and it felt solid. Taking a deep breath, Noraldo set one foot to following after the other and ascended the mighty staircase.

At the top of the stairs he stopped between two columns, facing the open portals. The palace was still silent. Not once had he heard the slightest sound of human habitation. "Perhaps they all died of the plague," thought Noraldo gloomily. He stepped up to the threshold. He sniffed the air inside. Far from smelling like rotting corpses, there was a fragrance of flowers, faint but intoxicating.

"Anybody home?" Noraldo called into the palace doorway. "Excuse me, but I've lost my way in the forest..."

There was no answer. The palace had the gloomy hush of a tomb.

"Fine," Noraldo thought to himself bleakly. "I'm certainly not going to get much help here. Might as well turn around right now and try someplace else."

Instead of turning around and heading back down the stairs, however, Noraldo timidly put one foot inside, hesitated only a moment, and then stepped all the way through, half-expecting some hidden mechanism to suddenly be activated, a portcullis to drop out of nowhere, the floor to drop away beneath him. But nothing happened. His footsteps echoed hollowly down the column-lined entranceway.

Something moved in the room at the end. There was a shift in the light. A crackling sound.

The Devil in Love

"Hello?" called Noraldo. "Is anyone there?"

No one answered.

With his heart pounding, Noraldo stepped into the doorway of the central chamber. Flames were snapping and leaping in the fireplace. Torches were lit on the walls. There were two comfortable-looking chairs before the fire, with a bowl of fresh fruit between them, as well as two glasses and wine. But no sign of a living host.

After his hardships in the forest, Noraldo didn't hesitate long before plucking a few grapes out of the bowl. Then he sank down into one of the chairs. It was even more comfortable than it looked. He put his feet up on the hearthstone and sighed. He stretched his toes, warming up nicely. He had a sip of wine. It was delicious. Noraldo abandoned all hesitation and poured himself a full glass.

"A toast to my invisible host," he said, raising his glass to the fire. "Thank you for everything a man could desire, except for human company. Well, you can't have everything. My heartfelt gratitude."

Noraldo drank. No one appeared.

"Could there possibly be a party tonight at someone else's castle?" he thought. "Or maybe they all go to bed early here. Well, it's certainly better than spending the night in the forest. Too bad I don't have my book with me."

Vaguely perplexed, Noraldo's curiosity at last overcame his reluctance to intrude upon someone else's home. "If he doesn't want visitors, he shouldn't leave his doors open,"

The Devil in Love

Noraldo reasoned. "He won't mind if I just take a peek inside."

He finished his wine, set the empty glass back down on the fruit table, and walked to the other end of the hallway. His footsteps seemed to echo. A double door opened into an exquisite dining-hall. The table in the middle of the gleaming chamber was lit by candlelight and set for two. He took a step closer to look at the candles. They hadn't been burning for long.

"Someone is obviously here, and yet he's hiding from me," thought Noraldo. "How very odd."

Never had Noraldo seen such costly finery. The handles of the knives were studded with pearls. The plates were made of silver, the goblets of gold. The candelabra and the chandeliers were of breathtaking detail and craftsmanship. The tablecloth was embroidered with gems. While in steaming platters down the middle of the table waited a row of covered platters. He lifted their lids, one by one, releasing a banquet of appetizing smells fit for a king – lasagna, raviolis, soups and salads, elaborate desserts of every description.

Not until then had Noraldo realized how very hungry he was. "Just look at this feast!" he exclaimed in wonder. "Hot and ready to be eaten. If only my host would arrive, so that we could begin."

Noraldo folded his hands behind his back and paced the dining-hall, tormented by mouth-watering aromas. Finally he

The Devil in Love

could hold himself back no longer. Drawing out one of the chairs, he picked up a golden plate and began serving himself hearty portions, scooping some from every platter, until his plate was filled to the edge. Then he sat down, tucked his silk napkin into his collar, and picked up a juicy chicken leg with his fingers.

The moment his mouth closed on the first bite, he heard the unmistakable sound of approaching footsteps.

The Devil in Love

Chapter 6
The Invisible Guest

Into the glittering dining-hall walked a well put-together young man dressed entirely in black, wearing a black leather mask. He was followed by two attractive boys of sixteen who were exchanging smiles with each other behind his back, smothering their rude giggles, making obscene gestures and otherwise scarcely repressing their snickering mirth. One of the boys was dressed in gold, the other in blue, and they were pretending to be his servants.

Noraldo at once stood up, his mouth full, nearly overturning his chair in an awkward rush to apologize.

"Please forgive me," he begged. "How rude of me to just sit down and help myself! I was lost in the forest, you see, and then I saw your light, I called but no one answered, and then…"

Not one of the three was paying him the slightest bit of attention. Without even deigning to look in his direction, they walked around to the other side of the table. Noraldo was flabbergasted. He had to remember to close his mouth. They were rudely pretending he wasn't there. Were they going to punish his forwardness by ignoring him?

The boy dressed in gold drew back the remaining chair, and the lean, black-clad figure sat down facing Noraldo. Eyes peering out of the slits in the mask stared as though they could see right through him.

The gold-clad boy began to serve the man in black.

"Thank you, Griffone," said a melancholy voice from inside the mask. He sounded educated, cultivated, civilized and young. "That's enough. More than enough."

"Wine, Your Grace?" asked the boy in blue, raising the decanter.

"Not tonight, Soranzo," said the youth in the mask.

"I hope I'm not intruding…" began Noraldo. But how could he have intruded, when no one was paying him the slightest bit of attention? Slowly he sank back down into his chair, thoroughly confused.

The boy in blue still held out the decanter. "Perhaps wine would ease your unhappiness, my Prince?"

"Who said I was unhappy?" replied the masked youth bitterly. "It's none of your business, Soranzo, how happy I am."

Though their master was obviously angry, the two servants were hard-pressed to restrain their giggles. The black leather mask turned away from them in contempt. The mysterious Prince began eating by lifting the food up under the mask.

"Leave him alone, Soranzo," said the boy in gold.

Soranzo rolled his eyes upward in mock despair. "Imagine being unhappy if you had all of this?" His extended arms included banquet, chandeliers, dining-hall, palace. "Some would call it ingratitude."

"Some," said Griffone, "would call it loneliness."

The masked Prince looked up in exasperation from his meal. "How could anyone be lonely," said the bitter voice behind the mask, "stuck here with the two of you for company?"

Soranzo guffawed.

"Lonely for your own kind," said Griffone, gently but with an unsettling smile. For one split second, Noraldo thought he caught Griffone looking right at him, winking. Noraldo looked again, and realized he had imagined it.

The voice from behind the mask was sad, indeed. "None of my own kind will ever find me here, that's for sure."

"Not if Vernaccio can help it," said Soranzo.

Both boys seemed to find the very mention of Vernaccio so amusing that they were immediately convulsed with silent laughter, clutching their sides and nearly doubling over with merriment. The Prince ignored them, and continued eating. The two servants wiped the tears from their eyes, and continued to attend him, winking and grinning at each other behind the Prince's chair.

Noraldo could make little of the entire conversation, though he paid attention to every word. The meal and the discussion, however, had come to an end. The Prince finished a last mouthful, pushed the remaining food about his plate nervously for a moment, and then rose to his feet.

The Devil in Love

Griffone was quick to draw back his chair. Noraldo wiped his mouth and was halfway to his feet, but no one noticed. The masked Prince walked out the door, followed by his two mysterious servants. Left alone at the table, Noraldo slowly sank back down into his seat, listening to their footsteps fade away.

He was dumbfounded by the strange behavior of his host. He would have immediately dismissed the entire occurrence as a dream, as some kind of madness brought on by the wine and his own recent terrors in the forest, had the irrefutable evidence not been staring him in the face – the Prince's half-finished meal in his plate, across a table littered with very real leftovers and very real bones.

"If I weren't getting so sleepy from this wine," thought Noraldo, "I'd be able to make more sense out of all this. Well, at least I certainly don't seem to be disturbing anyone by my presence here."

That much was reassuring. Noraldo would have hated to go back out into the forest in the middle of the night. "Since nobody seems to mind," he resolved, "I might as well find myself some reasonably comfortable corner where I can sleep until morning."

He wiped his mouth on the exquisite silk napkin and walked out the doors at the end of the dining-hall, heading deeper into the palace.

The Devil in Love

Chapter 7
"His Bed or Mine?"

Across a short corridor with a fountain sparkling in its center, Noraldo entered a chamber filled with harps, lutes, and musical instruments of all kinds. Beyond that opened an interior garden, lit with lanterns hung from the branches of lovely trees. Noraldo had never seen trees like those before, nor such immaculate banks of blossoming flowers. It would have taken an army of gardeners working day and night to maintain them, yet there was no one in sight. Marble stairs led down to a sunken, ivy-rimmed pool of water, so clear Noraldo could see the green and black tiles at the bottom. Beyond the luxurious bath stretched a gallery hung with masterpieces in gilded frames, all of them featuring naked youths in a variety of erotic poses depicting mythological scenes.

At the end of the corridor of paintings waited an open door.

Noraldo entered, to find himself in a bed-chamber more splendid than any he had ever imagined. A fire was lit in the hearth, and the covers had been folded back, lying open and ready. Noraldo's heart melted when he saw that bed. "How soft and comfortable that looks!" he thought. "I wonder, is it supposed to be his bed or mine? Well, I'm certainly not going to just invite myself, like I did at supper."

For what seemed like an hour, Noraldo wandered about the bedroom, warming himself by the fire, waiting courteously to make sure he wasn't taking someone else's bed. But there was no sign of the masked Prince, nor of anyone else. Noraldo was nodding by the hearth, and about to roll over onto the carpet and fall asleep, when his own drowsiness finally convinced him that the bed was intended to be his.

With a yawn he scrambled to his feet and began tugging off his clothes, which he dropped by the bedside. Then he slid his weary nakedness between the smooth, clean linen and drew the blankets snugly over him. Noraldo sighed with contentment. How much nicer that was than spending the night up in the branches of some tree in the forest!

As though he were getting ready to hibernate there all winter, Noraldo cuddled the blankets and pillows around him and with a sigh closed his eyes. He seemed to be falling asleep in the depths of a warm, fragrant cloud.

He heard a click across the room, too sharp and fine to be an ember in the fireplace. Noraldo's eyes blinked open. He lifted his head out of the blankets.

A secret door had swung open in the wall where there had been no door before. Shadows were entering the room. Noraldo sat up in bed, his mouth falling open. The masked Prince was looking straight into his eyes, without seeing him.

The Devil in Love

The two mocking boys who served him were right behind him. Griffone quietly closed the secret door. The wall appeared to become solid once again.

Noraldo desperately eyed his clothes scattered about the floor. He was on the verge of leaping out of bed and lunging for them, but neither the Prince nor his servants acted surprised to see him there, nor did he appear to be interrupting them in the least.

"Another night alone," sighed the masked Prince.

The two boys began to undress him.

With each garment they removed, Noraldo's eyes grew wider. The Prince's body was not simply attractive, not merely good-looking. It was a vision of human beauty, of such perfection that no single part of him was less than flawless. He was perhaps a year or two younger than Noraldo, satin-smooth skin over new, untested muscles, a statue come to life, the warm clay only just shaped by the hand of a master.

At last he stood by the bed wearing nothing but the black leather mask. That, however, the two boys did not remove.

Soranzo drew back the covers. There lay Noraldo, wearing nothing but a guilty blush.

The Prince lay down beside him, sliding up next to him as though he weren't there. Soranzo drew the covers over the two of them. Silently laughing, the servant boys left the bedchamber, opening and closing the secret door in the wall in the blink of an eye, leaving no trace of a door behind.

The Devil in Love

Noraldo was too amazed to budge.

"Surely, now at last, he'll have to say something," he thought. "He must feel me lying next to him. Besides, he can't possibly intend to sleep with that mask on." But if the Prince had anything to say, it was not forthcoming.

How Noraldo longed to snuggle up closer, to embrace that irresistible nakedness beside him! Hesitantly he slid one hand across the Prince's belly. It rose and fell beneath his palm with peaceful regularity. Too peaceful. Noraldo looked into the slits of the leather mask. The Prince's eyes were closed. He was lost in the depths of sleep.

"What?" thought Noraldo, doubting his own mind. "How could he have fallen asleep already? Is it possible I'm not really here? Could I have died in the forest?" How his fingers longed to end the mystery once and for all, to tear away that damned leather mask!

But while he lay there trying to get up the nerve to break his own spell of fear, to embrace the sleeping Prince, to roll over on top of him and ravish every tantalizing inch of that body, the wine at last overcame Noraldo and he fell into a deep slumber.

Chapter 8
Spellbound

He was awakened by the click of the secret door. The next thing he knew, the two servant boys were grinning beside the bed.

"It's dawn, Your Grace," said Griffone, folding back the covers. The moment the Prince was laid bare, his eyes blinked open inside the leather slits. He yawned, stretched, and rose up from the bed as though he'd been sleeping alone.

Propping himself up on one elbow, Noraldo watched from the bed in mute admiration as the two servants dressed the Prince in a whole new wardrobe. Then, without one of them giving a backward glance at the bed, the three of them went back out through the secret door and closed it behind them.

No sooner were they out of the room than Noraldo jumped out of bed and ran barefoot across the carpets to the place in the wall where they had disappeared. The door was no longer there. His fingers clawed the wall, trying to find a crack. There was none.

With a sigh of exasperation, Noraldo gave up his search and began picking up his dirty clothes off the floor and putting them on again. Dreading to find himself locked in, he approached the door by which he'd entered, but it opened without any difficulty.

Back he went again down that long gallery of masterpieces, past the sunken bath and through the lush gardens, no longer lit by lanterns but by the first touch of day. Through the music-room and beyond the splashing fountain, Noraldo re-entered the lavish dining-hall. A sumptuous breakfast was spread on the table before him, steaming, filling the room with delicious smells. The table was set for only one.

This time Noraldo didn't waste a moment hesitating. "No one seems to see me, anyway," he thought. "Might as well help myself."

No one joined him. He finished, and then lingered by the fire in the hallway to thank his mysterious host before departing. The masked Prince failed to appear. Noraldo's patience came to an end, and was replaced by curiosity. He went in search of him. Down one hallway after another he wandered, through chambers of breathtaking treasures. Not a single person did he discover. The Prince and his two young men-in-waiting were nowhere to be found.

Completely baffled by the whole experience, Noraldo at last gave up. With a sigh and a shrug of his shoulders, he walked out of the deserted palace and back into the depths of the forest, determined to find his way back to Valbrosa.

By the time the sun was directly overhead, Noraldo admitted to himself that he was even more lost than before.

The Devil in Love

How in the world could he have strayed so far from the right path? He began calling for Filandro, shouting his friend's name so that it rang through the trees. No one answered. If only he could find his own abandoned horse, with his beloved book in the saddle-bag! He found nothing. The trees seemed to be moving, so that it was impossible to find his way out of them. He found himself passing by the same landmarks over and over again.

The shadows began to lengthen. Noraldo's pace became more desperate. "I'm running in circles," he groaned. Twilight settled over the forest. Just as it was becoming too dark to see any longer, he noticed a familiar, shuddering light up ahead.

Noraldo felt a sudden chill. His entire day of searching had led him right back to where he'd started. Cautiously he drew closer, until he was parting branches on the edge of the clearing. The ghostly apparition of that silent, glowing palace seemed to float before him, filling the glade with its otherworldly radiance.

Those walls now seemed almost alive, intelligent, as though they were watching him, drawing him back. Noraldo whimpered in dread. But he was more afraid of wandering aimlessly through the forest in the dark. Besides, how could he forget the sight of the masked Prince standing naked by the side of the bed? The erotic longing that began to burn inside him heated his cold skin, beading his forehead with sweat.

The Devil in Love

One foot after another led him up those glowing stairs. Just as before, the palace doors yawned open. Just as before, there was no living person in sight. Without calling this time, knowing that no one would answer, Noraldo stepped through the doorway.

His footsteps echoed hollowly on the marble slabs. He crossed the entranceway. Beyond the shimmering columns he detected the subtle difference of firelight. The comfortable chairs and the bowl of fruit were just as he had found them the night before. The glasses and wine were waiting for him. He downed a quick glass to steady his nerves, and then half of another.

He entered the dining-hall. The platters were steaming, heaped with succulent fare. The table was set for two. The moment he sat down, he heard the approach of footsteps. His heart began hammering wildly. Toward him walked the masked Prince, dressed all in black, with his two servants following behind him, one in gold, one in blue.

"Hello, again," said Noraldo. "Remember me?"

He wasn't surprised when no one answered him.

The boy in gold drew out the remaining chair. The Prince sat down across from Noraldo. The boy began to serve him.

"Thank you, Griffone," said the Prince. "That's enough. More than enough."

"Wine, Your Grace?" asked Soranzo, lifting the decanter toward him.

"Not tonight…"

The Devil in Love

"Perhaps wine would ease your unhappiness, my Prince."

"Who said I was unhappy? It's none of your business, Soranzo, how happy I am."

Noraldo felt as though he had stepped into yesterday, as though somehow tonight had been transformed into last night all over again. Part of him wanted to leap up from his chair and flee for his life into the forest. He'd be safer out there than in that haunted palace. The other part of him tried desperately to rationalize.

"Well," he thought frantically, "people sometimes become very set in their ways." Meanwhile, every word that had been said the night before was repeated, so that Noraldo seriously wondered whether he had fallen asleep at the table last night and was still sitting there dreaming.

Though he knew in advance that it would be useless, for the sake of his sanity Noraldo tried to interrupt. "Thank you very much for your hospitality," he said loudly. His host not only failed to hear him, but apparently did not see him, either. Soranzo and Griffone were continuing in their prankish laughter, but there was no telling what they were laughing at.

Noraldo pinched himself. He slapped himself across the face. He felt his arms and legs to make sure he had not become invisible. He was still solid, still very much there.

"Then I've gone mad!" he concluded desperately. He tried to get a hold on himself. "Or can it possibly be that he's just used to eating alone every night?" Nervously, Noraldo

The Devil in Love

helped himself to some pasta. As he did so, he said loudly, in a voice that struggled to keep steady, "I hope you don't mind if I spend the night again. I can't seem to find my way out of this forest."

In answer, the Prince wiped his mouth with his napkin and rose to his feet. Griffone drew back his chair. Without so much as a glance in Noraldo's direction, the masked Prince walked out of the dining-hall, accompanied by his two snickering servants.

Noraldo jumped up from the table and ran out of the dining-hall after them. They were gone. He went gloomily back to the table, alone now with the remains of the feast. He finished his goblet of wine, and then another.

"What inexplicable behavior!" he thought. "If I hadn't felt his body beside me in bed last night, I'd swear he was a ghost." His mind scrambled in any direction which seemed to lead to an answer. It was a palace of dead ends. None of it made any sense.

Noraldo yawned and finished his wine, then rose to his feet. The floor tipped beneath him. His chair clattered over behind him.

"Well, I can tell you one thing that's not going to be the same," he said out loud to the walls. "This time if he climbs into bed with me, I'm not going to just lie there like a log. Once may be a whim, but twice is an invitation."

Chapter 9
Saved

Past the fountain he strode, his shoulders squared with a confidence he owed half to the wine and half to sheer bluff. On through the music-room he went, through the fragrant starlit gardens, under the bobbing lanterns, beyond the sunken bath, down the corridor of erotic paintings, toward the room at the end of the hall.

The door was open, as it had been before. The bed was turned down, looking just as soft and inviting. A fire crackled cozily in the hearth. Noraldo pulled off his clothes. No sooner was he comfortable in bed than the secret door opened once again. The masked Prince walked toward the bed, followed by his two servants. While Noraldo watched breathlessly, his heart thudding in his chest, they undressed the Prince until he was wearing nothing but the leather mask.

This time, however, there was one significant difference.

Noraldo stared wide-eyed, unable to believe what he was seeing. While everything else about the Prince seemed oblivious to Noraldo's presence in his bed, one part of him was no longer capable of deception.

Noraldo's amazement and exhilaration at the sight left him at once in the same condition. Then Griffone reached forward and drew back the covers, and the Prince climbed into bed beside him. Soranzo drew the covers up over them both, and the servants left the chamber.

For one tense, electrifying moment, Noraldo and the Prince both lay there side-by-side, each of them in a condition of aching excitement.

Then Noraldo rolled over on his side and eased up against him, cautiously slid one of his legs between the Prince's, and when his masked host made no attempt to push him away, took the Prince in his arms, and overcome with desire began covering his delectable body with kisses. The Prince didn't respond. His body was numb to Noraldo's lovemaking. His arms hung heavily, as though he were suddenly drugged. Through the slits of the leather mask, Noraldo saw what he feared. The Prince's eyes were already closed in a deep and senseless sleep. The Prince's manhood, only a moment before in a state of urgency, was already beginning to lose interest. His body had gone limp, his mouth hung open.

Noraldo tried to revive him, but only became more sleepy himself as he did so. Kissing the Prince's lips was like kissing a dead man. Halfway through the kiss, Noraldo fell asleep.

When he awoke, the bed beside him was empty.

Morning sunlight was streaming into the room. Noraldo leaped out of bed and pulled on his torn and soiled clothes. Down the gallery he ran without seeing the paintings, through the gardens without noticing the flowers. He flung open the door to the dining-hall. Breakfast was waiting for him. The table was set for one. The food was still hot.

Noraldo ran calling through the palace. There was no answer, no sign of life. He begged the Prince to stop torturing him. Only his own cries echoed back to him. Like a mausoleum guarding its dead, the palace refused to give up its secret. With a sob of despair, Noraldo ran down the column-lined entranceway and out the palace doors, down the glowing stairs, shouting frantically, hoarsely, into the trees.

That was how Filandro found him in the forest, scratched and soiled – babbling, calling, not making much sense of any kind. When Noraldo saw his friend standing there before him, he stopped in his tracks, gasping, blinking. It was as though he no longer recognized Filandro. Then he burst into tears.

Filandro embraced him, unable to bring him any comfort. "I've been looking for you, Noraldo, for the last three days. I'm here now. There's no need to worry anymore. Take it easy. Everything's going to be all right."

Unfortunately, Noraldo knew that everything wasn't.

Filandro tried to reassure him, in vain. Noraldo wept as though his heart were breaking. Filandro held him, begging him to tell why he was crying. Noraldo couldn't say. His lips tried to shape the words, but his mouth wouldn't supply any sounds. What he managed to choke out didn't make sense.

The Devil in Love

Helping Noraldo up onto the saddle of the spare horse, Filandro took the reins and led his friend slowly out of the forest back toward Valbrosa.

After a mile or so, Noraldo regained control of himself. Soon he could speak coherently on subjects like the weather and the forest around him. Finally he even dared to ask about his book. When Filandro assured him it was safe at home, Noraldo cast in his friend's direction a sad but hopeful smile.

Any mention of what happened to him in the forest, however, even the vaguest reference, brought that agonized look of confusion back into his eyes. Filandro stopped questioning him.

Outside the gates of the city, with the seven towers of the Duke's castle gleaming in the sun above him, Noraldo brought up the painful subject himself, on the condition that it be the last time they ever mentioned it.

"I owe you an explanation," he said to his best friend, "but I'm not sure what happened to me out there." His voice was tentative, insecure. "It was like a nightmare, and then it all happened over again. I don't know what was real. It scares me when I think about it. I found a place to spend the night, but I don't know whether it was real. I met someone, but maybe I didn't, and maybe he helped me, or maybe he didn't." Noraldo started crying. "I only know one thing – I don't want to ever think about it again. The sooner I forget about it, the better."

The Devil in Love

They said goodbye to each other in the narrow cobbled street beside the house on the piazza. Noraldo went in and closed the door, without looking back.

He tried to immerse himself in his old life again, stitching shoes in his father's shoeshop. He didn't entirely succeed. For the first few days he was easily distracted, trailing off in the middle of sentences, forgetting what he was looking for. After a while, he appeared to be recovering, but he never quite became again the same son that Petroccolo had lost.

Filandro stopped over most afternoons after finishing work at the bakery. Noraldo seemed fine, he seemed recovered, he was just distracted, unfocused.

Noraldo's gaze now had a habit of drifting away toward the nearest window, vacantly staring into space. He was too often daydreaming when he was supposed to be sewing leather. Needle in hand, he would forget about the shoe he was holding. His eyebrows would lower in a pensive scowl as he stared out the window and down the street, in the direction of that mysterious forest beyond the city walls, wondering what the secret could possibly be of the masked Prince and his two annoying servants in that lovely deserted palace.

He revealed his tortured thoughts to no one.

Chapter 10
"What Really Happened?"

"Noraldo, you're just staring at your needle again," barked the shoemaker, who'd finally had enough. "The cat could have sewed more shoes today than you have."

"I'm sorry, Father," said Noraldo with a blush, quickly setting his needle back to work again. "I don't know what I'm thinking about. I – I didn't sleep well last night."

"Nor the night before," thought the old shoemaker, but he didn't say anything. It was beginning to grow dark outside, anyway. "Go get some sleep, then," said Petroccolo out loud. "No more daydreaming tomorrow"

"Yes, Father," said Noraldo. "I'm sorry. I'll do better. You'll see."

"Not likely," thought Petroccolo gloomily.

A moment later the shoemaker heard his youngest son's obedient footsteps on the ladder leading up to his room. The shoemaker regretted his harsh words. He was plainly worried about his third boy, more so than usual. What was happening to him? Sweeping and setting the shop in order, Petroccolo was startled out of his fatherly ponderings by a rapping on the door behind him.

"Anybody home?" called Filandro from the doorway.

The Devil in Love

"Come in, come in," said the shoemaker. "Where have you been these last few days?"

"To tell you the truth," said Filandro sadly, "I've been keeping to myself. Noraldo doesn't make me feel very welcome. I don't know how to describe it exactly. His mind is somewhere else."

"That's exactly what it is!" said Petroccolo. "You've noticed it, too. Noraldo is becoming stranger with every day that passes. Ever since he was lost on that hunting trip with you, he hasn't been able to put his mind to anything. Filandro, you've got to tell me. What really happened to him out there?"

"You know as well as I do what he told us," said Filandro.

"I don't believe a word of it," replied the shoemaker. "There's something he's not telling. What could he be hiding? Whatever it is, he can't get it out of his mind, and he's not going to get any better until he talks about it. See if you can't get him to tell you, Filandro. Maybe he'll open up to you."

"If I find out anything, I'll let you know."

Noraldo hadn't gone to bed, as his father thought. He was lost in his usual melancholy fog, daydreaming by the upstairs window. Though his book lay open in front of him, he was staring out into the darkening piazza, and beyond. He looked up with a start.

"Filandro! I didn't hear you come in."

The Devil in Love

"I'm not surprised," said his friend, approaching him. "You were a million miles away." Filandro sat down beside him on the bed in front of the window, and closed Noraldo's book. "Now when are you going to tell me what really happened to you out there in the forest?"

"What are you talking about?" said Noraldo uncomfortably.

"You know very well what I'm talking about."

"But I already told you that..."

"I know you don't want to talk about it, but..."

"I don't even want to *think* about it!"

"But that's all you do!" exclaimed Filandro. "Night and day, you can't *stop* thinking about it."

Noraldo opened his mouth to argue, but could think of no defense. It was too painfully true.

"Now, tell me what happened," said Filandro. He put his arm around his friend's shoulders. "I care about you deeply, Noraldo. More than you know. I feel responsible. If only I hadn't run off after that stag! Please trust me enough to confide in me."

Noraldo could hold back no longer. It all came pouring out at once, in a torrent of pain, racked with sobs of doubt. "Maybe I'm going mad. Maybe it didn't happen. The second night was the same as the first, so I suppose I could have been dreaming. Nobody could see me. I was invisible. That sounds like a dream, doesn't it? They looked right through me, Filandro. Like I wasn't there. And maybe I wasn't. Except that…" He kept remembering that one exception on the second night, that one unbribable witness to his presence, with its silent, outspoken testimony. "But he was laying right next to me, touching me, and he couldn't feel me. The most beautiful creature I've ever seen…"

"The stag?" interrupted Filandro.

"No, not the stag," said Noraldo in exasperation. "I'm not talking about a stag. The Prince. The Prince with the leather mask."

"The what? Wait! Start at the beginning."

Filandro made him go back, back to their drunken lovemaking in the forest, their sleep in each other's arms before the arrival of the black stag. Noraldo relived it all. Once again he walked through the echoing halls of that spellbound palace, from room to room, unseen. Now that he had tapped all the pain bottled up in his heart, the words spilled out of him almost faster than he could say them. He left nothing out. His voice faltered as he tried to describe the Prince.

"I can't hide it. I'm in love with him. He's all I can think about. Day and night. Those eyes, looking through that leather mask. That splendid body. Every night I ache to be holding him in my arms, Filandro, and I don't even know his name, I've never seen his face. I don't think I could possibly find my way back there, yet that's all I want – to get him to break his silence, to return this passion that's eating me alive."

The Devil in Love

Unfortunately, Noraldo had become so intent now on spilling all the details and tortured emotions of his story that he failed to notice the effect he was having on Filandro. His friend's face had become haggard, as though he'd just seen a ghost. Slowly Filandro withdrew his comforting arm from around Noraldo's shoulders. Noraldo failed to notice his friend's eyes fill with pain. Noraldo wasn't looking. All he could see, hovering before him and filling his entire life, was a black leather mask.

"Yes, but why doesn't he show his face?" objected Filandro weakly. "What if he wears that mask because he's deformed, grotesque? Maybe that's why he doesn't take it off."

"I hadn't thought of that," said Noraldo uneasily. "I thought it was just to conceal his identity."

"There has to be more of a reason than that. Perhaps his face is eaten up with leprosy. Or syphilis. Or covered with a hairy birthmark. Or maybe..."

"Stop," said Noraldo.

"I'll tell you what I'd do," said Filandro, "if I were in your shoes." Noraldo didn't hear the bitterness. He didn't detect the knife-edge to Filandro's voice. "Go back to this magic palace of yours one more time. Do everything just the way you have been. But this time, when he climbs into bed with you, Noraldo, you must act quickly, the moment those two servants leave the room. Before you have time to fall asleep, tear that leather mask off his head and see for yourself why he doesn't show his face. One thing I can promise you – once that mask is off, this mysterious Prince of yours won't be able to pretend you aren't there anymore, and that's for sure."

Filandro's words were scarcely spoken before Noraldo knew in his heart that returning to the palace and removing the Prince's mask was exactly what he had to do. "But where will I get a horse?" he asked in a trembling voice.

"I'll get you a good one, without the least trouble," replied his friend.

"But how will I find the palace again?" A terrifying emptiness was opening up in the pit of Noraldo's stomach. Return to that lonely and terrifying forest?

"I'll guide you there myself, to the very place where you wandered off," said Filandro, taking his friend's hand coldly in his own. "Once you're back where we saw the stag, you'll be able to find your way."

Chapter 11
Without His Book

Noraldo woke long before his father and brothers. While they continued to snore and sigh in the depths of their dreams, Noraldo lit a candle, dressed, and then quietly climbed down the ladder with that single wavering light into the darkened shoeshop. He hadn't dared to tell his father, for fear that Petroccolo would object. Now that Noraldo had made up his mind, he couldn't have tolerated any other course. He had watched and hesitated as long as he could bear.

This time he was going to act.

Not until he was already downstairs did he remember his book, safely tucked away under his bed. He almost crept back up the ladder to get it, and then hesitated. His book seemed inappropriate.

"I'm setting off on an adventure as exciting and magical as any I've ever read about," Noraldo thought. "There'll be no time to read. I'll have to pay attention to everything around me. Besides, I might lose it." He turned his back as firmly as he could on the ladder leading back up to that book under his bed. Instead, he wrapped his cloak around his shoulders and wrote a brief apology note to his father, explaining that he would be back as soon as he could, and that he had taken the salami he found in the pantry with him.

Hooves clattered outside the shop on the cobblestones. Noraldo blew out the candle and slipped out of the shoeshop as quietly as he could. Dawn had not yet touched the piazza. Two horses and a shadowy mounted rider were waiting for him.

"Filandro?"

""Are you having second thoughts?"

"None." Noraldo climbed up onto the saddle eagerly, and patted his horse's neck. "Thanks for helping me."

"Never mind that," said Filandro. "Concentrate on what you've got to accomplish."

Noraldo took his friend's hand. "Thanks."

Across the still piazza they rode, the clip-clop of their horses echoing off the sleepy house-fronts. The guards at the gate were yawning, getting ready for the next shift to take their place.

"Off to do more hunting?" called one of them. "You boys are even earlier than before."

"Bigger game this time," replied Filandro. "Thought we'd catch him by surprise."

The guards laughed as they let them through.

Beyond the mighty gates of Valbrosa they rode, clattering over the bridge which spanned the Saluzzo. The first light of morning rippled and flickered on the water below. Beyond the wharves of the waterfront and the last few

The Devil in Love

clusters of cottages, the forest waited for them, without paths, without answers.

Deeper and deeper into the trees they went, ducking beneath the leafy boughs. With the sureness of a skillful hunter, Filandro led Noraldo from glade to glade, describing to him which bird or rabbit on that fateful day he had shot down in every spot, following as closely as he could the same route they had taken before.

Then Filandro stopped. They had come to a glade by the side of a shallow creek where once, so long ago it now seemed another lifetime, Noraldo and his friend had talked and laughed and lain in each other's arms. They were two very different young men now.

"From here I must go on alone," said Noraldo.

"Have the courage to do what you have to do," said Filandro in farewell. "You'll never be happy until you know what that mask is hiding."

Noraldo embraced him. The two of them clutched each other from saddle to saddle.

Something moved by the side of the creek. There was a soft splash. Several branches seemed to be moving. They were changing into antlers.

Noraldo saw it first in the expression of Filandro's eyes. He turned to look – the black stag stood with his hooves in the water, regarding them unafraid. Noraldo gasped. The proud, graceful creature stepped toward them. Filandro had already drawn an arrow silently from his quiver.

The Devil in Love

When Noraldo realized what was about to happen, he gave a cry and kicked his horse. The two horses collided. The arrow thudded into a tree. Then Noraldo was riding past Filandro, toward the glittering creek, across it, into the trees, after the stag, plunging recklessly deeper into the forest. The black creature leaped and bounded ahead of him. His horse crashed through the brambles in pursuit. They jumped a fallen trunk, splashed through a pond. They lunged through the underbrush, dodging trees on either side.

With his heart pounding at the same frantic pace as his horse's hooves, peering ahead through the branches to keep the stag in sight, Noraldo failed for one moment only to keep his mind on the lower branches. A sudden cracking blow to his head left his horse galloping on without him. Noraldo tumbled into the undergrowth of a forest suddenly very dark and still.

Chapter 12
Behind the Leather Mask

The throbbing ache finally woke him. He tried to lift his head off the dead leaves, groaned, and let it sink back down again. He was lying on the ground, stretched full-length on his back, looking up at the darkening sky through a grim lacery of darker branches.

An early star blinked at him. He blinked back.

Then Noraldo moved his head again. Flashing pain. Back to the dull throb. He groaned and sat up, holding his head with both hands as though it might fall apart in several pieces. Slowly he got to his feet.

How long had he been unconscious? Hours?

"Well, I knew it wasn't going to be easy," he thought, brushing off his clothes. Unfortunately, he had lost track of the black stag. He wondered if the mysterious creature would have led him right up to the palace stairs. "And to think that Filandro tried to shoot it!" He was aghast at his friend's behavior. Filandro had known well enough the importance of the black stag, and yet he had tried to kill it. What had possessed him?

Thinking about Filandro made him more aware of how alone he was. "Well, one thing's for sure," he thought bleakly. "I couldn't find my way back to Filandro now, even if I wanted to."

Slowly, feeling his way with arms extended before him, Noraldo faltered onward into the unfriendly forest. The trees crowded more closely together. Shadows lengthened into an encompassing blackness. Perhaps he would never find the palace again. Even if he did, would he really dare to unmask the Prince? What horrible secret would he uncover?

"But I'm going to do it," he repeated to himself with each step he took farther into the darkness. "I'm going to find him. I'm going to tear off that mask. I'm going to see his face, if it's the last thing I do."

Then he saw the spectral twinkling up ahead.

His heart began pounding so loudly, the sound seemed to fill the forest. He crept closer. He parted the branches. The enchanted palace shuddered before him at the other end of the clearing. The doors were open and unguarded. There was no living person in sight. Lights flickered and gleamed within.

He approached the staircase. The open doors beckoned him. Up those luminous stairs he walked, till he stood amid the ghostly columns. This time he didn't hesitate at the threshold. He entered and walked across the cold, white floor toward the firelit room where the wine and glasses would be waiting for him.

Noraldo found himself back on that very first night, all over again. The flames crackled warmly. He sank down into one of the chairs. His hand reached out for the wine – and stopped halfway there.

He rose to his feet. "This time," he thought, "I shall drink nothing." Leaving the wine and the bowl of fruit untouched, with his footsteps ringing hollowly through the deserted palace, Noraldo crossed the room and swung open the double doors leading into the dining-hall.

The table was set for two. Flames danced on the candles. A bowl of soup steamed beside meat-rolls and stuffed peppers, hot loaves of bread, as well as several different fruit pies. Noraldo walked around the table slowly, his mouth watering. The moment his hand touched the back of one chair, he heard the sound of footsteps in the hall behind him. Noraldo's back stiffened with fear, but he didn't turn around. He waited until the footsteps had entered the dining-hall, along with the smothered sound of boyish laughter.

"Good evening to you, my repetitious friend," said Noraldo to his masked host, knowing full well he would get no answer. "Another generous feast! Really, you do me too much honor. Unfortunately, your courtesy is wasted on me tonight, since I have already eaten. I'm so full I couldn't force myself to swallow one single bite."

The masked Prince stopped before the other place-setting. The boy in gold drew out the Prince's chair.

"Don't bother going through your whole performance again," said Noraldo, backing away from the table. "Twice is enough, thanks. In fact, I think I'll just retire for the night."

The Devil in Love

Noraldo bowed to him, turned around, and walked out of the dining-hall. Past the fountain perpetually splashing, past the lutes and harps which never made a sound, and on through those timeless gardens in which leaves never fell, blossoms never faded, went Noraldo bravely, step by step. His footfalls echoed down the corridor lined with those disturbing paintings, and on into the bed-chamber at the end of the hall, where he closed the door behind him.

He approached the bed. Firelight glimmered on the costly spread. Nothing had changed. Noraldo pulled off his clothes and dropped them at the bedside. His naked limbs slipped between clean sheets of the best linen. He sighed as he stretched out his aching body. He didn't have long to wait.

The secret door opened in the wall. The Prince entered the chamber. The two boys grinned behind him. They stopped at the bedside, where the servants began to undress the Prince, just as though Noraldo didn't exist. Open-mouthed with anticipation, he watched as they bared that perfect body in the firelight. In a moment, the Prince wore only his leather mask.

He looked down at Noraldo without seeing him. His manhood, however, was swollen with excitement. So was Noraldo's. The Prince slid blindly into bed with him. Griffone patted his pillows, while Soranzo folded the covers over him. Then both of them left the room.

Noraldo didn't wait one moment longer. At once he was on top of the Prince, and though he began with passionate kisses and amorous embraces he quickly seized the leather mask and pulled it away from the Prince's head with a snap.

Staring back at him, wide-eyed in amazement, was a youth so handsome Noraldo could only gasp in sheer disbelief. No sooner did the unmasked Prince realize what had happened than he shouted in horror, grabbed Noraldo by the shoulders, and shook him with exasperated frustration.

"You impatient fool!" he cried. "You've ruined everything! Just one more night, and the spell would have been broken. I could have finally left this prison. You would have been my lover forever. Now I'm doomed!"

Noraldo was horrified. Chilled with terror, he asked, "What do you mean, doomed? What have I done?"

The unmasked Prince sank down disconsolately on the side of the bed, and covered his face with his hands. "So close, so close, so very close. And now it's all lost!"

Noraldo was stammering in fear. "What do you mean, lost? Nothing's lost. We haven't lost anything. Put the mask back on, please, I'm so sorry…"

"I might as well tell you the whole story now, since it doesn't matter anymore. We have until dawn – just a few hours left. Then you're never going to see me again."

Noraldo crawled over and sat beside him. He put his arm around the Prince's shoulders. The Prince leaned against him, wetting Noraldo's chest with his tears. Then Noraldo eased him back down onto the bed, and they lay in each other's arms as the Prince began his sad tale.

The Devil in Love

Chapter 13
The Forbidden Chamber

My name is Prince Ippolito. My father is the King of Antichi. I suppose this whole thing is my fault to begin with. It never would have happened if I hadn't been so damned interested in sorcery.

My father used to employ an old wizard named Ambrogio. He must have been a hundred years old, but sharp as an owl. He was always very strict about keeping me away from things that didn't concern me. Ambrogio never let me pester him with questions, and kept me busy studying dusty old books about good government and kingship. I wasn't allowed to set foot in his study. But the few times he admitted me and showed me his magical skills, Ambrogio awakened in me a passion which has never diminished for all the thousand and one arts of enchantment.

Ambrogio, unfortunately, died when I was fifteen. My father hired another wizard to take his place. The new wizard wasn't as careful.

His name was Vernaccio.

You may have heard of him. Though he's still young as far as wizards go, not yet forty, he's already notorious, always courteous, always smiling, but genuinely scary, and more powerful when he's angry than any man I've ever known. To look at him, you'd think he was a plump, cheerful monk with a huge bald head. Let me tell you, that head is swollen enormous with brains so smart that you never, ever want to tangle with him. And those intense eyes of his can see right through you. Never, ever have dealings with Vernaccio. While he's laughing and hugging you, he's preparing to strangle you. He is more dangerous than you dream, and always three steps ahead of you. Stay away from Vernaccio. Run the other way. No ordinary man stands a chance.

Even then, Vernaccio was already very preoccupied with his own studies and experiments, only marginally interested in serving my father and Antichi. Things quickly got to the point that, whenever my father needed him, Vernaccio would put on the patient, wounded air of someone unjustly interrupted. He's worth putting up with, however, I assure you. Vernaccio is an exceptionally powerful wizard, utterly effective in everything he undertakes. He never settles for anything less than accomplishing his ends.

Before long, I began finding the door to Vernaccio's study left carelessly open when he wasn't there.

One day the temptation proved too much for me. While no one else was in sight, I dared to slip inside. I've never seen so much magical equipment in my life! Desks and counters piled almost to the ceiling with instruments whose names I didn't even know. Covering one wall was the library of a lifetime, row after row of priceless ancient books, and every one of them about the dark arts of enchantment. Finally I saw a chance to increase my knowledge of magic. I found a book that I could read without too much difficulty, concealed it under my cloak, and smuggled it out of the study and up to my room. The next time Vernaccio wasn't there, I put the book carefully back in its place, and took another.

I read secretly every night by candlelight. I began to learn.

Sooner or later, I was bound to get caught. One afternoon he pretended to be gone and was waiting for me. The door slammed behind me. When I spun around, there he was.

"Well, and what do we have here?" he said, like a hunter looking into his trap. "Have I surprised a thief red-handed? Or just a hungry little bookworm?" He chuckled and crossed the room toward me. I was so afraid I could hardly breathe.

"Poking around in someone else's room, my Prince, can be a dangerous sport," he counseled mockingly. "Especially when that room is the private study of a wizard. Do you value your life so cheaply? Had it been anyone else, there'd be nothing left of you now but smoking cinders."

He backed me up against the wall. He stroked my cheek. "If you ever enter my study alone again, dear boy, I won't be responsible for what happens." A tremble went through my body. His hand caressed my side, my front. "But since you're so curious about magic, and want to study it so desperately," he said, "there's no reason why we can't make some kind of arrangement. Just the two of us. Mutually beneficial. Do you find the thought attractive? If I were to instruct you in magic, would you be willing to teach me the joys of a young man's body?"

His suggestion took my breath away. Such an offer from a genius of sorcery was an irresistible temptation. As though he could read my mind, his hand slipped under my tunic, sliding down into the warm and private zones where no stranger's hand should go. I knew what the price of his lessons in magic would be, and yet... I could feel his hands memorizing every curve and bend of my body, lingering...

"My father will never approve," I objected weakly.

"Your father will never find out," smiled Vernaccio. "It won't be the first secret I've kept from him. There are spells, as I will show you, Prince, for every occasion."

That was how my secret meetings with the wizard began.

The Devil in Love

CHAPTER 14
The Wizard's Dream

I see everything differently now. None of it was an accident. No wizard as cunning and powerful as Vernaccio carelessly leaves his door open. Now I see that it was a baited snare. From the very beginning Vernaccio knew my secret passion, and lured me every step of the way. At the time, however, all of it just seemed to be happening. I thought I was making discoveries and choices, cleverly outwitting him. I was like a rat who thinks he's fooling the housekeeper, while he nibbles on the poisoned cheese.

We became inseparable. The more he taught me, the more eagerly I waited for each lesson. My desire for magical skills became the dominating drive of my life. I was a natural. I learned quickly. In short order I became his apprentice, assisting him through the nights on his strange and terrifying experiments. In exchange, I let him undress me, fondle me, embrace me. I lay on his bed and let him touch me wherever he chose. His hands were bold and insatiable. I tolerated his attentions, and got what I wanted.

At first I put up certain restrictions. I forbade some of his advances, granted only certain favors. My withdrawals infuriated him. The day came when he threatened to end my lessons, unless I granted him the honor of my manhood in his mouth. I refused. I allowed his hands to fondle whatever they would, but no more.

I didn't go up to his study that night. I stayed away all the next day. But without magical studies an emptiness opened up in my life that was unendurable. In the end I found his attentions easier to bear than a life without sorcery.

When he took my manhood into his mouth, I no longer objected. When I lay on the bed, I let him cover me with kisses. That night he taught me my first spell.

My father, unfortunately, had been noticing my behavior. Any interest I'd once had in becoming a good king had rapidly faded away to nothing. My mind was clearly elsewhere. Father took me aside into the royal gardens of Antichi, and I could tell he wasn't happy. He'd been losing weight, and was looking more frail than usual.

"My boy, my days are numbered and soon the throne of Antichi will be yours," he said, sitting beside me in the rose arbor and holding my hand in both of his. "You're not prepared. You've lost interest in kingship. All I see now is that you'd rather be a wizard than a king, and are spending so much time with Vernaccio that people are beginning to talk."

"Small minds will always talk, Father!" I objected.

But he had made up his mind. For my own good, for the good of the throne, for the good of the kingdom, he forbade me to ever visit Vernaccio's chamber again.

The Devil in Love

Vernaccio had foreseen as much, and when I told him in tears, he assured me that my lessons would continue. In the very next one, he taught me the spell of forgetting, it was as simple as that. My father's suspicions were unable to stop my magical studies, since whenever he tried, I made sure that he promptly forgot.

Everything proceeded according to Vernaccio's plan.

Then suddenly there was an unexpected complication, something not even Vernaccio had expected. Inexplicably, the wizard began suffering from terrible nightmares – not just one night, but every night he would wake up with a smothered cry, wet with sweat, as though he were in the grips of a fever. He refused to tell me about them. He appeared to grow several years older in a matter of days.

Shortly after they began I came upon an obscure passage one morning in the magical text I was studying, and impatient to know its meaning, I approached Vernaccio's door much earlier than usual. There were voices inside the room. I opened the door a crack. Vernaccio's back was toward me. All his attention was centered on his guest, and it wasn't hard to see why.

There before the wizard, in a pool of smoke, stood the Devil, fully eight feet tall and not wearing a stitch. It was a magnificent and terrifying sight.

"Every night I'm haunted by the same dream," complained Vernaccio. "An enormous book, as big as a

The Devil in Love

mountain, its binding carved out of rock. The pages are like cliffs, and covered with writing. The Hand of Fate emerges from a cloud. It points – there it is, on the page. It seems to happen before my eyes. Ippolito, clutching his side – an assassin's knife..."

"Surely the possibility has occurred to you," smiled the Devil. "Duke Federigo has taken Torello. Why not Antichi next? The King is old and weak, his son unprepared to rule. It seems only logical, since Ippolito stands in the Duke's path, he is doomed..."

"How can I save him?" interrupted Vernaccio. "Surely there must be a way. Some place I can hide him, take him. I'll do anything you ask – just don't let the Hand of Fate rob me of my one treasure."

I had never seen the wizard beg for anything. Vernaccio was powerful enough to take whatever he wanted – and here he was pleading, groveling, and what for? For my life to be spared.

"Do you promise to obey me?" asked the Devil. "To employ your magical powers in my service, to bring pain and confusion into the lives of all men?"

"Yes," whispered Vernaccio. "I promise. Now show me how I can save him from the Duke's assassins, and keep him for myself."

"Very well," said the Devil. There was a flash of light, and a rolled-up carpet appeared at the Devil's feet. Dusty and faded with age, it was marred by several large stains and the shag border had been nibbled by mice. The Devil kicked it, and in a puff of dust it unrolled at his feet. "I'm going to give you my old carpet. Not much to look at, but I'm sure you'll find it comes in handy. It will transport you through the air wherever you choose. You have only to place your left hand or foot over the griffin's eye and repeat the words of power, first aloud and then in your mind, focusing all your concentration on where you wish to go. There it will take you, swift as the wind. With the magic carpet, you should be able to capture and keep that silly young Prince with no problem at all.

"And that's not all. I'm also going to give you – this." He held out his hand. Nestled in his hot palm, still smoking, was a gleaming ring – ancient, ornately carved, and set with a blood-red stone. "Go ahead, take it. I'm sure it will fit just right."

Vernaccio did as he was told, and then held out his hand with the ring gleaming boldly.

"Inside this ring are imprisoned two demons," said the Devil. "They are the slaves of whoever wears the ring. You have only to release them with the secret word I teach you, and they will do your bidding. Together they will create a splendid palace for you to keep your Prince, luxurious rooms with every comfort and pleasure. Out of the smoke of Hell they will forge it, strong enough to withstand all enemies, yet light enough for the demons to carry through the air as though the palace weighed no more than a feather. There you'll be able to keep young Ippolito all to yourself, in endless splendor and happiness, safe from all other jealous eyes as well as from Duke Federigo."

"Perfect!" sighed Vernaccio.

"Probably not," said the Devil, "but then, nothing is."

He then leaned forward and whispered the magic words in Vernaccio's ear. As he did so, for one horrible moment the Devil seemed to look through the crack in the door, right at me. He laughed. There was a flash, and he was gone.

Chapter 15
Master of the Game

I fled from the doorway where I had been eavesdropping. I was terrified, ashamed, and feeling desperately alone. Needless to say, the thought of being murdered any moment by the Duke's secret agents made me unbearably nervous. But I was equally determined not to be carried off into the clouds by a lovesick wizard. I now saw that my entire education in magic had been nothing more than a seduction. I had fallen almost completely under his spell. I no longer saw any of my friends, or thought about anything other than my magical studies. I had become utterly dependent on him.

Fear made me act rashly. I decided to flee that night. When my father summoned Vernaccio to his council-chamber for their evening conference, I saw my chance. I packed my belongings, not knowing where I would hide, knowing only that I had to escape while I still could. I slipped out of the castle through a side door which led into the courtyard. There I mounted one of the guard's horses, galloped down a narrow alley to the city walls, and commanded that the gate be opened. From there I rode out of Antichi into the night.

I didn't get far.

There was a strange sound behind me, a mysterious whirring which I could hear over the clattering hooves, a sound I'd never heard before. I turned around in the saddle. Hovering in the air behind me floated Vernaccio with a triumphant cackle, standing in the middle of a radiant, gloriously-colored magic carpet, his robes billowing behind him.

"Where are you off to in such a hurry, sweet boy?" he said, and he held out his ring.

A beacon of red light flooded out of it, so bright that I couldn't see a thing. Desperately I pleaded with my horse to run faster, but his legs were already thundering down the road as fast as he could go. I heard laughter behind me. Demons were floating out of the ring, swimming up to the surface out of the depths of that beacon of blazing red light. Their terrible, cold hands closed around me. They lifted me up out of the saddle. Suspended between them, kicking at the air, with my horse no longer beneath me, I cried out in fear as

The Devil in Love

they carried me back toward the carpet. A cold hand closed over my mouth. Their maddening laughter rang in my ears. No matter how I kicked and struggled, I couldn't pull away from those demons or loosen their hold in the slightest.

They handed me to Vernaccio. His arms closed around me. Gripped in his embrace, as though he were never going to let go of me again, with a demon flying on either side, I found myself catapulting headlong into the night. I remember flying over a forest, plunging down into the trees, and an empty meadow of grass. I remember the carpet landing on a grassy hill, and the two demons in the air on either side of the carpet crying out words I didn't understand, and then a sound like thunder as arches of blue and gold reared up overhead, turrets thrust into the sky, corridors stretched out before me, chandeliers and cressets of fire seemed to explode into more colors than I ever knew existed. That's how I found myself in this beautiful prison.

Ever since, Vernaccio has kept me captive here. Those two servants you saw with me are really the two demons of the ring. They watch over me whenever the wizard is away, going about the Devil's business. This palace is entirely their creation. I can enjoy almost any form of entertainment I wish here – but I am no longer allowed to study magic, my life's one passion.

The loss of that pleasure made me so despondent at first that the wizard feared I would take my own life. That's how he came to devise this game for me. I'm kinder to him now,

The Devil in Love

and in exchange he has allowed me this one opportunity to escape – I can change myself into the shape of a black stag to lure men here to this palace. The wizard has given me one year's time to find a man who will sleep with me for three nights, without my speaking a single word to him or letting him see my face unmasked. That man would break the spell, and set me free.

The year is almost over. There are only a few days left. So far, no man has had the courage to come back for even a second visit. Not until you came here. You passed the test on the first night, and the second night, too. You gave me hope. I nearly went out of my mind waiting for you to return. And then tonight, there you were again. My one chance for freedom. And now...

Now you've looked under the leather mask. It's too late for anyone else. My last hope is gone. I'm condemned to spend the rest of my days with Vernaccio, wherever he chooses, in this enchanted palace. There's no way to escape now. No one can protect me or hide me. Vernaccio has granted me one last wish, to say farewell to my father in Antichi, which is where I must go now. It will break his heart. How bitterly this has ended! How I dared to hope that one day I could be happy with you. I would never have stopped showing you my gratitude. Ever...

Prince Ippolito's lips sought Noraldo's. Their tender, desperate lovemaking lasted only a few brief moments.

The Devil in Love

Then the doors of the bedroom were flung open. The lovers leaped apart, trembling. The two young servants stood in the doorway. This time they weren't laughing. They strode angrily to the bed. Griffone seized Noraldo before he could squirm away, pinning his arms behind his back. Soranzo dragged Prince Ippolito toward the balcony. There was a roaring outside. A flying carpet heaved itself out of the night, in the middle of which stood a sinister man dressed entirely in black, his cape swirling around him.

"Vernaccio!" cried the Prince, backing away from the wizard in terror, struggling to escape from the demon servants' hold. He twisted and flailed in vain. Soranzo lifted him up to Vernaccio as though the Prince were as light as a child. Black-robed arms enfolded the kicking white body of Ippolito. There was a roaring outside, and both the wizard and Ippolito were gone.

Noraldo found himself alone in that haunted bedroom, facing the two angry demons. His heart pounded wildly. The two boys grinned at him. Then they stamped their feet in unison, and with a spout of fiendish laughter, both of them began growing larger and larger, bursting out of their pageboy uniforms which flew apart into flapping rags of colored smoke.

The floor shifted. Noraldo gasped. The marble tiles beneath his feet began to tremble. The walls shuddered. Noraldo's eyes opened wider and wider. Then he bolted

The Devil in Love

toward the window in three long leaps, and took a desperate sailing lunge out into the darkness.

He hit the ground with a stunning thud. The breath was knocked out of him. Behind him, there was a thunderous explosion. Slowly, with a vast rumbling, the palace began to rise up off the ground.

It was lifted by those titanic boys, each now as tall as the palace itself. They grunted as they reached their hands underneath it. Up onto their vast, bare shoulders they heaved it. Then demons and palace all rose up into the turbulent night.

In a moment, Noraldo found himself standing alone and trembling amidst the dark, silent trees of the forest. Where once the magnificent palace had stood, there was only an empty, windblown clearing.

Chapter 16
Running Out of Time

Blundering through the forest without any sense of east or west, Noraldo somehow managed to wander in the general direction of Valbrosa. Before morning was too far advanced, he stumbled out of a last thicket and heard to his surprise the sound of the mighty Saluzzo roaring up ahead.

He ran the rest of the way to the bridge. He found himself crying as he ran. On through the city gates he hurried, dodging vendors and loaded donkeys and baskets of fruit, through the market-place, down one narrow, cobbled street after another, until he could see his father's shoeshop across the piazza.

Noraldo burst through the doorway so suddenly that one of his brothers stabbed his thumb with his needle. He shouted. The startled cat leaped down off the counter, taking several pairs of new shoes with him. Petroccolo cursed, and kicked. The cat expertly avoided his foot and lunged for the door. Noraldo tripped over him, and fell into his father's arms.

"Well!" said Petroccolo in exasperation, hiding his relief. "How thoughtful of you to drop in. I don't suppose you have time to do a little sewing? We have orders to fill piled up to our ears."

The Devil in Love

"Father," said Noraldo, catching his breath, "can you loan me some money?"

"What?" exclaimed the shoemaker, his face turning red. "That's how you greet me? That's all a father is good for? After all that I've…"

"I've got to get to Antichi as soon as possible," said Noraldo. He pulled away from his father and started toward the ladder leading up to the living quarters. Petroccolo seized him by the arm before he got three steps away, and spun him around.

"Antichi!" he cried. "What do you mean, Antichi? Where have you been since yesterday morning, I'd like to know?"

Noraldo looked the old shoemaker in the eye. His own were desperate, determined. Without explaining, with a stubbornness that exasperated and somewhat frightened Petroccolo, he ignored the shoemaker's questions. Instead, he hugged his father – earnestly, as though he might never hug him again.

"You mean so much to me, Father, and I hate to disappoint you," said Noraldo. "Just trust in me that I'm doing the right thing. I don't have any choice. I'm doing what I have to do. I don't have time to tell you right now, Father, but I will," said Noraldo, squirming toward the ladder. "Please just trust me with some money and let me pack up a few clothes. If I don't hurry, it will be too late. I'll lose him forever."

The Devil in Love

"Lose him?" repeated Petroccolo. "Lose him? Why can't you talk sense to me? Who are you talking about?"

But Noraldo had managed to worm out of his hold and was already halfway up the ladder. Petroccolo almost chased him up, then remembered his bad knee and stopped at the bottom. Gripping a rung of the ladder, he called up after Noraldo, "You're not getting a single coin out of me until I get a few answers."

There was no reply. Just the sound of Noraldo's footfalls hurrying about the floor.

"Do you hear me?" shouted the old shoemaker. "I mean it, Noraldo. It's time you started showing a little responsibility. What about the shoeshop? What reason could you possibly have for…?"

Noraldo's feet were coming back down the ladder. Petroccolo got out of his way, and stood blocking his passage to the door, his arms folded sternly across his chest. Noraldo had a sack of clothes slung over his shoulder. He jumped from the third rung down, and advanced upon his father.

"Please."

"Now, wait just a minute," objected Petroccolo.

"It's now or never, Father," said Noraldo, trying to push past him toward the door.

"Surely you can spare a few minutes to tell me…"

Noraldo gripped the old shoemaker by the shoulders. "We're almost out of time, Father. Please don't hold me back."

The Devil in Love

The shoemaker let him go with a sigh. "How much do you need?"

"Enough for three days. Maybe four."

The shoemaker went to unlock his strongbox. Noraldo hugged his brothers and bid them farewell. Then Petroccolo handed him a small leather bag containing a handful of sliding and clinking coins.

"May the Hand of Fate guide you," said the old shoemaker. "I hope this isn't a mistake."

Noraldo embraced his father with real gratitude, kissed him, and then lunged for the door of the shoeshop, calling goodbye over his shoulder. They watched him run across the piazza through a squawking flurry of pigeons toward the door of the bakery.

Hot air came belching toward him as he entered from the brick oven at the back. Along with the stifling heat came clouds of mouth-watering smells. Two men in white with flushed, wet faces and flour-covered arms were sliding out a tray of freshly-baked bread. Noraldo pushed past several waiting customers toward familiar white shoulders bent over a rolling-pin, beyond the bread counter.

"Filandro!"

Recognizing the sound of his friend's voice, the young baker looked up sharply.

"I need a horse," said Noraldo urgently, without giving his friend a chance to say a word.

"*A horse?* But, Noraldo…"

The Devil in Love

"I've got to go to Antichi. He's there."

Filandro's features changed subtly. The hope went out of them. "This Prince of yours," he asked. "Did you pull the mask off his face?"

"Yes, and I almost ruined everything. There's still a chance, though. If I hurry." Noraldo made no attempt to conceal his impatience.

"He wasn't ugly? He wasn't deformed?"

"Ugly as the dawn," said Noraldo. "Deformed as a rose. Listen, can you help me? I need a horse now."

"I can get one for you tonight after work," said Filandro. "I'm sure father will agree. I'll go with you, Noraldo. You'll never find the way there, otherwise. We can leave tomorrow morning."

Noraldo shook his head. "No," he said. "I'm leaving this very hour."

"But why?"

"It might already be too late. I'm not waiting. Not for anyone. Not for anything. I'll run if I have to."

Filandro was getting angry. Didn't Noraldo ever think about anyone else but himself? He felt like saying, "Fine. Don't wait. Go ahead and run." What's more, he felt like telling Noraldo he could go to Hell for all he cared. Something made Filandro hold back. He knew that look in his friend's eyes. It was fear. Noraldo needed him, and was trying hard not to admit it.

The Devil in Love

The young baker could see, then, that he was going to have to decide, there on the spot, in the middle of the hot and crowded bakery, just how much he was willing to endure in the name of their friendship. There was nothing in it for him. Filandro clenched his teeth.

A customer poked his head between them.

"How much is the sesame loaf?" he asked, pointing.

Filandro didn't hear him. He was listening to his heart. He wiped his hands on his apron. "Just give me long enough to tell Father I have to take the afternoon off," he said. "I know where we can get two horses."

An hour later, the two of them were mounted on horseback and galloping out of the stable behind the bakery. Dogs and children scrambled out of their way. Soon they were riding for all they were worth, leaving gate and bridge behind them, away from the seven gleaming towers of Duke Federigo's thriving city.

Instead of plunging into the unknown forests of the east, however, as they had done before, this time they turned their mounts to the north, galloping out the wide and level way along the Saluzzo which had become known as the Duke's Road. They rode like the wind, reaching Torello, galloping on beyond where the Duke's Road ended, and only a rough roadway accompanied the shores of the Saluzzo, sometimes little more than a muddy trail. The waters of the river flowed faster, through rougher terrain. On either side of them rose the cold, forbidding peaks of the White Demons. Wind-twisted bushes climbed the slopes. Higher up there was snow. The two travelers wrapped themselves in their cloaks.

It began to rain. Their hoods hid their faces from each other. Both of them were deep in thought, each intensely preoccupied with his own private desires.

"When the year is up, the wizard wins," said Noraldo miserably.

"You mentioned that," said Filandro.

Again and again Noraldo started talking about the Prince, and every time Filandro managed to change the subject. He had heard enough about the Prince to last a lifetime.

Soon, as the mountains darkened with approaching nightfall, Filandro pointed out up ahead the first of the steep, cliffhanging villages of the oldest kingdom of the all – misty, legend-wrapped Antichi.

The Devil in Love

Chapter 17
Sign of the Hanged Man

They had still not reached the Antichi walls, however, when it became too dark to go any farther. It was raining harder now, and the road through the White Demons was sometimes haphazard at best and not frequently taken. It was anything but straight, full of unexpected bends and set-backs. Filandro could see that Noraldo was determined to push onward in spite of the weather, and knew his friend well enough to remain silent until even impatient Noraldo was ready to admit it was time to look for shelter – they were both completely drenched and their horses exhausted from slogging through the mud.

Up ahead, through the rain, Filandro saw a flickering light. He waited until Noraldo said, "Let's turn up here." The closer they rode, the clearer they could see that the light was coming from the open shutters of a large inn set back from the main roadway in the trees. A signboard was creaking over the door.

"We could spend the night over there," said Noraldo.

"Sounds like a good idea to me," said Filandro, relieved to hear his friend finally talking sense. "We can get back on the road at dawn. By tomorrow morning we'll be in Antichi."

The Devil in Love

"That should be fine," agreed Noraldo reluctantly. It was just as well. He was exhausted, and they certainly couldn't call on the Prince at this late hour, looking the way they looked now.

They rode up the winding horse path toward the inn. A chill wind tore at the hill, lashed the grass. Old tombstones clustered on one bank, leaning this way and that, at whatever tilt that relentless wind had tipped them. One grave was still fresh. Out of the corner of his eye, Noraldo thought he saw someone move away from the grave. He peered into the blurring sheets of rain.

"Look!" he called to Filandro.

A child of no more than seven or eight was walking through the nearby tombstones. The boy was weeping bitterly, oblivious to the rain, and there was a hangman's noose around his young neck.

"What the Devil...?" gasped Noraldo.

Then their horses carried them past him. When he twisted around in the saddle looking back, the boy was no longer there. The two of them looked at each other in amazement, unable to believe they had really seen such a morbid sight.

"Come on, let's get out of this rain," said Filandro. They rode up to the front of the inn. Smoke billowed up from the chimney. Firelight shuddered within through cracks in the shutters, accompanied by the fragrant smells of a hearty stew. They could hear voices, and someone laughed. "We couldn't make much progress in this weather, even if we wanted to," he said. "This place ought to at least cheer us up."

Noraldo took one look at the signboard suspended over the door, and grabbed his friend's arm. Part of the weathered paint had peeled away, but it wasn't hard to make out the figure of a man hanging from a rope.

"What's that supposed to mean?"

"It's just the name of the inn," said Filandro. "Hopefully a name isn't enough to make you change your mind."

"On the other hand, maybe the Sign of the Hanged Man isn't the best place to find cheer," said Noraldo. "Let's ride on to Antichi. We can make it. We can stay at an inn there."

"Too dangerous to keep riding in this weather," said Filandro. "It would be so easy to go over the side. Don't let that old signboard bother you. Lots of inns have dreadful names. Believe me, we're safer here than going on in the dark and the rain."

"But what about that strange little boy?"

"We can ask someone inside about it," said Filandro. "Probably just some little mischief-maker stirring up trouble. Nothing to get nervous about. Come on. Let's get some dinner and a dry bed."

They had scarcely swung their legs down to the ground, however, when the door of the inn opened and a young man wearing an apron said, "Can I help you gentlemen?"

"Yes," said Filandro, before his friend could object. "We'd like to spend the night."

The Devil in Love

"Not much of a night to spend outdoors, is it?" laughed the young man. There some something vaguely insolent about him. "Welcome to the Sign of the Hanged Man. Consider yourselves spending the night."

"But first," interrupted Noraldo, "would you mind explaining something to us, the curious sight we just beheld down the road – a mere boy walking through the tombstones in the rain, with a noose around his neck."

"So that's where he is!" growled the man in the apron. He was actually a good-looking fellow, but with a sullen look, as though he were getting ready to complain about something, attractive enough not to worry about whether his hair were well-brushed or his cheeks well-shaved. With the scruffy, sweaty look of someone in charge, he assessed both Noraldo and Filandro up and down boldly, as though they were horses to be sold. "That weird little boy you saw is my son," he said. "My father died last week. The boy adored his Grandpa. He keeps going back out to my father's grave."

"I'm sorry," said Filandro.

"May your father rest in peace," said Noraldo.

Filandro persisted, "But why the rope around the boy's neck?"

The young man laughed. "Not from around here, are you? Otherwise you'd know about the Hanged Man. That's where this inn gets its name. Up on that hill behind us there used to be a scaffold. Did you know that? Little bit of local history. Fellow was hung there who they found out later was innocent. It happened back when my father was a boy. What a tragedy! Everyone liked the lad, too. They say the ghost still walks these hills. Old-timers swear the only way to be safe from him is to wear a rope around your neck. Then he won't touch you. Renzo was just afraid to go out to his Grandpa's grave in the dark. Here he comes now." His voice became harsh, angry. He shouted, "Didn't you hear me call?"

"I saw the Hanged Man tonight!" cried the boy.

"You're not answering my question."

"But I saw him!"

The boy ran toward his father, and clutched his legs in fear.

"Don't lie to me, Renzo," snarled the young man, giving the boy a solid smack with his hand across the side of his head. "You know what I told you about lying. There's no such thing as the Hanged Man."

The boy's eyes grew wide. "But I saw him, Papa!" he protested. "In the graves."

"From now on, you come when I call you, whether a ghost is there or not," growled the young father, poking his finger into the boy's chest for emphasis. "Now, help these men. Take their horses to the stable and feed them. And take that ridiculous rope off your neck before you hang yourself or scare away any more customers."

Embarrassed, eyes downcast, the boy pulled off the noose, took the reins from Noraldo and Filandro, and led their horse away around the side of the inn.

The Devil in Love

"This way, now," the young innkeeper said to them. "I'll get you a room and something to eat." He held out a greasy hand. "My name is Troilo. Now that Papa's gone, this inn is mine. If you need anything, let me know."

He shrugged his shoulder against the door, nudging it open with the help of his foot. Noraldo gave his friend an uncomfortable look. Filandro ignored him and followed the young innkeeper inside. Noraldo uneasily went after them.

Chapter 18
The Innkeeper's News

Filandro arranged for supper and a room for the night. Perhaps a dozen other men, of various ages, were scattered in clusters about the large central room, most of them near the crackling hearth. He and Noraldo brought their bags upstairs and changed their clothes. The room was small, dusty and so old the wood was half-soft with rot, but at least it was dry. The old bed took up most of the space, and had a slept-in look, as though the hired help took naps there. The sheets weren't clean. The flickering candle only managed to highlight mouse turds in the corners. Still, it was better than being out in the rain.

Noraldo was restless. "Let's go down and get something to eat," he said. "I feel like talking to that innkeeper. Maybe he'll have heard something. If the Prince has really come back to Antichi..."

"If he really *is* the Prince," added Filandro. "Sure, let's go. I could stand a bite to eat."

They went back down the stairs. It was supper-time at the Sign of the Hanged Man. Little Renzo and a skinny apprentice were carrying trenchers of hot food to the tables. The boy glanced up at Noraldo and quickly looked away.

Troilo tapped wine from the barrel into their mugs. Filandro carried his over to sip by the hearth. Noraldo, however, lingered by the young innkeeper.

"Busy night?"

"Hardly. These are regulars. Men who would rather be here than at home. They've all got their reasons, believe me, and I've heard all about them. Real customers have been slacking off a little since the rains started."

"You get mostly travelers?"

"Now and then, and these locals," said the innkeeper, picking at something between his teeth with a sliver of wood. "Mostly honest folks just hurrying through to Antichi. Like yourself."

"What's the talk these days?" asked Noraldo, trying to sound as casual as he could. "Any news?"

Troilo glanced at him out of the corner of his eye. "Not much. Been pretty quiet up here in the mountains. Rain's the only news up here, and in Antichi rain is no news." He flipped away his makeshift toothpick, and gave Noraldo another one of those long, assessing looks, as though he were thinking about buying him. "What kind of news are you looking for, stranger?"

"Nothing in particular," said Noraldo quickly, taking a long drink of wine in order to give himself time to think. "I just figured you must hear plenty, what with folks coming and going, the way folks talk. There must be some rich old families having a feud? Or some strange local feast-day coming up? Or somebody who just fell in love? Somebody returning after a long, mysterious absence? Or maybe somebody important who disappeared and then came back...?"

"Say, now that you mention it," said Troilo, his eyes widening brightly, slapping the table with his hand at the memory, "somebody did fall in love. And a more unlikely couple..."

Noraldo groaned. The last thing he wanted to do was get Troilo talking on the wrong subject. Filandro was looking across the room at the two of them with a melancholy face. Troilo was obviously enjoying Noraldo's attention, and was standing closer to him than necessary. "How about anybody who was missing and then suddenly shows up again..."

"No, let me tell you about this couple who fell in love," interrupted Troilo. "It's a real piece of news!"

"Actually, I'd rather know if anyone had returned after..."

Troilo laughed. "Well, that's part of it, too."

The Devil in Love

That brought Noraldo up short. "It is?"

"You probably didn't realize, being an outsider, that Prince Ippolito has been missing for almost a year."

Noraldo tried to keep his features still, to reveal no expression. He cleared his throat. "No, um, I didn't."

"The King has been trying to keep it quiet," said Troilo, lowering his voice and moving his lips closer to Noraldo's ear. "When word finally leaked out that the Prince had mysteriously vanished, the King pretended that the boy was just traveling, visiting cousins. Well, there were soon rumors that the real explanation was being suppressed. Some servant with a loose tongue said that the boy had fallen head over heels in love with the King's wizard, Vernaccio. And there was no denying that the wizard was very definitely missing, too."

"You don't say," said Noraldo.

"Well, guess who just returned to Antichi? The long-lost Prince Ippolito himself, with none other than his boyfriend, the missing wizard, Vernaccio. Off on a year-long holiday together, without a word to anyone. Not only that, but in just three days, Ippolito has announced that he's going away to live with Vernaccio in some gorgeous palace the Devil knows where. He says they're in love! Can you believe it? There's no accounting for taste, is there? Good-looking young Prince like Ippolito could have just about anybody, and he chooses to give up the throne of Antichi – why? Out of love for a man

The Devil in Love

old enough to be his father! Why, every time I see that Prince's handsome face..."

Noraldo gripped Troilo's arm. "See his face?" he exclaimed. Realizing his voice had squeaked, he tried to regain his composure. "What I mean to say is, this doesn't look like the kind of inn where you'd find a Prince."

Troilo glanced at him with mild surprise, but didn't pull away from Noraldo's hand. Instead, the young innkeeper let himself be drawn even closer to his excited guest.

"You have a problem with this inn?"

Noraldo deftly changed the subject. "You saw his face?"

"As clearly as I see yours. Yesterday and today. Right out there by those trees over the river. You can almost see the spot from the window here. Yesterday I just watched him, but today I went up to him and asked him what he was looking for. He said he just enjoyed getting away from his servants once in a while, and that he liked that place by the water, under the trees. I wouldn't be surprised at all to see him walking around down there by the river again tomorrow."

"And his servants weren't with him?" said Noraldo. "How mysterious! How fortunate! And you actually saw his face clearly in the daylight?"

"What's so hard to believe about that?" asked the innkeeper with a grin. "Haven't you ever seen a Prince before? They're just like you and me. And when they walk by, anybody who's looking at them can see their face." Troilo laughed, and one of his arms slipped quietly around

Noraldo's waist, drawing him closer. "If he's got eyes to see with!"

Noraldo had eyes enough to see that Filandro had finished his wine and was scowling at him.

"Well, that is interesting news," he said. "I certainly must thank you for your company this evening. You'll have to excuse me now – I'm starving, and it looks like my friend over there is, too. We'd better order our supper soon, if we want any. Can't tell you how glad I am that we found this place! We may end up staying longer than we thought, who knows? Oh, and another thing – can I buy a jug of wine from you tomorrow morning…?"

He was interrupted by a scream.

A crash caused the other men in the inn to jump to their feet. The door of the inn swung lifelessly open, revealing an empty porch and downpouring rain. Wine-flushed faces strained to see in panic. Little Renzo backed away from the storm-lashed doorway, out of a mess of spilled trenchers and splattered stew, pointing out into the night and the rain, his entire body so shaken with fear that he was shuddering uncontrollably.

"The Hanged Man!" he shrieked. "He was there! I saw him – watching us!"

Chapter 19
Desire and Treachery

Troilo quickly pulled his son out of earshot of his customers, into an empty room upstairs where he cuffed and spanked the boy out of his fears. Before long Renzo was whimpering softly and denying that he had seen anything, his young face wet from crying, sniffling but at least somewhat composed, preferring his father's ill humor over whatever terrifying unknown was walking around out there undead.

He was more composed than his father. Troilo was now pacing the room, back and forth. He was just as disturbed as the boy, but his turmoil sprang from desire rather than fear, and it was not the Hanged Man he was thinking about. He couldn't get Noraldo out of his mind. Not that the shoemaker's son was so unbearably good-looking or superbly built – he wasn't. Though there was something vaguely attractive about Noraldo's physical mass and proportions, what most seduced the young innkeeper was Noraldo's complete indifference to him.

Troilo was not used to being ignored. He and his inn were popular for good reason. He was easy on the eyes, and had been sought and pursued by some of the handsomest youths between Torello and Antichi. He had been faithful to none. He was passionately courted for his looks, even though everyone knew he was utterly unscrupulous and untrustworthy. He was selfish, ruthless, and made a fool of every lover in public at least once, yet he was tolerated and indulged because of his fetching body, low standards, easy physical affection and easy access to wine. Now that Troilo was turning thirty, he was sensitive about someone resisting his charms. It aroused him.

"Don't you ever embarrass me that way in front of customers again," he scolded his son, giving the boy a last whack on the behind.

"I'm sorry, Papa, I'm sorry," Renzo sobbed miserably. He tried so hard to make his father love him.

"What are you going to say if someone asks you about the Hanged Man?"

"I'll say that.. . I'll say that…"

Troilo shook him. "*What* are you going to say?"

"He wasn't there." To insist that he'd really seen the Hanged Man would only infuriate his Papa more and result in more spanking. "There's no such thing. I didn't see anything."

Troilo let go of him. "Now, do you think you can do your Papa a favor, and do it right?"

Renzo sniffed, and nodded solemnly.

"All right, then," said Troilo, crouching down in front of his son and taking the boy's two shoulders in his hands, looking him squarely in the eye and lowering his voice. "I want you to go to the strangers' room, and ask if either of them would like you to prepare a bath for them. If one does, come and tell me which one…"

Renzo hurried off to do as he'd been told.

Filandro was beginning to regret having ever come along. It was all turning into one long humiliation. Listening to Noraldo talk on and on about this Prince of his, watching him flirt with the innkeeper, was starting to give Filandro one continuous headache which showed no sign of going away. He was ready to get on his horse and ride back to his father's bakery. His bitterness spilled over into words.

"I hope I'm not being – in the way?"

"What are you talking about?"

"Well, if you and that innkeeper want to spend some time alone together…"

"Filandro, you've got to be joking."

"Joking? Have you seen the way he looks at you?"

A rapping at the door interrupted them. Noraldo opened it, and smiled to see who was standing there. Renzo didn't look up high enough to see the smile. He delivered his message directly to Noraldo's belt. "My father wants to know if either of you would like a hot bath?"

"Not me," said Filandro. He rolled over on the bed and faced the wall.

"And you, sir?"

"Actually," said Noraldo, "that sounds very tempting. Yes, maybe I will."

The Devil in Love

"Upstairs, at the end of the hall, sir," said Renzo. "I'll have the tub filled with hot water in half an hour, sir. I'll come back and fetch you."

Noraldo thanked him, but the boy was already gone.

He swiftly returned to his father, who couldn't conceal his pleasure at the news. Troilo would see to the bath himself, and if his guest wanted privacy, Troilo knew about a small hole in the wall just large enough to afford a satisfying view. He had good reason to know – he had drilled it there himself. He always enjoyed watching his oblivious guests in their natural states.

"Well done, Renzo," said the innkeeper. "Now, hurry up and get that water heated, like a good boy. And once he's in the tub, I want you to mop up the kitchen."

The boy hurried about his task. He remembered to be very careful not to burn himself. Soon the water had been heated and the tub was filled and steaming. Then he went to Noraldo's room and led the kind stranger back to the bathtub. He didn't know about the hole in the wall, or he would have seen his father's eye watching everything that happened.

"Will there be anything else, sir?" asked the boy.

"No," said Noraldo. "Thank you."

Renzo slipped out the door.

Noraldo undressed. The eye pressed up against the hole. When he was wearing nothing, Noraldo folded his clothes on a chair and then tested the water. It was very hot. He flinched and drew back. His every movement was scrutinized by the eye. Noraldo lowered one leg into the water again, and then the other. Slowly he lowered himself down into the tub, like a plucked chicken sinking into the soup. He sighed, and let his head sink back against the rim.

The door opened.

"Ah," said Troilo, entering the room uninvited and pretending to be surprised. "I see my son has already taken care of everything."

"Yes," smiled Noraldo awkwardly. "He was very quick and quite polite. A good boy. Thank you."

Instead of ducking back out again, however, the young innkeeper moved closer to the tub, so that he was looking down into the hot water. "I have a feeling you're going to like Antichi," he said, giving Noraldo a sly wink. "Know what I mean? Lots of good-looking boys around these parts, I can tell you that. Just let me know if either you or your friend would like a companion for the night. It's easily arranged."

Noraldo could feel himself being stared at. It was giving him an erection.

"Not for me," said Noraldo. "I appear to have already found what I was looking for right here at your inn."

Troilo grinned in satisfaction, like a cat who has just cornered a mouse. He naturally assumed that this was a reference to himself. Beaming with pleasure, he idly rubbed his knuckles over his belly muscles in a way which he knew was provocative, already feeling somewhat less interested in an admirer so easily won. He was about to give Noraldo the opportunity of blowing him then and there when Noraldo added, "I've been so deeply in love this last month that I probably won't even notice the good-looking boys of Antichi. The only one I have eyes for now is – well, I suppose there's no hiding it – I'm in love with Prince Ippolito. That's why I'm here."

Troilo froze. His eyes darkened. He couldn't believe what he'd just heard. "Oh, really?" he managed to choke out.

Noraldo mistook his words for encouragement to continue. Filandro hadn't been much interested in talking about the Prince lately, and since that was all Noraldo thought about, he was not only passionately interested in the subject, but just waiting to find a sympathetic ear.

"Actually we've only slept together twice," said Noraldo, exaggerating a bit. "But I've never felt this way before about anyone. Until now, I thought I'd lost him. Now I've found him again here, at your inn. Surely the Hand of Fate is guiding me. By tomorrow, I'll be holding him again in my arms."

"Sorry to disturb you," mumbled Troilo, backing toward the door and out of the room. "I'll leave you to bathe in peace."

The door slammed abruptly behind him.

As he stepped out into the dim corridor of the inn, however, Troilo turned around to find himself facing a shadow in the shape of a man. The figure stepped toward him, blocking his path. It was Filandro. His eyes weren't friendly.

"Is Noraldo in there?"

"Taking his bath," said Troilo, in his most courteous and soothing voice. "And you, sir? Have you changed your mind?"

"No," said Filandro. "Just wondering."

He retreated down the hall, back into the room. But not before Troilo had detected the sad look in Filandro's eyes, the ache which not even Noraldo had yet discovered there. Before closing the door, Filandro gave the innkeeper one last, suspicious glance.

"Pathetic," growled Troilo, his breath escaping in a hiss. His desire, unbearable a moment ago, had already been twisted into anger and contempt. "So he thinks he's going to meet the Prince tomorrow?" he laughed bitterly. Obviously the innkeeper had another opinion.

Lighting a lantern, Troilo used a small key attached to his belt to open a low door behind the kitchen. Holding the lantern out into the darkness, he descended a crooked, very narrow staircase into the pantry. Beyond the pantry were the wine barrels. There he reached behind a dust-covered barrel in a far corner of the cellar, and withdrew a small black jar.

"I think the Prince is going to be very surprised tomorrow," smirked the innkeeper, "at what he discovers about his dear friend."

The Devil in Love

Opening the jar, Troilo carefully poured some of the contents down into the mouth of a wine jug. Then he filled the jug at the barrel of his best red wine. He swirled around the wine in the jug to conceal the taste, and then smiled as he hid the black jar back where he'd found it. "I think someone's plans are about to change."

The young innkeeper was so intent on his treachery that he failed to notice a small iron grill missing, high up in a dim corner of the cellar. He didn't feel the chill of the rainy night blowing in through the opening, nor did he see the eyes, steady and unblinking, watching him in deathly silence.

Chapter 20
Red Wine

After breakfast, Noraldo and Filandro bought a jug of wine from the innkeeper and walked down to the trees by the river, to the place where the innkeeper said he's seen Prince Ippolito wandering for the last two days. It was a quiet, removed spot, with no one else in sight. The leaning trees appeared to be falling asleep on their feet. Wildflowers peeked at the two intruders out of the tall grass. There, in peaceful seclusion, lulled by the sound of the river and the warmth of the sun, the two friends lay on the grassy banks talking and sharing the jug.

After the first sip, both heartily agreed that the bitter wine was far from the best they had ever tasted, but the wine's poor quality was only in keeping with the rest of the inn where they had bought it. Besides, the more they drank of the stuff, the less the taste seemed to matter.

The sun became hotter. The water in the river began to sparkle. Every minute Noraldo expected Prince Ippolito to appear. The sighing of the warm breeze through the branches overhead caused the leaves to murmur and stir. Noraldo thought he heard footsteps approaching through the tall wild grass. He looked up. All around him, the silent, ancient trees seemed to have awakened, and to be watching him.

The Devil in Love

"Must have been the leaves rustling," he thought.

He had another drink and stretched out closer to Filandro, who was in the midst of talking about something as though his friend were listening. Noraldo hadn't been paying attention. He tried to concentrate on Filandro's words.

"…though the way he treats him, it's not at all surprising. Poor little fellow is probably so shaken up by his Grandpa dying that his nerves are raw…"

"But did you see that boy's face?" interrupted Noraldo. "He sure looked like he'd really seen something to me."

"And who exactly do you think he saw?" laughed Filandro somewhat sharply. "This Prince of yours, I suppose? Or maybe the Hanged Man himself?"

Noraldo put out his hand to shush Filandro, and instead his hand brushed his friend's cheek. It lingered there. "Let's not argue." They both gave up trying to talk. Noraldo's head rolled back on the grassy earth. His eyes became lost in watching the clouds changing shape in the blue, blue sky, where no trace of rain remained. He no longer felt the earth beneath him. He was floating, light as a cloud, out into that bright, infinite blueness…

"Must have had a little more to drink than I thought," he murmured in Filandro's direction. Filandro didn't answer. Where had he gone? Someone's lips brushed a light kiss on his cheek. "Are you getting as drowsy as I am? I can hardly keep my eyes open."

The Devil in Love

As though in answer, Filandro's hand slid under Noraldo's clothes. At least he thought it was Filandro's hand. Until he opened his eyes and saw instead someone else crouching over him, his face darkened by the shadowy branches overhead. A man with a rope around his... Noraldo blinked in the bright sun. No one.

But where was Filandro? No longer beside him. His eyes closed. They had become so heavy they refused to stay open. Footsteps approached him through the tall grass. Noraldo smiled, but his eyelids wouldn't budge. Too bright, much too brightness. He felt hands caressing his body, pulling open his clothes. "Where have you been?" he asked. He opened his eyes, squinting up at Filandro. But it wasn't Filandro. He was looking up into the face of the Prince.

"At last," said Ippolito. His voice had a curious echo, as though he were speaking in a hollow cave. "At last..."

Noraldo smiled sleepily. His search was over. He felt the Prince's arms close around him. He felt the Prince's naked body sliding on top of him. He managed to open his heavy eyes one last time, fluttering weakly. For some reason which he couldn't understand, the handsome, laughing face above him belonged to the innkeeper. But when he closed his eyes again, the mouth that kissed him belonged to the Prince.

Noraldo woke himself by the sound of his own snoring. He shivered. He wasn't wearing any clothes. His head jerked up from the ground in bewilderment. "Where am I?" he thought. "Why am I undressed? What am I doing here?"

It was almost dusk. He lay in the tree-sheltered grass by the river, where they had gone to wait for the Prince. Filandro lay sprawling in front of him, sleeping like a log. Noraldo's clothes lay scattered about, crumpled, where they had apparently been flung. He struggled to reassemble his foggy memories. They didn't fit. Pieces were missing. Where, for instance, was the Prince?

Had Ippolito gone? Had he ever been there at all? Noraldo was no longer quite so certain. He and Filandro appeared to be very much alone. Was it possible that the two of them, in their drunken state, had...? Because if not the Prince, and not Filandro, then who...?

He shook Filandro awake.

"What? what?" murmured his friend, as his eyes fluttered open. Filandro, too, seemed surprised to find himself asleep under the trees. He looked up at his naked friend for an explanation. But all Noraldo had were questions.

"What happened?" he demanded in fear.

"How should I know?" said Filandro. "I just woke up. I should be asking you."

"How long have we been sleeping?"

"All day, it looks like." Filandro rubbed his eyes, trying to clear away the sleepy blur. "I don't know about you, but I've been having some very strange dreams."

The Devil in Love

"Me, too," said Noraldo. "At least, I didn't think they were dreams until just now. But what else could they be? That damned wine! It went right to my head."

Noraldo began pulling on his clothes.

"For a while I almost thought," said Filandro, "that your Prince Ippolito was really here."

"I thought so, too!" cried Noraldo. "Then maybe he really *was* here. Maybe it wasn't a dream. I know this much – I was holding him in my arms."

"Not the way I saw it, you weren't."

"What do you mean?"

"He was holding *you*," said Filandro. "You weren't in any condition to be holding *anyone*. Either I was dreaming, Noraldo, or you slept right through your Prince's entire visit, without waking up once."

"Slept through it?" repeated Noraldo in horror. "But I thought I was awake. You mean I was just dreaming?"

"One of us must have been. I woke up before the Prince got here. You were sound asleep, and not wearing a stitch."

"*Before* the Prince even got here?" exclaimed Noraldo. "That doesn't make any sense."

"Stop interrupting me," said Filandro. "Yes, before he got here. It doesn't make sense to me, either. I got up and left you for a minute, to relieve myself. I walked over past that tree, there. I was just coming back when a man stepped out over there by the water. It was your Prince, or whoever he is.

The Devil in Love

He didn't see me, so I stayed where I was. All he could see was you, sprawling there in all your glory.

"He knew you the minute he saw you. He shouted your name, shook you by the shoulders, kissed you, hugged you. He slapped you on the cheeks, cried over you. But it was useless. You were dead to the world. A naked corpse."

Noraldo couldn't believe his ears. "You can't be telling the truth!" he groaned. "Please tell me you're just pulling some kind of cruel joke on me." He couldn't stop shuddering over the very thought of lying there in a drunken stupor in front of the Prince. "What he must think of me!"

"He gave you kisses that were so tender, I hated him," said Filandro. "But he didn't get the slightest response from you. He was ready to cry, and fighting back the tears."

"That damned wine!" Noraldo shouted. He grabbed the jug impulsively and heaved it out into the river, where it disappeared with a dull splash. "Then what happened?"

"Then he pulled out a dagger."

"What" Noraldo knew for certain now that he was hearing things. He sank weakly back down again.

"I thought he was going to kill you. In another moment, I would have dashed out of the trees and struck him down. Instead of trying to stab you, though, he lifted the dagger up to his own head and sliced off a lock of his hair. He pressed the lock into one of your hands."

"A lock of hair?" interjected Noraldo. "What lock of hair?"

The Devil in Love

"Just listen," said Filandro. "This is what he said to you. 'When the odds are a thousand to one, Noraldo, throw this lock of hair at your enemies.' Then he took a ring off his finger, a dazzling ring with a blood-red stone, and put it into your other hand.

"What ring? Where's the lock of hair?"

"Noraldo, listen to me. He said, 'This is the real Demon Ring. The wizard is wearing an imitation, and doesn't know it yet. I switched rings while he was asleep. Whoever wears the real ring, controls the demons. My love for you continues, even if you don't return it. If the wizard discovers what I've given you, he will kill me. But without this ring and this lock of hair, you'll never be able to rescue me. Just in case you ever want to try.'

"Then he started crying like his heart was going to break, and he ran off into those trees over there by the water."

"But tell me," cried Noraldo, "where are the lock of hair and the Demon Ring?"

"That's the part I don't understand," said Filandro.

"Why?"

"After the Prince left, there was – someone else."

"Someone else?" gasped Noraldo. "But who?"

"I don't know. I was hardly awake myself, and my eyes weren't focusing very well. At first I thought it was the Prince coming back again. But then I saw that he was barefoot. Wearing a ragged black robe. With a rope around his neck. He moved very quietly, like a shadow. He leaned over you. Before I realized what he was doing, he took the lock of hair out of one hand and the ring out of the other. By the time I'd jumped up, there wasn't a sign of him. Just a couple of footprints on a stretch of muddy ground. Left by bare foot. If it weren't for those footprints, I'd have sworn it was the Hanged Man himself!"

"And so the Prince's two gifts have both been stolen!" groaned Noraldo. "Snatched by a phantom. And without them, rescue is impossible? What horrible luck! Things couldn't have turned out worse. Well, I can tell you one thing. Tomorrow I'm going to be down here by the river again, waiting. The Prince has only one day left. This time I won't fall asleep. I only hope it's not too late."

They walked back to the inn without saying another word, sunk in gloomy silence. The moment they walked through the door, Troilo looked up from the cauldron of stew he was stirring, and called out, "Well, did you get a chance to share a drink with your friend, the Prince?"

Noraldo didn't want to discuss it. "No," he said bluntly, heading in the direction of their room.

"Surely you at least saw him go by?"

"Why?" asked Noraldo, his curiosity aroused. "Did you?"

"Of course!" said the innkeeper. "Right from this window. How could you have missed him? He must have walked right over you. Weren't you in that grove of trees by the river, like I told you?"

The Devil in Love

"Yes, we were there," admitted Noraldo gloomily. "Unfortunately, that red wine you gave us was so powerful that it put us both to sleep."

"You boys aren't used to Antichi wine, eh?" The innkeeper thought that was funny.

Noraldo didn't. "Tomorrow, my good man, I want you to find us a light, white wine to take with us – just something to wet our lips and calm our nerves, nothing more. Please, now, make sure this time that it's not too strong."

"A white wine, yes," promised Troilo. "Very light."

He smiled bitterly as the two of them walked past him, staring down into the stew he was stirring. He silently resolved that Noraldo would get his white wine, all right, with a little something added. Only this time he would put in twice as much.

Chapter 21
White Wine

That night Noraldo lay awake long after Filandro was sound asleep beside him. He felt wretched. "Can't I ever do anything right?" he repeated to himself bitterly. Every time he thought about the Prince finding him passed out in a drunken stupor, he groaned. Now, for all he knew, it was too late, and besides, he had lost the two very things he needed most for the rescue. What in the world had happened to him that afternoon? That mysterious drowsiness...

Tomorrow would be the Prince's last day in Antichi, before being swept away into that elusive, spellbound palace. "I've got to see him again!" he swore fervently in the darkness. His fists were knotted, his teeth clenched. "I've got to!" No matter how dangerous it was, he was determined. Somehow he had to free the Prince from Vernaccio and those two demons, even if he had to do so with his last breath. Tomorrow he was not going to fall asleep by the river!

Filandro moaned in his sleep, shifted position, nudged up against him. Noraldo looked over at him. "Is it possible," he wondered, "that Filandro may not be the loyal friend I take him to be? It was by following Filandro's advice to tear off the mask that I lost the Prince in the first place. Then Filandro tried to kill the black stag. Now he tells me I slept through the

The Devil in Love

Prince's visit. Could he have gotten me drunk on purpose? Could *he* be the one who stole the lock of hair and the ring? Or is the whole thing a lie, in the first place? Could Filandro have come along just to make sure that everything goes wrong? But why? Why would my best friend…? Unless…? What if Filandro, himself, is in love with the Prince? What if the two of them, while I was unconscious…?"

Thus Noraldo went on worrying and imagining the worst, unable to see the truth that was right in front of his nose, until he had himself convinced that he couldn't trust anyone.

The next morning, while they were dressing, Noraldo put one hand on Filandro's shoulder, looked him straight in the eye, and said, "My friend, today you must not fail me. No matter how long we end up waiting by the river for the Prince, I've got to stay awake. You mustn't, under any circumstances, let me fall asleep. Not even so much as close my eyes for a minute. Do you understand?"

"I'll make sure you don't," promised Filandro.

"Prove your friendship to me in this. Don't let me fall asleep."

"You can trust me."

They had breakfast downstairs. Little Renzo didn't look like he'd managed to get any sleep at all. His eyes had a haunted, nightmare look. His father hadn't rested much, either. Troilo yawned as Noraldo paid him for their meal.

The Devil in Love

"And here's your wine," said Troilo. He produced a jug half the size of yesterday's. "Light, white wine, just like you asked for. Have a taste."

"I'll take your word for it," said Noraldo. He thought he could smell wine on the innkeeper's breath.

Troilo grinned as Noraldo counted the coins into his hand. "Going out to see the Prince again?"

Noraldo ignored him.

He shouldn't have. Troilo watched the two friends from the inn window, his eyes glittering with fascination and malice, as they walked down toward the river.

They came to the grove of trees overlooking the water. They spread a blanket under one of the trees, just as they had done the day before. Filandro settled the jug of wine in between two rocks of the river to give it a chill, and together they tried to relax in the morning sunshine.

It was a very hot day. Soon they retreated into the shadows of the wide-spreading branches. The air seemed to stop moving, to grow thick with heat. They were sweating, even in the shade.

"Time for a drink," said Filandro, heading toward the water. Returning to the blanket with the wet jug, he could see the uneasiness in Noraldo's face. "Listen, I promised I wouldn't let you fall asleep, and I won't. But my throat is like dust. Just a small one."

He tipped his head back, upended the jug, and took a deep swallow, wiping his mouth with the back of his hand.

The Devil in Love

He puckered his lips. "Bitter again, but nice and cold." He had another swallow, and then held out the cold, dripping jug to his friend. Noraldo looked as though he were being handed a poisonous snake.

But it was hot, and he was getting nervous. He took hold of the jug reluctantly, and tipped back his head, taking only enough to wet his lips. It was icy, refreshing. He took a small swallow, and then another quick one, and passed the jug back.

"That'll do for me," he said. "The rest is yours."

They stretched out beside each other on the blanket, listening to the birds and the breeze stirring through the leaves, and the endless rumble of the river. They talked about old times. Noraldo relaxed. He stopped distrusting his friend. He took Filandro's hand. Half an hour later, Filandro had another drink of wine. Noraldo joined him. This time they didn't put the jug back in the river, but kept it there with them on the blanket...

Before Filandro sank hopelessly down into the depths of sleep, he managed to open his eyes weakly one last time. There was Noraldo, slumped over on the blanket beside him and breathing deeply, regularly, eyes closed, lost to the world. The sight was enough to make Filandro groan and struggle up into a sitting position. "I promised," he mumbled groggily to himself. "Noraldo must not fall asleep."

The Devil in Love

Filandro took hold of his own head with both hands. It felt like it was about to roll off his neck. Was the ground subtly moving, shifting, beneath him? "I can't be this drunk," thought Filandro desperately.

He leaned over Noraldo's limp body and shook him. Noraldo wobbled about bonelessly beneath his entreaties. "Wake up, Noraldo, come on," he pleaded. "I'm trying to be a good friend, remember? I promised I wouldn't let you fall asleep, and I'm not going to let you."

His unheeding friend, however, seemed to have no intention of waking up. He was little more than a placid bundle of clothes, without any will of his own, lost in distant dreams and floppy as a rag doll. What was worse, Filandro's own eyelids were growing heavy, sliding down. In a frantic attempt to keep from falling asleep, Filandro began slapping himself across the cheeks, pinching himself.

Why were his eyelids sliding shut?

"I promised," he groaned, staggering up onto legs that were determined to fold out from under him, remaining upright only with difficulty. "I've got to stay awake," he thought. "I'll throw myself in the river. That ought to wake me up."

Filandro lurched across the grove, determined to do just that. He didn't make it. His feet became tangled in a fall of dead branches. He hit the ground hard. It took him a while to get his breath back, and a little longer to clamber back up onto his legs. Halfway upright, he discovered that the two of them were no longer alone in the grove. He remained where he was, sinking back down again in hiding, unable to believe what he now saw happening before his eyes.

An intruder was crouching over Noraldo, pulling open his clothes and covering him with passionate fondlings. Instead of the Prince, however, Filandro saw the insolent young innkeeper clutching his friend in the wildest frenzy, while Noraldo lay in his arms, oblivious.

A branch snapped nearby.

Troilo jerked away from Noraldo and scrambled up onto his feet, eyes scanning the nearby trees as he tucked himself back into his clothes. A crunching of footsteps nearby. Troilo bolted across the grove and into the forest, heading back toward the inn.

The innkeeper wasn't gone long before his voice rang through the trees in a piercing scream, which was followed by a crashing away through distant, unseen underbrush, and then silence.

A figure stepped into the sunlight through the golden leaves. It was the Prince. He did not appear to have heard Troilo's cry. His attention was elsewhere. Noraldo lay before him, half-bared and senseless, sprawling across the blanket. The Prince sank to his knees. He kissed Noraldo urgently, shook him by the shoulders, shouted in his ear. Noraldo smiled back blandly from another world, insensible, unreachable. Prince Ippolito's heart seemed to break. He began weeping, his shoulders hunched forward and shaking.

The Devil in Love

Even Filandro was moved at the sight of so much sorrow, and he tried to shout, to wave his arm, to explain to the Prince that his friend had accidentally drunk too much wine, but none of that happened. He tried to call out, to do the right thing for Noraldo, who had always been his best friend, but no words came out of his mouth.

Then he saw something that was impossible, so Filandro knew he must be dreaming. Holding the limp body of Noraldo in his arms, the Prince looked up wretchedly at the moon, wailing his grief, and Filandro clearly saw that instead of tears, two lines of red were dripping down the Prince's cheeks. He was weeping blood.

"Now I know I'm asleep," Filandro thought feverishly. "No one weeps blood. I've got to be dreaming."

The Prince took out a white silk handkerchief and touched it to his face, wiping away the red. Then he tucked the bloody handkerchief into one of Noraldo's lifeless hands.

"Never part with this handkerchief," he said sadly into Noraldo's ear, "for without it, you don't stand a chance against Vernaccio." Noraldo didn't hear a word of it. Filandro, however, listened intently even if he couldn't move or speak.

"Tonight, my sleepy friend," said the Prince, caressing him tenderly, "my time is up. At midnight the wizard will make me his own. I've lost the game. I have no choice. I must go through with our bargain. All the legions of Hell have been invited to the palace to celebrate our union. How I wish you were awake, so that I could say goodbye to you! How I wish I could just say to you once that I'll always love you."

The bell in the distant tower of Antichi began tolling midnight.

A sudden tension crackled through the air, causing the Prince to look up uneasily. Out of the hush of the afternoon, a wind was beginning to rise. Suddenly a howling blast shook the branches of the forest, sweeping down out of nowhere. The wild grass began to lash about, as though the stalks were trying to uproot themselves and flee headlong. From out of the sky over the darkening river approached a black shape, rapidly growing larger. Birds screamed and lunged for cover. Clouds were blasted into streaming white ribbons. With his cape swirling out behind him, Vernaccio hurtled relentless toward them on the flying carpet, with a demon flapping on either side.

The Prince leaped to his feet in terror, letting Noraldo's unconscious head thud upon the ground. With a cry, he tried to run. He got halfway across the grove before demon wings engulfed him. He was swept off his feet, kicking. The two laughing demons presented him to the wizard. Vernaccio's arms closed around him.

"My dear boy," said Vernaccio, "you mustn't wander far from home, tonight of all nights." He kissed Prince Ippolito tenderly on the cheek. "Come now, it's time you took your bath and started getting ready. Our guests will soon be arriving."

The Devil in Love

For one brief moment, Filandro glimpsed the determination of crazed love in Vernaccio's eyes, he recognized that private agony of longing and need carved into the lines of the wizard's face. Then a wind howled through the grove. The carpet was gone. The wind was abruptly still. No Prince, no wizard, no demons. Sprawling unconscious, with the bloody handkerchief tucked into one fist, Noraldo remained unaware of the entire incident.

Filandro's heart was hammering like a mad blacksmith. He was too terrified to move. A frightened hush settled over the forest, and then he began to weep. "Noraldo, Noraldo, I'm so sorry I failed you!" he sobbed. "I was not a good friend."

Then a bare foot crunched cautiously out of the undergrowth. A black-clad figure with a rope around his neck glided out of the leaves. A hand reached out and snatched away the bloody handkerchief before Filandro could get his legs to cooperate.

"No!" cried Filandro. "Give that back...!"

Always the faithful friend, he staggered to his feet and lurched toward the apparition. He almost got there, before the ground rushed up and hit him in the face. That was his last memory.

Chapter 22
The Secret Watcher

When his eyes snapped open, Noraldo was looking up into a gray, twilit sky. He gasped and rose up onto his elbows. The grove all around him was shadowy and dim. His worst fears had come true. He had slept through his last chance to meet with Ippolito. Drunk and half-undressed again, Noraldo was horrified – and furious. Filandro lay deep in slumber beside him on the blanket. Noraldo rudely shook him into consciousness.

"You've betrayed me again!" cried Noraldo. He struck his friend angrily. "You're a liar! And you got me drunk on purpose!" His fists began to pummel Filandro.

"What are you talking about? Hey, stop that!" gasped Filandro, scrambling away from him on wobbly legs. Stunned by his friend's rage, Filandro stumbled backwards, holding out his arms to fend off Noraldo, frantically trying to sort out the dozens of lurid memories clogging his mind, to find the truth behind what had just happened. His mind was far from up to such a task, being still half-asleep. His thoughts were whirling with all the unbelievable things he had witnessed. What he remembered could be nothing but impossible nightmares. How could the Prince have wept blood? And if he did, then where was the bloody handkerchief?

The Devil in Love

Pain thudded into his shoulder. Noraldo, again.

"How can you pretend to be my friend?" shouted Noraldo. "You scheming, two-faced liar! I thought you promised to make sure I didn't fall asleep?"

It was only too clear that night was falling.

"But I hardly drank anything!" cried Filandro in self-defense. "I'm sorry I fell asleep. You don't know how hard I tried. I don't understand what happened to me."

"I understand it perfectly," shouted Noraldo, only inches from Filandro's face. "You *wanted* me to fall asleep."

Filandro couldn't believe his ears. He tried to pull loose from Noraldo's hands, but they weren't letting go. "Wait a minute – you don't understand. I couldn't wake you up, but I tried…"

Noraldo's hands closed around Filandro's throat. Through clenched teeth, Noraldo hissed, "Stop – lying – to – me!" Tears of disappointment and betrayal ran down his cheeks. Filandro couldn't bear the sight. He wanted to explain. He would have told him everything, if he could have gotten a breath, if he could have forced Noraldo to listen. Though he was stronger than Noraldo, he couldn't pry loose that grief-maddened stranglehold.

"How could you stab me in the back like that?" cried Noraldo, so angry he was crying. "I'll never be happy with anyone in the world but him, and now I've lost him! Thanks to you…!"

The Devil in Love

Then arms grabbed Noraldo from behind, pulling him off of his friend and jerking him backwards off his feet, so that Filandro was able to stumble weakly away from him, gasping. In a moment, both of them forgot their quarrel completely. They found themselves staring up at a hooded, black-robed figure whose feet were bare. Around his neck coiled a thick rope knotted into a noose.

"Your friend is innocent," said the Hanged Man, in a voice which seemed to fill and echo through the silent grove. "Save your anger for the innkeeper."

Noraldo and Filandro were both speechless with terror. They gaped up at the apparition looming before them with bulging eyes. The more they regarded their spectral informer, however, the less he looked like some ghostly revenger from beyond the grave.

"Who are you?" cried Noraldo.

"A defender of the innocent," said the Hanged Man. Then he pulled back his hood. He looked surprisingly like a man of flesh and blood with curly brown hair and a serious, sun-browned face. "Your friend is faithful. If you got that wine from Troilo, you can be sure he put something else in those jugs besides wine."

"But, why?" said Noraldo.

"Because you resisted him," said the Hanged Man. "Troilo doesn't take no for an answer. He enjoyed you anyway, while you were unconscious."

The Devil in Love

"He what?" cried Noraldo. "The innkeeper? Drugged the wine? I thought he liked us. Why would he do that?"

"You aren't the first good-looking boys I've found drugged and undressed on these hills," said the Hanged Man. "I keep my eyes on him, but he's always up to trouble. I watch just about everything that goes on around here. Everything is revealed to a man in time, who can open his eyes wide enough to see."

"Who are you, anyway?" interrupted Filandro.

"My name is Lodovico," said the black-robed man. "I've lived as a hermit in these hills for the last fifteen years. My father was the good man who was hung by mistake, over there on the old gallows that used to stand on that hill. I burned down that gallows on the night they proved his innocence.

"I've never had much to do with people, not since they took my father away. Let's say I'm not overly fond of my fellow men. To me they seem lazy, greedy, and vicious. I wear this noose around my neck just to keep people out of my way. The only Hanged Man who haunts these hills is me. My father rests just as peacefully in death as he did in life. This noose gives me a chance to make sure that no one forgets how easily they judged and killed an innocent man."

The hermit looked directly into Noraldo's eyes. "As you, yourself, judged your innocent friend a moment ago."

Noraldo hung his head, casting a guilty glance at Filandro. "How can you ever forgive me? I've been wrongheaded before, but never as bad as this! I'm so ashamed."

In answer, Filandro took hold of his hand.

"I live not far from here," continued Lodovico, "in a secret cave that I call my hermitage. I make a point of seeing as much as I can. I saw everything that happened here both yesterday and today. I should never have let Troilo get out of my sight.

"Just a few minutes ago, I surprised him as he was running back to the inn. I think I scared him half to death. He'll be a little less hasty to take out his frustrations on little Renzo now, the next time the boy tells him he saw the Hanged Man."

"And so it was all just a drugged dream!" groaned Noraldo bitterly. "My Prince never arrived, just that damned innkeeper…"

"Not true," said the hermit. "Both yesterday and today, after you fell asleep, your Prince Ippolito himself was really here, in the flesh, holding you in his arms, begging you to rescue him, leaving you magic talismans to help you do so."

"He was?" Noraldo's eyes opened wider, filling with hope.

"Yesterday he left you an enchanted lock of hair and the Demon Ring itself," said Lodovico. "Today he left you a handkerchief wet with his own tears of blood."

"Tears of blood?" Noraldo thought he was going to faint.

The Devil in Love

"And now the time has come," interrupted Filandro, "for you to tell us what you've done with those talismans, because you're the one who took them, aren't you?"

Lodovico reached into the side of his robe, and withdrew the white handkerchief with red stains, the lock of hair, and the ring with the gleaming red stone. "Though I seldom interfere in the schemes of men, I couldn't bear to see such treasures left exposed to any passing thief." He held them out to Noraldo. "They're yours," he said, as Noraldo took them carefully into his hands. "You're going to need them."

"He wants me to have these?" said Noraldo.

"The Prince cares for you deeply. He may be a young fool at times, but he has a good heart. He's worth trying to rescue. Take very good care of these. They can never be replaced. You have only one chance left. Without them, you'll never be able to defeat those demons, and get that boy away from Vernaccio."

Noraldo looked at him in amazement. "You know all about it, don't you?"

"As I told you, I'm a watcher. I watch everything that happens in these hills. Very seldom do I interfere, as I am doing now. But I've seen the Prince grow up. I know his love for sorcery, and I've watched him with that wizard. I want Ippolito to be happy. Now that's going to be up to you. Save him."

With trembling fingers, Noraldo slid the Demon Ring onto his right hand. He folded the lock of hair carefully into a dry corner of the handkerchief, tucking the rest of it around the hair into a small square of folded silk, which he poked safely down into a leather pocket attached to his belt.

"You who watch everything," said Noraldo, "tell me what I should do now."

Lodovico smiled grimly. "Ippolito will officially lose his game with the wizard when the year of the contest ends at midnight. Vernaccio will immediately sweep him off in that enchanted palace, and by morning they'll be far, far away. Tonight will be your only opportunity. Unfortunately, many other demons will be haunting the palace tonight, to celebrate the wizard's triumph. Still, you have no choice. You must trust the talismans, and take the chance. If you conduct yourself with care, Ippolito may still have one slim hope to escape that wizard."

"But where am I ever going to find that enchanted palace again?" interjected Noraldo. "It used to be back in the forest outside Valbrosa, but I watched those two demons carry it away into the sky the last time I was there,."

"Ah," said the hermit. "I thought you knew. The magic palace is on the other side of that hill, just west of my cave. With my own eyes, I watched those two demons lower it out of the sky and set it down there." Lodovico pointed up beyond the darkening treetops, toward the silent crags and peaks of the White Demons. "The wizard is there now with Prince Ippolito."

The Devil in Love

"Can you take me there?" whispered Noraldo, trying not to think of the mortal danger into which he was going.

"At once," said Lodovico. "Follow me."

Noraldo and Filandro looked at each other, an unspoken question hovering between them.

Then the time for choices was over, and the choice had been made. The hermit raised his hood so that it consumed his face in darkness, adjusted the rope noose that hung down from his neck, and led the way up into the hills, with Noraldo right behind him. At Noraldo's side walked Filandro, far too loyal a friend to abandon him now. As long as there was breath left inside the young baker, Noraldo would not be fighting for the Prince alone.

Chapter 23
The Wizard's Triumph

"Up on that cliff," said Lodovico.

Noraldo looked up where the hermit was pointing. There, on a high rocky ledge suspended over the chasm, perched that breathtaking, shimmering illusion of marble columns and stairways, galleries and gardens, just as it had looked in the forest not long ago. This time, however, the spellbound palace was not deserted. Even from the distant path where they were standing, they could hear the nightmarish fiddling and the maddened drums. Noraldo felt a cold sinking in the pit of his stomach.

"Do you know how to get up there?" asked Filandro.

"These hills are like the chambers of my mind," said the hermit. "I know every corner of them. This way."

Lodovico slipped into the shadows of twilight. Noraldo followed him into the darkness, and then up the side of the mountain, with Filandro close beside him. Once again Noraldo found himself approaching that demonic palace where he had already lost his heart. This time, however, the wizard was not going to be conveniently off somewhere else, bringing misery into the world. This time Vernaccio would be at home.

"Me against a wizard?" thought Noraldo bleakly.

The Devil in Love

He began to get the uncomfortable feeling that he might be setting out on the very last night of his life. He tried to follow after the hermit with a brave step and a forthright heart, but he only felt more and more like a condemned man walking to his execution. They didn't stand a chance against the Devil's own wizard and a palace full of demons. Who were they fooling? They were marching to their deaths. The closer they got to that gleaming palace, the more Noraldo knew in his heart that he would be entering it that night for the last time.

The cliffs and crags around the palace were lit with its shuddering radiance. The walls and towers flickered, as though they were made of nothing more substantial than mist and candlelight. The hermit led them stealthily closer and closer, until they could see the majestic stairs and the open doors at the top. Instead of entering there, however, as Noraldo had done twice before, Lodovico led them around to the side of the palace, where they could see down from the hillside over the steep, sheer walls, into the luxurious gardens beyond the rows of slender white columns.

All three of them stopped in their tracks and stared in terror.

Before them surged a ghastly celebration in full swing, a gathering of fiends and capering ghouls all flinging themselves unrestrainedly through the twists and contortions of a hideous dance. Demons of every kind and description had converged there from the farthest corners of the seven worlds, among the most illustrious and terrifying of the Devil's children. With chilling howls and shrieks of laughter, they shared in Vernaccio's triumphant wedding-night, dancing through the gardens in a celebration of such ear-splitting noise and bone-shivering music that the Devil himself would have felt at home.

On an elevated walkway spanning the gardens stood the wizard in his long, black robes. He raised his arms. Trumpets rang through the gardens in a minor key. The din hushed. The revelers looked up.

Griffone, clad in his handsome gold livery, stepped out onto one end of the walkway. "Prince Ippolito has been bathed in scented oils as you requested, Master," said the demon servant.

He drew the Prince out onto the walkway before them. The appearance of Ippolito caused great excitement. Except for several artificial leaves of paper-thin gold to conceal his manhood, with similar leaves encircling his head in a crown, Ippolito wore only a cape of the finest black silk. Eager cries rang out below. Griffone escorted the Prince down the length of the walkway to the middle of the span, where Vernaccio waited for him. The wizard at once slipped a black-sleeved arm around the pale, perfect body of the defeated Prince, while the demons leered up at Ippolito on all sides with hungry, impatient looks.

Soranzo stepped out onto the walkway from the other direction, attired in blue, and bowed deeply. "Master," said

The Devil in Love

the demon servant with a grin, "your bed has been scattered with rose petals from India, as you requested."

The demons roared their approval. They knew what was going to happen on those rose petals. They had been invited there that night to watch. Well might they howl and stamp the floor with their hooves, claws, and feet. They were about to banquet on a visual feast.

Vernaccio's face was bright and flushed, helplessly smiling. He had never been happier. He could hardly keep his hands off Ippolito. How he longed to finally satisfy that aching desire! The very mention of those rose petals seemed to make the wizard feverish with anticipation. He could wait no longer.

"My notorious friends," he said in a voice which filled the gardens, "thank you for coming to share with me this glorious wedding-night."

The demons roared their approval.

Vernaccio held up his arms for quiet, sweeping the air dramatically with his long sleeves. "Let me introduce to you, my friends, my own beloved Ippolito, Prince of Antichi."

The fiends stomped and shrieked with anticipation.

"Tonight I have invited you to share in my glory, for tonight this beautiful boy –snatched away from the Hand of Fate – shall be mine!"

The demonic roar

Vernaccio raised his arms, in a booming voice that was louder even than the cacophony of demonic glee. "Come now, my friends. The bell is about to toll midnight. This way to the bed-chamber."

Enchanted trumpets gave a blast. The wizard took Ippolito's hand and led him in a grand ceremonial across the walkway. The two demon servants followed, smirking. The Prince proudly looked straight ahead, but his resistance had been broken. He stood straight and strong, his shoulders unbowed by defeat, but he made no struggle to prevent Vernaccio's eager hand from slipping around his waist beneath the black cape, those fingers so eager to be unleashed upon his body.

The demons surged after them, roaring for the consummation.

Both Noraldo and Filandro were in shock, open-mouthed at the horrors they had witnessed. Lodovico could see that. He put a hand on each of their shoulders. "There's only one way we can rescue Ippolito," he said grimly, "and we've got to act now, or it will be too late. We've got to go in there, and just hope that those three talismans can do what the Prince said they would. We could be committing suicide. It's now or never. Are you willing to risk it?"

Noraldo's head was spinning, and he was feeling faint from lack of air. "Let's go," he said.

Echoing down from the bell tower came the deep, echoing bong of the first stroke of midnight.

Chapter 24
The Three Talismans

They hurried around the side of the palace, to the wide flight of marble stairs leading up to the open doorway. With Filandro on one side and the hermit on the other, Noraldo mounted the stairs one by one, walking back into a yesterday which would never be quite the same again. As they approached the open doors, with the Demon Ring on his finger, Noraldo withdrew from his leather pocket the bloody handkerchief and the lock of Ippolito's hair. The three of them stopped at the palace threshold, staring inside.

The bell in the tower tolled two – three – four...

There were no demons in sight. They passed into the room beyond. No demons yet, though this time plenty of evidence of their passing – glasses of wine littered about everywhere, fragments of broken glass, grape stems, peach pits, orange peelings, and bones, bones everywhere, gnawed bones. Wine had been spilled on the chairs and floor. Everything remained just where it had been flung when the demonic revelers had all rushed off to the bed-chamber, abandoning the room to disorder.

The bell in the tower tolled five – six – seven...

On into the dining-room slipped the intruders. A dozen long tables were heaped with the remains of an epic banquet.

The Devil in Love

Platters of leftover scraps testified to the food that was no longer there. Neither were the guests who had eaten and rushed on.

After them came those three trespassers, dashing quickly between the tables and beyond, past the fountain, past the music-room strewn with lutes and viols, and out into the lantern-lit gardens. Through the trampled flowers they ran. Beyond the tiles of the sunken bath waited that long gallery of disturbing paintings, at the end of which loomed a shadowy door that for the first time in Noraldo's visits to the palace was closed.

Nine – ten – eleven…

Noraldo had taken no more than three running bounds down that corridor of masterpieces when the door of the bedchamber at the end of the hall was flung open. Out of that room burst a horde of fiends that should never have seen the light of day. They were horrible enough by torchlight. They were not at all happy about being interrupted. They were, in fact, quite furious and apparently determined, by the looks on their faces, to tear the tree intruders apart, limb by limb.

The bell struck twelve.

Noraldo's knees turned to water. He found himself running back out into the gardens after Lodovico and Filandro, but too slow, far too slow.

"Throw the lock of hair at them!" cried the hermit.

Noraldo's terror had become so great that he'd almost forgotten about it. He unfolded it out of the bloody handkerchief with shaking fingers, and flung it toward the pursuing demons.

The lock of hair blew apart. Each strand became a whirring, glowing filament of light. Swirling through the gardens in a storm of fiery threads, they began looping around the demons' arms and legs, clinging to their hair, tripping them, entangling them in a vast and sticky net. Shouting furiously, their beating and kicking only made things worse, as the demons tumbled on top of each other in the flower-beds, bound and tied. In a moment, the gardens were half-buried in legions of demons all roped together in a knot of thrashing limbs. They set up a howl of rage.

That howl was answered.

Out of the bed-chamber stormed the two demon servants, Griffone and Soranzo, growing larger and larger as they strode down the corridor toward the gardens, now eight feet tall, now nine, now ten, no longer snickering and giggling, both of them furious, glowering down at the three uninvited guests who were so rudely disturbing the night's crowning moment.

"You are no longer welcome here," said Griffone malevolently.

"We've had just about enough of you," growled Soranzo.

Their enormous hands reached down on either side, ripping apart the magic threads which bound their cousins, freeing them left and right. Demons jumped to their feet, tearing off their bonds, Leaving the freed demons to liberate the others, those two titanic boys loomed over the intruders, hands reaching down to crush and break. Noraldo was wide-eyed in horror.

"The ring!" shouted Lodovico. "Hold out the ring!"

Noraldo was just sensible enough to do as he'd been told. The moment he stretched out the Demon Ring toward them, the blood-red stone began to emit a pale glow, which shot out from the ring in a beacon of light. Soranzo and Griffone shouted. That pulsing ray no sooner fell upon them than, with a cry, the two towering youths began to shrink and were swept off their feet into the light, around and around, as though into a blazing whirlpool.

"Master, have mercy!" shouted Soranzo. "We'll give you endless nights of pleasure!"

"Master, we will serve you alone!" wailed Griffone.

But Noraldo had had quite enough of demons. "Into the ring with you!" he cried.

"No!" they protested in an echoing wail. They apparently had little say in the matter, however, since down and down into the light they spun, shrinking smaller and smaller, until they were imprisoned, kicking mad and reduced to the size of ants, within the solid red rock of the ring.

Deprived of the demonic magic upon which it fed, the enchanted palace could no longer sustain itself. A rumbling shudder caused the columns to crack and the floor tiles to snap. The walls began to lean, as though about to buckle inward. Paintings slid to the floor with shattering crashes.

The Devil in Love

The slabs of marble jiggled underfoot, their edges cracking, no longer in alignment.

With a crack, the walls began to topple. Surrounded by tumbling debris, horrified by the fate of Griffone and Soranzo, the remaining demons flew howling away in all directions. The columns sagged and snapped. The roof folded inward. All of it dissolved into dust and billowing smoke, which collapsed on top of the three intruders and left them doubled over, coughing and gasping for air.

They weren't the only ones.

The dust cleared away to reveal the wizard and Ippolito, coughing and choking in the middle of the magic carpet, which hovered several inches above the bare rock of the cliff. It was littered with artificial leaves of gold and burned rose petals. Vernaccio shrieked in rage, and climbed off the boy. He leaped to his feet and strode toward Noraldo with flaming red eyes, his black robes swirling around him.

"Irritating little meddler!" hissed the wizard. "If you think I'm going to let you ruin everything…"

Noraldo didn't need the hermit to tell him what to do next. Before Vernaccio could mutter more than the first few words of a fatal spell, Noraldo threw the blood-stained handkerchief toward him. It leaped flapping into the air, swelling to the size of a billowing sail. Vernaccio's mouth fell open. Before he could scream, the gigantic handkerchief had swallowed up the wizard completely in a blur of crackling and snapping folds, now white, now red.

The Devil in Love

A blinding flash!

When they could see again, there was no sign of the wizard except for a charred stretch of ground where Ippolito's blood-stained handkerchief had imploded in a blinding blaze.

Chapter 25
The Disenchanted

At last Noraldo and the Prince were forced to pause long enough in their embraces to take a couple of deep breaths.

"There's something I want to ask you," said Ippolito, "but I don't know if now's the right time."

"Go ahead," smiled Noraldo weakly.

"Will you be my companion for life, Noraldo? And share with me the throne of Antichi?"

Noraldo, who was near exhaustion anyway, simply fainted. Filandro had to lift his friend up under the armpits, and Ippolito got him under the knees.

"This way," said the hermit. "My secret cave is just around the side of this hill."

They carried him slowly, stopping now and then to rest. Noraldo moaned a couple times, and once called out deliriously for his book. Otherwise he was oblivious to the entire journey, and did not even wake up when they stretched him out in front of the hermit's hearth.

"Don't worry," said Lodovico. "He'll be fine. I know just the thing for him."

There, in that humble and lonely retreat devoted to prayer and meditation, Lodovico brewed a soup over the fire with roots, wild vegetables, and healing herbs. He added rosemary, oregano, and sweet basil to the cauldron, from dried branches hanging from the crossbeams of the simple, rough-hewn porch. When the soup was bubbling, he scooped some into a wooden spoon, blew on it, and then tipped it into Noraldo's mouth. Spoonful by spoonful, Noraldo sputtered and revived.

"I didn't die, after all," he said in wonder. He had been expecting the worst. He took Lodovico's hand, and the hand of his friend, Filandro. Then he looked up into Ippolito's eyes, and seemed to regain his senses.

"Thank you for your three gifts, my Prince," he said. "We could never have succeeded without you." Ippolito answered him with a kiss. Noraldo remembered more, and it awakened him completely. His face clouded over as he recalled the horrible way he had defeated the wizard. "Whatever really happened, though, to Vernaccio inside that – that handkerchief?"

Ippolito avoided Noraldo's eyes. "You don't want to know," he said simply. "Vernaccio will never bother us again."

The Devil in Love

Lodovico then handed steaming bowls of soup to Filandro and the Prince, serving up a hearty portion for himself as well. Everyone agreed that it was exceptionally tasty, especially when sprinkled with grated goat's cheese. No one refused second helpings, and the hermit's soup renewed the strength and lifted the spirits of them all.

Unfortunately, when Noraldo was sufficiently recovered and it came time for them to depart, they could not persuade Lodovico to accompany them back to Antichi.

"I don't belong in a city," said the hermit, "though it's kind of you to invite me. No, I wouldn't last more than a few hours, I'm afraid. Just not that fond of my fellow men, to be rubbing shoulders with them all day long. I've seen their ugly side, and it's a hard thing to forget. You go ahead. Live a good life. Love each other. Come visit me whenever you pass nearby."

Noraldo hugged the hermit gratefully, and wept a little on his shoulder. "Thanks for your help, Lodovico. I would have made some terrible mistakes without you."

Then Prince Ippolito said, "The kingdom of Antichi owes you a great debt, Lodovico. How can I ever repay you?"

"Come visit me sometimes in my cave," said the hermit. "You are an exception among men. I've known that all along. I've watched you grow up, Your Highness, and I'm proud of you."

The Devil in Love

Ippolito joined Noraldo in the middle of the magic carpet while Filandro and the hermit said goodbye. Though they had said very little to each other throughout the adventure, they took longer than Noraldo expected to take leave of each other now. Then Filandro bounded aboard the carpet to join his best friend and the Prince.

Though Ippolito's knowledge of sorcery was limited, he had a sharp eye and a good memory, and had ridden on the carpet often enough with the wizard to help him guess how to animate the carpet's magical powers. Up off the ground it soared and into the sky, bearing the three of them swiftly away from the cave, while Lodovico shrank to the size of a beetle, his arm raised in sad farewell.

Down they swooped over the walls of Antichi, and into the courtyard of Prince Ippolito's castle, causing screams, cries, and shouts of joy. Guards and servants came running. Trumpet fanfares erupted from the walls. In relief and rejoicing, that ancient kingdom came back to life and launched into a solid week of festivity, with banquets every night and dancing in the streets.

Their beloved Prince had come home.

No sooner had Noraldo eaten breakfast on his first morning in Antichi than he wrote a letter to his father and brothers, explaining what had happened to him and inviting them to join him. The poor shoemaker had already abandoned all hope for Noraldo. Furthermore, he had taken to dressing in black and speaking about his third son in the past tense. Imagine his joy! No sooner did he receive Noraldo's letter by royal messenger than Petroccolo hammered a notice on the shoeshop door, announcing that it was closed until further notice.

When at last the shoemaker and his two older sons stood shuffling in awe before the throne of Antichi, gaping at the wonders all around them, Noraldo introduced his family members to the Prince, one by one.

Taking Ippolito's hand, Noraldo told his father the whole story.

"What a clever son I have!" cried Petroccolo.

Noraldo shook his head. "The whole thing was an accident, Father. I had no idea I was falling in love with a Prince. When I first encountered him, he was an unfriendly masked host in a haunted palace, always ignoring me and disappearing. And then I ruined everything by unmasking him. Twice he found me passed out drunk – how that must have disappointed him! But now, at last, I've finally managed to do things right, somehow I've saved the missing Prince of Antichi, and things are starting to look rosy."

Petroccolo was delighted. "Just think!" he marveled. "You rescued a Prince from a wizard!" He shook his head in surprise and paternal admiration. "Whoever would have guessed you had it in you? Well, I always suspected you had a little something special."

The Devil in Love

Then the shoemaker caught a glimpse of Filandro standing a short distance away. After a last few words with the Prince, he hurried over to his son's best friend. With much clapping on the back and clasping of hands, Petroccolo tried to thank Filandro for how well things had turned out.

The young baker was glad to see the shoemaker in such good spirits, but longed to be alone. As soon as Petroccolo's attention had wandered elsewhere for a moment, Filandro slipped away from the merrymaking.

No one noticed him leaving.

Filandro paced unhappily through the gardens. He sat down on a far-removed stone bench, and sighed with a heavy heart. Things had not turned out so terribly well as far as he was concerned.

A shadow seemed to stop out of a nearby tree, stealthy as an animal. The brittle remains of a dead leaf cracked in two. Filandro's sharp ears detected it, and he turned quickly toward the sound.

The lanky shadow of Lodovico stood beside him. The hermit sat down, took one of Filandro's hands. They talked through the night. The next morning they were gone. Neither of them ever returned to Antichi.

Soon after, a letter from Filandro arrived at his father's bakery, explaining that he had renounced all life in the city, and had gone to live with Lodovico in his lonely, rocky hermitage. There the baker's son and the hermit loved each other in seclusion from the rest of the world, while at the same time keeping an eye on Troilo, to make sure he caused no one any more trouble. Unable to find a man who ever satisfied him for long, the dissolute young innkeeper began drinking more than was good for him, in larger and larger quantities. In spite of his derelict father, Renzo somehow managed to grow up healthy and strong, kind and fair-hearted, though he was always unusually thoughtful and somewhat serious for a child.

Noraldo continued to live happily with the Prince in the castle at Antichi. While Ippolito trained himself daily in the virtues of government, memorizing laws and tax systems, Noraldo was perfectly content to slip quietly away into some forgotten corner of the castle and continue reading that long and endlessly fascinating book.

Yet on warm, sultry evenings, Prince Ippolito would sometimes set aside his statecraft and close Noraldo's thick volume on its velvet bookmark. Then he would whisper the words of power while he and Noraldo were lying in each other's arms in the middle of the carpet. Up from the roof of Antichi's single tower they would soar, straight up into the clouds of sunset, until the carpet was swallowed in thick, red billows and the last blaze of day, up where no one could disturb them, to enjoy a sweet, stolen hour together.

*

The Devil in Love

BOOK THREE
TERROR ISLAND

CHAPTER 1
Noraldo's Obsession

"Beppo!"

The plump young pageboy, halfway out of the royal bedchamber, froze at the sound of the Prince's voice.

"Yes, Your Excellence?"

"Are you sure there weren't more candied almonds in this bowl when you got it?"

Beppo's cheeks, pink and pudgy in the first place, grew slightly redder. "No-no, of course not, Your Grace." He was all but trembling.

The Devil in Love

"Come closer, here," said Prince Ippolito, from where he reclined on his bed. Beside him, Noraldo was reading his book, which he had propped open against the bolster. Noraldo did not look up. The Prince studied the nervous pageboy as he timidly approached. His clothes were too tight for him, and his livery made him look uncomfortable.

Ippolito's sharp eyes quickly spotted an ill-concealed bulge which he recognized at once as the multiple lumps of stolen candy. Beppo's forehead was lined with sweat. The Prince felt sorry for him, in spite of himself. He decided to let the pageboy off with a warning.

"If I ever thought you were stealing candies from my very platter," said Ippolito, "I would put you on a diet of beans-and-water for a month. I hope I never have reason to suspect you again. Now, on your way."

Beppo hurried out the door. Two minutes later, when he dug the candied almonds out of their hiding-place, they were wet with nervous sweat and sticky with melted sugar.

He ate them anyway.

Meanwhile, Prince Ippolito had completely forgotten about him as he watched Noraldo intently reading beside him. Oblivious to Beppo and the Prince alike, he was gripping the open book in both hands and utterly lost in the story. Then he turned the page, groaned in dismay and struck the bed with his fist.

"A surprising twist in the plot?"

"I only wish it were! It's another missing page."

The Devil in Love

"Would a candied almond help?

"Maybe later."

Ippolito wrapped his arms around his upset friend and managed to draw him away from his reading with a series of well-placed kisses. "I know how much you love your book, but you do realize, don't you, that you haven't been yourself lately. When are you going to tell me what's troubling you?"

Noraldo let go of the last threads of the story, and closed his book in frustration. He was about to deny any such thing, but the Prince gave him another kiss and said, "Tell me the truth. What are you brooding over all the time? Don't you trust me enough to tell me what's on your mind?"

Noraldo's face underwent a change, in which emotions seemed to be battling for control. "All right," he said, "I'll admit it, I'm unhappy, and I'm not doing a very good job of hiding it."

"No, you aren't," said Ippolito, kissing him.

"And the reason I haven't told you," Noraldo tried to go on, "is that – well, when I put it into words it sounds ridiculous, but it's all I can think about lately, it completely frustrates me, and there's no use pouring out my sorrows to you because I just don't think anyone else will be able to understand."

"Try me," said the Prince.

"Well, to tell you the truth, it's about my book," said Noraldo, checking to see if the least trace of amusement had appeared on the Prince's face, and then continuing, "You know how I feel about it."

"I certainly do," said Prince Ippolito. "It's taken over your life. I think it means more to you than I do."

Noraldo kissed him, and said, "Nonsense!" but they both knew his words were close to the truth.

"I've never read anything like it," said Noraldo, trying to explain. "It's been a revelation to me. It's changed my thinking. I've memorized parts. And now I've come to another place where – well, once again there are pages missing. Bad enough that the title page is gone, and the opening chapters, and who knows what else, and then I come to gaps, holes in the story. I can't tell if pages fell out from poor binding or were torn out for some reason, but another chunk of the story is gone, and it's driving me crazy."

"Surely there is another copy of the book in some other kingdom," said the Prince, in his most reassuring voice.

"I don't think so," sighed Noraldo. "I really think there's only this one copy. My father and his brothers invented the story themselves when they were young. My uncle wrote it all down before he ran away from home. As far as I know, he only wrote it down once. But how could I find out if there *were* another copy somewhere? And if there isn't, who would know what the missing pages contained? And how the story began? And the name of the book? That's what I need to know! What was in those pages? Who could tell me?"

The Devil in Love

"Well," said the Prince guardedly, "it sounds to me like one of those questions where there's only one way to find out the answer, but you don't even want to consider that."

Noraldo looked at him curiously. "And what is that?"

"Well, you can be sure that the Sfinge would know, since he knows everything."

"The what?"

"The Sfinge," repeated Ippolito. "But you would never want to ask him anything, he's such a dreadful creature. Although they do say he's got the head and upper body of a really gorgeous boy – quite a sight I hear, that part, but he's got these eight-foot wings instead of arms, they're like bat wings, and instead of legs, the long tail of a serpent. The Sfinge knows the answer to every question. But it's much too dangerous to ask him anything. He lives on an island of horrors, deadly man-eating creatures you don't even want to hear about, much less even *think* about going there. Besides, for every question he answers, the Sfinge has a price – you have to answer one of his riddles, and if you can't guess the right answer, you die."

Noraldo was nodding his head, but he was no longer listening. He had heard all he needed to hear.

He kissed Ippolito, they fell into doing what boys fall into doing, and for the moment, Noraldo appeared to have forgotten all about his book. But from that day on, he was preoccupied with only one thing – how to reach the Sfinge, and ask him about the missing pages.

CHAPTER 2
A Pool in the Forest

If Noraldo ever thought of his best friend, Filandro, anymore, it was not very often. The baker's son, his childhood companion, was far from his thoughts now, far away from the rest of the world, in Lodovico's secluded cave high in the wild hills of the White Demon Mountains. There the young baker lived with the good hermit, and since Filandro was an expert hunter, provided the meat for their meals. Filandro had adjusted his simple wants and needs easily to the life of a hermit. The solitude suited him. Much of his day he spent alone in the forest with the silent trees. His nights he spent with Lodovico, wrapped in the hermit's arms at the mouth of the cave. There, in that rough hermitage, the two of them lived together in peace and contentment.

Then one afternoon Filandro wandered into a part of the forest he did not remember having seen before. He loved to explore new places, but he was already far from home, and was just about to turn around and retrace his steps, when a ghostly voice reached his ears, softly singing in the midst of the hushed trees.

Filandro crept closer without making a sound, and quietly drew aside the lower branches at the end of a still forest pond. A boy stood up to his thighs in the water, bathing himself. He could not have been more than fifteen years old, his body just hardening and ripening into that of a young man. His face was serious and shy, his eyes deep pools of darkness and not innocent. Those eyes drew Filandro like the currents of a river.

"Stay away," said the boy. "I'm not allowed to talk to strangers. Father says all men are liars." The boy drew back a step, deeper into the pond.

"Wait," said Filandro. "I promise I won't lie to you."

"Do you promise to tell the truth until dawn tomorrow?" asked the boy, retreating.

"Yes, yes, I promise," called Filandro after him. "Come back."

The moment Filandro had promised, the boy's attitude totally changed. He was no longer afraid. He stopped backing deeper into the pool. The fear left his eyes, to be replaced by curiosity and frank attraction. He smiled. His member poked its head up out of the water. He blushed.

"You're all covered with sweat and dust from your day in the forest," said the boy. "Why don't you take off your clothes and bathe in the pool with me?"

How could Filandro resist? His clothes seemed to pull off by themselves. He was in the same condition as the boy by the time he waded into the pool. The water was refreshing. He splashed it up over his arms and shoulders. He washed the dust from his face. Then Filandro's wet arms were sliding around the boy. His lips found the boy's lips. Their two erections pressed up against their two bellies, crushed between them. Not until twilight began to darken the trees at the water's edge did Filandro realize how long they had been making love. Reluctantly he pulled away from the amorous boy and rose to his feet, reaching out for his clothes.

"I've got to get back to the cave," he said hurriedly. "I didn't realize it was so late." He groaned at the sight of the boy's delicious body, lying there by the water's edge, where only a moment before he had enjoyed every pleasure that flesh can offer. How he longed to throw himself down upon the boy again, and cover that young body with another deluge of kisses. "Goodbye," he said, brushing his lips one last time over the boy's lips. Then Filandro ran back through the sheltering branches toward the familiar wooded hills near Lodovico's hermitage.

Halfway there, on the windswept side of a moonlit hill, another figure lurched into sight. Filandro came to an abrupt stop. "Who are you?" he called out sharply, trying to conceal the alarm in his voice. "Get out of my way."

"Filandro, it's only me," said the voice of the hermit. Lodovico hurried toward him through the shadows. "Are you all right? You didn't come home. I thought something might have happened to you." Then the hermit's strong arms were around him.

"Yes – yes, of course I'm all right," he stammered, caught off-guard.

The Devil in Love

"Where were you?" asked Lodovico. His eyes were large with worry and concern.

"Hunting," said Filandro.

No sooner had the lie slipped out through his lips than a terrible pain and coldness crept over his whole body. He could no longer move. His limbs were stiffening. Half of a scream escaped from his mouth, only to end in an abrupt silence. Slowly his face turned gray, and then his whole body. As Lodovico watched helplessly in horror, his living and breathing Filandro was transformed into a lifeless statue of stone.

The Devil in Love

Chapter 3
The Hermit's Search

Unable to believe the testimony of his eyes and hands, terrified to think that he might have gone mad, Lodovico clung to the statue. Though he wept and pleaded for mercy from the Hand of Fate, the cold statue did not move. The miserable hermit did not return to his rocky cave that night, but slept at the feet of his transformed friend. When he woke up the next morning, he prayed desperately that he might find it had all been a dream. But the morning light only confirmed the nightmare. Filandro was no longer flesh, but solid rock.

With his heart half-broken inside him, Lodovico returned to his high, secluded hermitage only long enough to pack up a few clothes, set everything in order, and lock the door. Then he walked down through the wild grass and out of the lonely hills, until he came to a small village on a cliff overlooking the Saluzzo and the southern walls of Antichi.

At one end of the village was a mud hovel which seemed scarcely large enough for a child. A line of blue smoke rose up into the sky out of the narrow chimney. Lodovico had to crouch down almost into a squat to get through the low doorway. Inside, half-hidden in the shadows, was a very old man.

"Have mercy on me, Your Reverence," said the hermit. "A cruel enchantment has come over my friend in the forest.

The Devil in Love

Once he was flesh and blood like I am. Now he no longer moves or breathes, but stands like a statue of stone. What can I do to restore him?"

Flies buzzed around the old man. His crippled fingers scratched in his long, matted hair. He appeared to be chewing something, but there was nothing in his mouth but his gums.

"Ah," he sighed. A hissing breath escaped from his dry, cracked lips. "The Devil is up to his tricks again." He made a strange sound which could have been laughter, or perhaps he was only choking. "Turned to stone, eh? Only one thing can help you now. You'll have to find the water of life to break that enchantment." The old man wheezed and crumpled forward, as though the air had gone out of him.

"The water of life?" repeated Lodovico. "But where?"

The old man didn't move.

"I beg you, Your Reverence," pleaded the hermit. "Where can I find this water of life?"

"Don't ask me," mumbled the old man without looking up. "Only the Devil knows that. But I'd look to the west…"

"The west?" questioned Lodovico. Why would anyone want to go farther into those treacherous mountains? Antichi lay to the east, Valbrosa and civilization to the south.

"The west…" he repeated. The last word was a whisper, after which he no longer spoke.

Lodovico crawled out of the mud hovel. It was an hour before nightfall. He set off into the west, toward the cold, rocky crags of the White Demons.

The Devil in Love

That night he was tormented by vivid and terrifying dreams, of raging waterfalls, dangerous mountain rivers, boulders the size of houses, and twisted vegetation. The next day, however, the hermit began to recognize in the unfamiliar landscape around him certain places which he had glimpsed in his dreams the night before. The same thing happened on the following night. Slowly those lurid, unsettling visions led him steadily deeper and deeper into the west, winding through narrow passes between the high reaches of the White Demons. At last Lodovico came to the mountain wall, decayed and moss-covered, forged of bricks the size of a man's coffin, built so long ago that no one remembered who built it.

The Devil was waiting for him.

The hermit didn't need to be introduced. The moment he saw that seven-foot colossus, standing before him in a blaze of sunlight which he seemed to wear upon his broad shoulders like a cloak, Lodovico knew that his search had come to an end. He came to a faltering stop. He tried to swallow, but his throat was too dry. The hermit had never seen anyone or anything quite so beautiful. The Devil grinned at him, radiating so much charm and self-confidence that it took Lodovico's breath away.

"Good morning, Lodovico," said the Devil.

The hermit dropped to his knees, weak with fear. He looked down at the rocky ledge on which he knelt, no longer able to bear looking at the Devil's achingly perfect body. "You know why I'm here," said the hermit.

"Yes, I was expecting you," smiled the Devil.

"You know what has happened to Filandro."

"Yes, what a shame. Never make a promise to one of my boys that you can't keep. Still Filandro does make a beautiful statue."

"Show me, then, where I can find the water of life," begged the hermit. "Help me restore Filandro to a breathing man again."

"I suppose I could do that," said the Devil with a grin. "But if I do, would you be willing to do a little favor for me in return? Instead of hiding from the world up in that cave of yours, meditating all day on the Hand of Fate, would you be willing to serve your fellow men? There's very important task that needs doing, and I think you're the very one to do it."

"Yes, of course," said Lodovico. "If only you show me where I can find…"

"Perfect," said the Devil, reaching out his hand toward the hermit. "I was hoping you would. Come with me, and I think we'll be able to make a bargain."

Chapter 4
Shoemaker's Holiday

"If I knew the missing part of the story," Noraldo said one night as they lay in bed together, "all the rest of it would make so much more sense."

"Still, it's only a story," said the Prince. "Some crazy fairytale your father and brothers threw together, isn't it? Just an old family heirloom, with all your old family legends in it, spiced up with a lot of wild imagination."

"No, it's more than that," argued Noraldo. "You don't understand."

"I understand this much," said Prince Ippolito. "You've let those missing pages bring you far too much unhappiness."

"But what you don't understand," insisted Noraldo, "is that this book is more than just some crazy fairytale. It seems to be about – well, about more than that, about everything that's important. About goodness, and loving, and the truth…"

"I give up," sighed Ippolito. He slid over on top of Noraldo, pinning one of Noraldo's wrists in each of his hands, covering Noraldo's protesting mouth with his own. When Noraldo had at last stopped squirming and submitted to the kiss, Ippolito drew his lips just far enough away to be able to speak. "I can't bear to see you unhappy like this anymore.

The Devil in Love

Vernaccio's carpet is locked in the tower. I'm going to take you to the island of Maligna, where you can talk to the Sfinge and set your heart at rest. And if you answer the Sfinge's riddle with the wrong answer and have to die, then I'll die with you, and that's the end of that."

Noraldo looked at him in wonder. "Would you really do that?"

"Tomorrow," said Ippolito. "And now shut up, because I'm going to make love to you like I never have before."

The next morning they began making plans. The Prince took him up into the damp, drafty tower, to a chamber packed to the ceiling with old furniture, chairs no longer in use, tables piled on top of tables, and a rolled-up carpet in the corner, propped up against the wall and draped in spider webs.

Together they unrolled the carpet in the middle of the cold floor. There, before him once again, Ippolito looked down on the intricate woven beauty of that golden griffin with its enormous spread of wings, appearing to fly out of the very heart of an angry red sun. He stepped onto the carpet so that his left foot covered the griffin's eye. Then he slowly and painstakingly taught Noraldo the magic words that unleashed the carpet's powers.

With Noraldo and Ippolito standing in the middle of it, Vernaccio's carpet rose up off the floor. Ippolito taught him the other words, and the carpet slowly and rather unsteadily

The Devil in Love

lowered itself to the floor. Noraldo had repeated both raising and lowering the carpet, and was embracing Ippolito in excitement and affection as the carpet settled to the floor when there was a knock at the door.

"Yes?" said the Prince impatiently.

Beppo's round face poked through the half-open door. "Forgive me, Your Excellence," said the pageboy. "A shoemaker of Valbrosa is requesting to see you. He says his name is Petroccolo."

"Father!" cried Noraldo in amazement. "My father is here in Bolgaro? What on earth could bring him here?"

"Tell him we'll be right down," said the Prince.

They found Petroccolo contentedly waiting for them in a high-backed chair before the fire, sipping at a goblet of hot spiced wine, his traveling bags beside him, and a benevolent, fatherly smile wrinkling his face.

"It's so good to see you, my boy!" he cried, giving Noraldo a hearty squeeze. "You look wonderful, so healthy and happy. I'm so glad I came. This is the best idea I've had in years."

"What idea is that, Father?" asked Noraldo uneasily.

"Why, taking this vacation, of course!" laughed the shoemaker. "Your two brothers can manage the shoeshop just fine without me for a couple weeks."

"A couple weeks!"

The happiness almost faded from the shoemaker's face. "Unless I'd be in the way," he added.

The Devil in Love

"Not in the way – exactly," faltered Noraldo. "It's just that Prince Ippolito and I were just getting ready to leave in a day or two on a holiday of our own."

Petroccolo beamed. "Perfect," he said. "What excellent timing! We can all go somewhere together."

Noraldo gasped in horror. "Out of the question."

"We're going on a rather difficult mission, I'm afraid," explained the Prince.

"I don't mind a little scramble now and then," said the shoemaker. "Besides, it will be good for me to get some exercise. Sewing all day isn't good for anyone. Why, I'm half-blind from threading so many needles."

"It isn't safe, Father," said Noraldo. "We're flying there on a magic carpet."

The old man's eyes glowed like a boy's. "Wonderful!" he sighed. "I've wanted to fly on a magic carpet since I was that high." He put his arm around Noraldo's shoulders. "You're such a good son – I can see you're worried that I'll strain myself. I know I'm not as young as I used to be. But I can be useful. Once we get there, I'll take care of the cooking and the washing. I promise not to get in the way." Petroccolo winked at him. "And whenever you two want a little privacy, all you have to do is drop me a hint and I'll take walk."

"You don't understand, Father," groaned Noraldo. "There's a chance that this trip might be dangerous, and just in case…"

The Devil in Love

"Dangerous?" interrupted Petroccolo. His fatherly instincts were alerted. "What do you mean, dangerous? Just where is it, son, that you're planning on going?"

"It's an island far to the north of here," explained Ippolito vaguely. "On the other side of the mountains."

The shoemaker's face turned pale. "Of course, I know you're not talking about – the island of Maligna?"

"Well, actually, Father, as a matter of fact, funny you should mention…"

"Yes, we are," said the Prince. "We're going there to ask the Sfinge an important question. Then we'll be flying directly home…"

"That's all I needed to hear," said the shoemaker bluntly, rising to his feet. "You can save your breath. Either I'm going with you, or Noraldo isn't going, and that's the end of that."

Chapter 5
Hour of the Assassin

Noraldo and his father sat silently together in the royal library, neither of them speaking to each other, or even so much as looking in the other's direction. Through the open window, the full moon stared in at them, unnoticed. The magic carpet, spread out in a pool of that moonlight, mutely awaited the outcome.

Beppo entered carrying a golden platter heaped with fruit. First he offered the platter to the shoemaker, and then to Noraldo. Both of them ignored him. Beppo set the platter down on a low table nearby, plucking off a few fat grapes as he did so and popping them into his mouth.

Noraldo's book was open in his lap, but he was too angry to read. His father was being such a stubborn nuisance.

"I'm going," said Noraldo firmly, through clenched teeth.

"Over my dead body," said Petroccolo.

Silence froze the room again. Beppo stole a couple more grapes. He had just plopped the first one onto his tongue when he looked up in alarm. Rapid, uneven footsteps pattered down the corridor. Noraldo heard them, too. He closed the book in his lap, and started to rise from his chair. Then the door swung open and Prince Ippolito stumbled through it, his face pale, clutching his side where it was sopping red with blood.

So absorbed was the Prince in his struggle to remain on his feet that he failed to see either Noraldo or his father in the library. It took all of his strength and concentration to get the library door closed behind him. He began fumbling desperately with the lock. Then, with a cry, Noraldo was beside him, supporting the Prince in his arms.

"Twelve years old," mumbled Ippolito. "Couldn't have been more than twelve." He braced himself against Noraldo, wrapping one arm around Noraldo's neck. Then he blinked his eyes and seemed to realize who was holding him up for the first time. "You've got to get out of here," he groaned.

Ippolito pulled away from Noraldo, dragging his friend over toward the magic carpet. There was a sopping red stain down Noraldo's front now where the Prince had leaned against him. Noraldo sobbed at the sight of it.

"Beppo!" cried the Prince weakly. The boy was standing speechless with horror. "Those chairs. Push them over in front of the door. We've got to block it."

"Help him, Father!" cried Noraldo. "Quickly!"

"Only twelve years old," murmured the Prince, clamping his hand over the wound to try to keep the blood inside. It ran out between his fingers. "I've never seen him before. A new pageboy, I thought. He said he had to show me something." He gasped with pain, remembering the child assassin's cold and glittering eyes, the sudden flash of the stiletto in his hand.

The Devil in Love

"But there are more. Federigo's agents – more than I dreamed…"

Distantly, from some other part of the castle, they could hear the sound of cries and running feet, distant shouts of alarm, a scream. Beppo and Petroccolo were sliding a heavy table across the floor toward the doorway.

"Hurry," whispered the Prince. His face was wet with sweat, his skin almost white. "The carpet. Noraldo, you must fly the carpet. The spell has been set to take you straight to Maligna. You'll be safer there than here, believe me."

"Father! Beppo! Get on the carpet," ordered Noraldo.

"He's in the library!" cried a triumphant voice outside in the corridor.

The shoemaker and the pageboy hurried across the room and huddled in the middle of the carpet. Outside the open window, trumpets were sounding. There were shouts and the clanging of swords. The gates of Antichi were groaning open, and the soldiers of Valbrosa forcing their way inside. In a single blow, the ancient city had been taken.

Fists began hammering on the door. Then shoulders rammed against it, causing the table and chairs blockading the door to rattle. There was a smashing, ripping sound, and the edge of an ax sliced through the wooden door.

"Out the window!" gasped the Prince. "Before it's too late."

Again the ax thudded into the panels of the door, and again. Then, with a sudden splintering, it gave way. Pulling

The Devil in Love

free of Noraldo's arms, Prince Ippolito seized his book, forced it into Noraldo's arms, pushed him backward onto the carpet next to Beppo and the old shoemaker, and then seized a sword off the wall and turned to face the splintering doorway.

"Get on the carpet!" screamed Noraldo at the Prince, but as men he had never seen before broke through the door at last, with his terrified father clinging to him for dear life, Noraldo gave a sob and, with one foot over the griffin's eye, said the words of power.

The carpet rippled, and gave a lurch. Then in one smooth motion it lifted all three of them off the floor as though they weighed nothing at all. Soldiers shouted and backed away before Ippolito's swinging sword, and then Noraldo found himself sailing out the window, out over the heads of the invading troops, out over the castle walls and the river, with the pageboy weeping with fear and his old father chattering in terror, into the wild hills and mountains of the north, into the surging winds, heading straight for the island of Maligna.

Chapter 6
Bargain with the Devil

The Devil led the hermit along a rocky ledge which entered a fissure and then burrowed down into the rock of the mountain wall itself, into a cavern lit with a warm fire. Though the blaze was crackling when they arrived, there was no sign of anyone else in the cave. A cauldron of steaming soup was waiting for them. Though the Devil had none himself, Lodovico had two bowlfuls. Then the Devil led him to a soft bed of moss. No sooner did he lie down than the hermit sank into an exhausted sleep far too deep for dreams.

He was awakened by a wet kiss. His eyes snapped open. He was looking up into a face that seemed to be all nose, the entire thing covered with fur. Lodovico would have unleashed a cry to echo and rebound through the cave, if the Devil had not appeared beside him at that moment.

"I thought you might appreciate a helper on your new job," chuckled the Devil. "This is Placido." It was a gentle, gray donkey. Beside the donkey was a saddle and a pile of straps and wicker-baskets.

"My new job?" repeated Lodovico in bewilderment.

"Since you're going to be travelling night and day, from one end of my kingdom to the other, I thought Placido might come in handy," said the Devil. "At least you won't wear out quite so many pairs of sandals."

"Travelling night and day?"

"Don't worry," laughed the Devil. "This little donkey is strong as an ox and sure-footed as a mountain goat. He's so sweet-tempered he'll never scare the children."

"The children?" echoed Lodovico. "I don't understand."

"Each of these wicker-baskets is just big enough for one little boy," explained the Devil with a smile. "As time goes by, you'll need every one of them. Each morning at dawn you will go to a particular rock I'm going to show you on the other side of the mountain wall. You will gather up all the infant boys you find waiting there…"

"Waiting there?" interrupted Lodovico. "How did…?"

"That's not your concern," smiled the Devil. "You will simply tuck the little fellows into the baskets on Placido's back, and take them to the magic cave which I have created for them. There all the boy babies will be nourished by streams of milk, cared for by invisible hands, entertained by the most delightful dreams until you carry them down into my new domain and deliver them to the fathers there to be raised as their sons."

Lodovico's mind was spinning. He drew several breaths to speak, but said nothing, floundering to even conceive of what he had just been told. "But how will I know where to take all these babies?"

The Devil in Love

"All you have to do is watch for signs and omens," said the Devil. "Believe me, the Hand of Fate will be quite clear. You'll never have any doubt about finding the right father's door. From this day onward, every man in my domain shall be handed his sons by you, the bringer of fatherhood. You alone shall know the secret way through the mountain wall, and the cave of sleeping infants."

"But why me?" interrupted Lodovico.

"Because you're exactly right for the position," said the Devil. "Honorable, dependable, hard-working, not particularly error-prone. And also because, unless you cooperate, your friend Filandro will remain a statue until the end of time."

"Very well, then," said Lodovico. "I'll do as you ask. As long as you show me how to restore Filandro to life."

"Saddle up your donkey," said the Devil.

When the hermit was mounted on Placido's back, the Devil took hold of the donkey's reins and led them through one dark tunnel after another. The last tunnel opened out onto a forest glade, in the middle of which, surrounded by colorful wildflowers, was a slab of rock as smooth and flat as a tabletop.

"This is where you'll find them," said the Devil. "You're to check this rock every morning at dawn. Now I'll show you the enchanted cave."

Back into the tunnel they went, down one rocky corridor after another. At every junction, the Devil showed him how to feel the marks on the wall by which he could always find his way. Emerging from underground, the Devil led them out along a narrow stone bridge across a gap between two mountains, and then through a fissure in the side of the next mountain, down a dim tunnel opening into a cavern lit with a soft blue light.

The mysterious glow came from a rose bush in the middle of the cavern. The thorny branches were sagging with heavy blossoms, which appeared to be made of pale blue glass.

"This is the Ice Rose," said the Devil. "The only one in existence. It was created by a powerful rival of mine – who is no longer with us. Its powers are many – far too terrifying for the mortal mind. It governs this cave. Just take my word for it."

White rivulets gurgled over the cavern floor, trickling out of cracks in the walls and winding between dozens of comfortable-looking nooks and dells which covered the moss-lined floor of the cave in a honeycomb of green crannies and narrow white creeks extending up the sides of the cave walls.

"Each nook is the perfect size for a little boy," said the Devil. "And the milk of this cave is more nourishing than anything they will drink for the rest of their lives."

"Where does it come from?" asked Lodovico uneasily.

The Devil winked at him and ignored his question. "Here they'll sleep and dream and wait to be delivered," he said.

"After that it's up to their fathers. Now, come this way, and I'll show you the passage through the mountain wall that leads down into my domain."

"No, the time has come for you to show me where to find the water of life," said Lodovico firmly. "Once Filandro has been restored to life, you can employ me however you choose, and I will obey all your commands, but until then, I have one mission, and that is to give my good friend, Filandro, the life he deserves."

"Have it your way," said the Devil with his most charming smile. "Follow me"

Lodovico rode on Placido's back right behind the Devil, following him across the glowing cave and out through the mouth of a tunnel on the other side, leaving the hazy blue light of the Ice Rose behind. They continued on for almost an hour down a dozen burrowing passageways, through turnings and twistings in the rock, until the tunnel ended in a rocky wall, at an awesome gray doorway with a paneled frame around it of burnished gold.

"Tell me, Prince of Darkness," said the hermit, "what door is this? Where does it lead?"

"This is the door you are seeking, Lodovico," said the Devil. "You will have to pass through this door if you ever hope to restore Filandro to life. But you might be happier if you turned back, and went to work for me. Beyond that doorway lies a cruel and terrible land."

The Devil in Love

But Lodovico had already slid down from the donkey's back, his feet were already leading him right up to the slabs of rock that framed the doorway.

"Where does it lead?" he repeated, drawn relentlessly toward that gold-framed door by some kind of helpless instinct. "Is this where I can find the water that will bring Filandro back to life?"

Chapter 7
Doorway of the Ancients

"This," said the Devil, "is the Doorway of the Ancients. No one knows how long ago it was made. Many are the brave and foolish people who have opened it and stepped through it. I advise you to turn around right now, though of course I don't expect you to heed my warning."

The hermit didn't even seem to have heard him. "What's on the other side?" he persisted. He stared at the door as though at any moment he expected it to groan open, so that he could see through it. The door didn't budge.

"An irresistible temptation, I'm afraid," said the Devil. "That's where you'll find the water of life. Unfortunately, the well is guarded by horrors beyond belief."

Lodovico didn't hesitate. His hand, of his own accord, left his side and reached out for the doorknob, which seemed to pulse with a molten inner fire.

The Devil in Love

"Don't touch it," cautioned the Devil.

The hermit's hand closed around it. The doorknob was scorching hot. Lodovico's scream echoed down the twisting tunnels. He jerked his hand away. With a shudder, the door began to slowly swing open, groaning ponderously on its ancient hinges.

"Too late," sighed the Devil. "But then good advice always is. You see, pain unlocks the door."

The towering gray door thudded back against the wall of the cave. Beyond the threshold swirled vague, shapeless mists across a gray expanse, which seemed to stretch away deep into the interior of the rock without limits or definition, as far as he could see.

The Devil, too, was staring into that perpetually shifting wilderness of fog. "That's where you'll find the well," said the Devil. "Every last one of us is born with a desire to taste that water."

"The water of life?" asked the hermit eagerly.

"That's the one," said the Devil. "The water of healing. The water of redemption. The water of life eternal."

No sooner did Lodovico hear what it was that drew him, than it seemed as though he had always known, and his need became urgent. "Prince of Darkness," he whispered, "this is the well for which I've been searching. I must pass through this door." The hermit climbed back up onto Placido's back.

"It's an exhausting and treacherous journey," warned the Devil.

The Devil in Love

"Whatever the price, I'll pay it," said the hermit. He nudged Placido forward. The donkey stepped across the threshold. His hoof sank into the gray lake of smoke. "Where will I find this well?"

"On the island of Maligna," said the Devil. "You must find it for yourself. But before you reach the well, you will have to pass by the terrible creatures who guard the way – the hideous Sfinge, two nightmarish giants, and my awful one-eyed brother, Polifemo, who has many repulsive habits, the least of which is his preference for barbequed men. I assure you, Lodovico, you will never survive to find the well – without this."

A flash temporarily blinded Lodovico, and when he opened his eyes he saw the Devil holding upright in one hand a gleaming sword. He pushed it into Lodovico's hand before the gentle hermit could refuse to touch it.

"The name of this sword is Durindana. It once belonged to the great Orlando himself. They say it was forged by the fairy folk. It never fails."

"No, thank you," said the hermit.

"Take it," said the Devil.

"I have nothing to do with weapons of any kind."

"Without this sword," said the Devil, "you're a dead man, and Filandro will remain a statue forever."

"I have sworn an oath never to take life," said Lodovico. "And I'm not going to start now."

The Devil in Love

"Fine," said the Devil, strapping Durindana securely to the back of the donkey. "Then don't use it."

With that, Lodovico nudged his donkey forward, and Placido crossed over the threshold, stepping cautiously into a shallow lake of swirling mist. "Keep your promise, and I will keep mine."

"Do not linger for any reason," he advised the hermit. "Let nothing distract you from your goal. Beyond this door, Time knows no law. An hour is not an hour there. The closer you get to the well, Lodovico, the more swiftly the currents of Time will flow against you. Who knows how many months may slip past you in a minute? Many have died before they could find it. Do not linger, and be vigilant, for there are dangers, many dangers…"

But Lodovico was making his way farther and farther out into the swirling mists beyond the door. Placido was up to his knees in smoke, leaving a wake behind him which closed together swiftly, erasing all trace of their passage.

The Devil's voice echoed through the hollow reaches after them, but the hermit could no longer hear what he was saying.

Chapter 8
The Castaways

"There!" said Beppo, pointing down through the gloomy clouds toward that barren, hostile little island. "Down there!" he cried to the others.

"That must be it, all right," said the old shoemaker grimly, peering nervously over the edge. "Not the friendliest looking place."

He might have gone on to describe the crippled-looking branches of the trees and the clogged stream and brutal, sharp rocks below but at that moment the carpet gave an unexpected jerk and veered abruptly to the left. Then it rippled, buckled, sagged in the middle, and began to spin.

"Noraldo!" cried the old man, clutching his son.

By a desperate act of will, Noraldo had managed to keep his presence of mind in spite of what had happened before his very eyes in Antichi. Inside he was howling inconsolably over his loss, and now he had passed his limits. Suddenly the sight of Ippolito's bloodstains down the front of his own tunic was enough to make Noraldo sag forward in shocked grief, his aching head slumped and nodding, his burning eyes closed, the words of power fading from his mind. His need to question the Sfinge no longer seemed so urgent. Within a few short moments, he had lost both his lover and his new home.

The Devil in Love

His life had been torn up by the roots. All he had left was his book, which he clutched in his arms. When he saw that he had smeared bloodstains on the front of the book, he gave a plaintive cry and lost his last bit of control over the flying carpet.

The shoemaker screeched. The pageboy lost his balance. The island seemed to rush up toward them. Then the sky turned over, and they found themselves riding on air, clutching at nothing, the carpet suddenly crumpled and dropping, lifeless as a dish-rag.

They hit the water like stones.

Abruptly Noraldo found himself sloshing and thrashing in oily wet blackness, gasping for air, taking in mouthfuls of water, kicking and flaying out his arms in an attempt to find the surface. His head broke through into the day. First he could see only spray and gleaming rocks. Then he spotted his father's bald head bobbing on the water, as the old shoemaker desperately dog-paddled toward shore. Splashing and sloshing, Beppo clung to the side of a jagged rock, trying to drag the waterlogged carpet up out of that heaving wet blackness. The sight made Noraldo suddenly frantic.

His book! Where was it?

He was nearly weeping in distress before he spotted it high above him, dangling in the branches of a tree overhanging the water. With alternating cries of relieved joy at the book's precarious holding and anxious moans of apprehension that it might tear loose at any moment and

The Devil in Love

plunge into the water, Noraldo splashed as fast as he could toward shore. He never suspected, as he clambered as fast as he could up the wet rocks onto the island toward where he could see his exhausted father stretched on the sand, that he had only just escaped the hungry jaws of a lurking denizen of the deep, which had been following him along the bottom through the muck.

Noraldo climbed up into the tree's branches, and worked his way higher and higher, hand over hand, until he was within reach of the book.

Below him sloshed and lapped the black waters of the bays. After several attempts, he managed to dislodge the book from the tangle of branches and twigs which had broken the old volume's fall. Though the cover had been partly torn and several pages were loose and threatening to slide out, the book was still miraculously in one piece.

Weak with relief, it took Noraldo twice as long to get down out of the tree as it had taken him to climb up, since one arm was clutching his book to his side. Then he joined his father and Beppo on the beach, where they were stretching the soaked carpet out to dry in the sun.

"Is the carpet ruined, do you think?" asked Beppo fearfully, as Noraldo came up to them.

"No, of course not," said Noraldo with more confidence than he really felt. "It was my fault, not the carpet's. I must have stopped concentrating on the words of power. I'm all right now." But when Noraldo stepped onto the drenched carpet and put his foot over the griffin's eye, nothing happened. "I don't understand what's wrong," said Noraldo uneasily. "It probably just needs to dry out."

"Does that mean we're stranded here?" asked his father. The old shoemaker didn't like the looks of that island one bit.

"For the time being, I'm afraid so," said Noraldo.

"I'm hungry," said Beppo.

"Doesn't look like there's much to eat around here," said Noraldo, regarding the bleak, inhospitable terrain.

"We can at least make a fire," said the shoemaker with a wet shiver.

"That might help the carpet to dry out, too," agreed his son. "Beppo and I will gather some wood. You stay here, Father, and try to stay warm. Come on, Beppo."

"Maybe we could try fishing?" suggested the pageboy as he hurried along beside Noraldo, hunting for dry driftwood.

"Wouldn't want to see what kind of fish could live in black, oily water like that," said Noraldo with a shudder. "Much less eat one."

"Look over there!" cried Beppo, running a few steps ahead. "Beyond those boulders. Are those berry briars up there on the edge of those trees?" Without waiting to hear what Noraldo thought, the pageboy scrambled up the rocks much faster than his plump legs were used to moving. By the time Noraldo joined him, Beppo's mouth and lips were red with berry juice.

The Devil in Love

"A little on the bitter side," said Beppo, puckering his lips. "But it's food. That's all that matters." He popped several more berries into his mouth, then gave a cry of delight as he spotted an even larger briar of berries just a short way into the trees. "Look – more over there," he called back over his shoulder as he ran off in the direction he was pointing.

"Don't go too far away," cautioned Noraldo. He was about to follow after Beppo, just to make sure he didn't get lost, when Noraldo caught a glimpse of something beyond the trees in the other direction which captured his attention totally. At once he forgot all about Beppo and his berries. All he could see or think about was the red crag of rock thrusting up before him between two forks of a waterfall. Across the tumbling water stretched a narrow bridgeway that ended in the mouth of a cave at the top of the red crag.

"The cavern of the Sfinge," he whispered to himself.

It was not until he actually saw it there before him that Noraldo realized he was not going to leave that island until he had asked the Sfinge the one question which alone seemed to matter anymore. He backed away two steps, then turned around and ran headlong back down the shoreline again, toward where he had left his father by the drenched carpet.

The old shoemaker was asleep. He didn't hear his son approach. There beside him was Noraldo's battered and blood-stained book. Noraldo gently picked it up and retreated without making a sound. It was not until he broke into a run that his foot dislodged the rock which woke Petroccolo up.

The Devil in Love

The old man blinked, trying to remember where he was. Then he noticed his son clutching his book and racing toward the trees. Petroccolo gave a cry of dread, scrambled up onto his feet, and took off in pursuit.

Noraldo didn't seem to hear his father's shrill voice begging him to come back. His destination before him was all that mattered, and the question waiting silently on his lips to be asked. The bitter ache inside him caused by the death of Ippolito made him reckless. Like many a hero, he felt certain that sheer determination would be enough. He was going to get an answer out of the Sfinge. There was the bridge before him, and he was going across. If he noticed the stone tower beside the bridge at all, it was only in passing. Striding past it out onto the narrow span, he certainly failed to notice the door swinging open in the tower wall behind him.

Then something was lifting Noraldo up off his feet. For a moment he was suspended, kicking in terror, out over the bridgeway and waterfall alike, dangling above the roaring cascade. Then Noraldo looked up and screamed, all but dropping his book at the sight.

A grinning giant the size of a walking tree was gripping Noraldo by the back of his tunic in one mighty hand. Noraldo screamed again, and kept screaming, but he couldn't wake up. He bucked and flailed. He sobbed in despair. Why hadn't he been more careful? Coming here had been the worst mistake of his short life.

Chapter 9
The Shores of Maligna

Placido's hooves broke their way through the rippling gray fog, which lapped around the donkey like a shallow ocean of smoke. Lodovico's lanky legs hung over the donkey's sides, so that his sandals trailed through the mist. Though he peered about in all directions, the hermit couldn't tell whether he was crossing a vast cavern, with rocky walls and ceiling too far away to be seen, or whether that foggy ocean lay stretched beneath some unknown, starless night sky. In either case, there was only darkness above and swirling mist below, as far as he could see.

Although sometimes he thought he could perceive, in the coiling gray billows, other human beings like himself, as soon as he looked closer they would fade and withdraw. Lodovico never knew for certain whether he went alone through that nebulous realm, or whether he was only one of a vast phantom army of searchers.

At last the endless monotony of the smoky landscape began to be interrupted by the gnarled, twisted branches of some strange variety of leafless bushes. At first they were widely scattered about, but soon those crooked, crippled-looking growths were more and more closely gathered together, until Placido was winding his way through a low forest of contorted boughs and dry, brittle branches.

The fog and the leafless forest both came to an abrupt end at the shore of a weed-choked bay. Beyond the stagnant waters, half-concealed in mist, waited a single, bleak island. Before him, on a crude raft, crouched a scrawny twelve-year-old boy, little more than skin and bone, clad in a few rags. A metal collar around his neck chained him to the raft.

"Good day," said Lodovico kindly. The boy didn't look up, or even glance in his direction. "Tell me," continued the hermit, "who has been so cruel as to chain you to this raft?" The boy looked out across the bay toward the island, as though the hermit had not spoken.

"Can you tell me if this is the island of Maligna?" Lodovico continued, wondering if the boy was deaf. The surly boy said nothing, but spat into the water. "Would you at least be kind enough to get us across?" asked Lodovico. He offered the boy a few coins. At last he was speaking a language the boy understood. The young ferryman greedily snatched them out of his hand.

Then the boy opened his mouth and pointed inside. Where his tongue should have been, there was only a chopped-off stump. Lodovico shuddered. The boy gestured for the hermit and his donkey to come quickly aboard. No sooner had they steadied themselves on the raft than the boy poled them out onto the black, turgid waters.

The island lurched closer and closer, stroke by stroke.

The Devil in Love

Maligna was a desolate, windblown series of plateaus, all barren rock, surrounded by dark and troubled waters. No sooner had Lodovico led his donkey ashore than the tongueless boy poled his raft quickly away, and was soon back on the other side.

For an hour Placido made his way from one cold ledge or slab of stone to the next. They encountered no one. Toward nightfall, however, Lodovico began to hear snuffling sounds coming from behind a cluster of boulders. There they came upon an old man, crumpled on the rocks and weeping bitterly.

Lodovico dismounted and approached the old man, putting his hand comfortingly on the old man's shoulder. The poor wretch flinched, gasping and drawing away from Lodovico with wide, frightened eyes. A moment later, able to see that the hermit meant him no harm, the old fellow crumpled forward on the rocks and began weeping again.

"Why? Why?" he sobbed miserably. "What have I done to deserve such punishment? Why would the Hand of Fate snatch away my sweetest happiness, my dearest treasure? My youngest boy, give him back to me! I am pleading for mercy before an empty throne!"

"Tell me what assistance you need from the Hand of Fate," said Lodovico, "for it was the Hand of Fate that guided me this way to overhear you, good man."

The wretch redoubled his lamentations.

The Devil in Love

"No man knows what evil fate may be waiting for him until the hour arrives," he groaned. "Today my evil fortune came to meet me."

"Tell me the whole story," said Lodovico.

"I'll try," said the old man, "but I don't know whether you'll be able to understand me. In the first place, I had no idea – you see, I tried to talk him out of it. He wouldn't listen to me. Now it's too late. Maligna, bitter island! He was trying to get up to that mountain, there. Little did he dream what a horrible destiny was waiting for..." He broke down in sobs.

"Leave off your tears, good man, so that perhaps I can help you," said Lodovico. "Now, what about this mountain?"

"It's not very far from here, in that direction," stammered the old man, wiping away his tears with the back of his sleeve, "though it might as well be in Bolgaro for all I can see. I don't see as well as I used to. It's old age, though crying so much hasn't helped any, either. But I can tell you that the color of the mountain is red as brick, and that it stands on the edge of a cliff overlooking a waterfall.

"From the peak of that red crag you can hear a voice cry out more terrible than any the world has ever heard, but as to what the voice is screaming, that I can't say. The sound of the waterfall is too loud. The water tumbles down from the cliff on both sides, leaving the rock in the middle carved in the shape of a jagged crown. A narrow bridge stretches over the falls to an open door in the rock. Why did he go? Because he's stubborn and crazy! That's where my boy was heading.

The Devil in Love

"He was convinced, you see, that all he had to do was enter that doorway and he would know the answer to all questions. He got as far as the bridge. I was about to rush out onto that narrow span after him, when a giant stepped in front of me and blocked my way. I've never seen any living thing so tall. That creature heaved my son up off his feet, and threw my boy over his shoulder like a bag of potatoes. My poor son kicked and struggled, to no avail. That foul giant intends to eat my boy, I know it. Now you know why I'm crying. Take my advice – turn around and escape from this island before it's too late."

"This island holds no fear for me," said Lodovico. "And neither does that giant. I'm heading for the bridge."

"Then I wish you joy in the Afterworld," said the old man, "for you have lost the desire to live. Believe me. I'm speaking the truth. When you're standing before him, looking up at that fierce face high above you, not even the bravest hero could help but tremble."

"Don't worry about me," said Lodovico. "You just kneel down and say a few prayers, thanking the Hand of Fate for sending help in your need. I'll be back with your son as soon as I can."

"If only that were possible!" cried the old man.

"Give me till twilight," said Lodovico. "If I'm not back by then, get away from here and don't look back."

The Devil in Love

Chapter 10
The Giant at the Bridge

As Lodovico rode closer to that mountain of red rock, he began to hear the roar of the waterfall. Then, half-drowned in that roar, he heard a harsh animal scream, the scream of a killing beast from somewhere up above. The sound made Lodovico cold inside, and he shuddered.

Up the rocky path he rode, leaving the shores behind. Then the trees ahead parted, and he saw the bridge over the waterfall. A rock tower loomed at the near end of the span, and on the other side of the thundering water was a cavernous doorway, leading into the red rock which rose up in the middle of the torrent.

Lodovico drew Placido to a stop near the bridge, by the edge of the cliff. Then a doorway in the tower nearly as tall as the tower itself swung open, and a giant stepped out to block Lodovico's way. Though he towered several feet over Lodovico in a fierce and threatening way, he looked immature as far as giants went, a youth among titans, with a huge pumpkin head on a broad-shouldered, monstrous dolt of a body, young and dangerous and stupid.

"Turn around, foolish hermit," said the giant. "You have no business here, and you don't want to die. No man is allowed to cross here."

The Devil in Love

"Who are you?" asked Lodovico. "And in whose name do you block my way across this bridge?"

"They call me Nazzo," announced the giant proudly in his booming voice. "That's short for Draghinazzo, but nobody calls me that but the Devil." He thought that was funny. His laugh shook a couple rocks loose from the hillside. For sheer physical impact, the towering fellow resembled a slab of mountain come to life. His enormous, strapping limbs were the size of tree-trunks and bare as sun-bleached rock, save a black mane of tangled hair on his head which looked as though it had never known a comb, and the skin of some monstrous beast which the giant had tied around his loins. In one hand he held a massive lance, as tall as a pine tree. "I guard this bridge in the name of the great Polifemo of the One Eye, King of Maligna. Polifemo has ordered me to let no one pass."

"But why would anyone want to cross the bridge?" asked Lodovico.

"To speak with the terrible creature of the rock," answered Nazzo. "They call him the Sfinge. Whatever question anyone may ask, the Sfinge can answer. He possesses all secret knowledge. But once the Sfinge has spoken, then he too asks a riddle. Whoever cannot answer that riddle he tears to pieces and flings into the waterfall below. Men without number the Sfinge has lured to their death."

The Devil in Love

"So he can answer any question?" mused Lodovico, his heart surging with renewed hope. Then, through the tower's open doorway, Lodovico caught a glimpse of a bound young man lying on an earthen floor covered with dirty straw. He blinked, unable to believe his eyes.

"Noraldo!" shouted the hermit.

The bound prisoner looked up and gasped in amazement. "Lodovico!" he cried desperately, half out of his mind with fear. "How did you find me here? Watch out – keep away from him. Don't come any closer."

But Lodovico was undaunted. He stood before the giant firmly. "Why is my friend a prisoner here? Untie him at once!"

Nazzo regarded the bossy hermit with amusement. "Your friend has no business on this island. I'm keeping him. He entertains me. He reads to me from his book. When I get tired of him, I'll eat him."

"His father wants him back, and so do I," said the hermit stubbornly.

"Too bad for his father, and too bad for you," said the giant. "It's lonely here, and the little fellow amuses me."

"Nevertheless," said Lodovico, "you must set him free."

The giant scowled. His eyebrows drew together in anger. "Must?" he said with a mocking snort. "No one but King Polifemo himself tells Draghinazzo what he must do. I tell you, this puny human being is mine, and I intend to keep him. Now, run for your life, or lose it."

The Devil in Love

"I'm not leaving without him," said Lodovico.

A menacing growl rumbled in the giant's throat. "You are really determined to die, aren't you? Well, I've had enough of you. Human beings can be so annoying."

With that, the giant lowered his mighty lance, with its deadly sharp point on which he had skewered many a stubborn traveler. In one swift movement he rammed the lance toward Lodovico's middle, but to his amazement Lodovico seized it, jerked it out of the giant's grip, and heaved it over the edge of the cliff into the tumbling water below.

Nazzo gave a furious roar at his impudent snatching of the lance, and down came his huge hands, closing around Lodovico to crush the life out of him. He had crushed many pilgrims that way before, and he would have crushed the life out of Lodovico, but just as the giant jerked him up and away from his donkey, the hermit's hand closed over the handle of the sword strapped to his saddle.

Up flashed Durindana into the sun.

A hissing blur sliced through the air. One of the giant's ears leaped off his head and fell to the ground twitching. With a shriek, Nazzo clutched his bleeding head and backed away from Lodovico.

"Do you want me to cut off the other one, too?" said the hermit grimly. "Now, set him free at once."

The mighty Draghinazzo could see that the man before him meant what he said. Holding his bleeding head with one hand, with the other he yanked loose the rope which had been tightly wrapped around both Noraldo and his book. Noraldo scrambled whimpering to his feet, staggering, his legs numb and not working correctly, brushing the grime and filth off his book, trembling from his sheer proximity to death.

"Enough," begged Nazzo. "Take your friend here and go. He has suffered no harm."

"My friend has suffered extremely and I will be kind enough to spare your life on one condition," said Lodovico. "Go and tell your King Polifemo that, since I have travelled far to talk with the Sfinge, I thank him for the use of his bridge. Also tell him that I do not approve of chaining boys to rafts, nor in cutting out their tongues, and I shall personally deal with anyone who perpetuates such crimes."

"But who will guard the bridge?" asked Nazzo.

"There will be no need," said the hermit. "While I am visiting with the Sfinge, my friend Noraldo will wait for me here and advise anyone who comes this way that we are not to be disturbed."

"But how will you answer the Sfinge's riddle?" asked the giant. "He'll tear you to shreds."

"There I must trust to my wits," said the hermit. "Should they fail me, then I will soon know the answer to all riddles."

The giant was amazed at the hermit's courage, and regarded him with a grudging respect.

"I will tell Polifemo what I have seen and heard," said the giant. Clutching his bleeding head, with a last glance down at his severed ear cupped in his palm, Draghinazzo turned his back on the tower and the bridge and lumbered away miserably, pushing his way through the trees like a farmer through his cornfield.

Chapter 11
Brief Reunion

Noraldo's face was streaked with dust and tears. Bits of straw were tangled in his hair. His torn clothes were filthy. He threw his arms around the hermit's neck in gratitude. "Lodovico, you've saved my life again!" he sobbed in exhausted relief. "What brings you to this island just in time to rescue me?"

"An unhappy quest, I'm afraid," said Lodovico. "Your dear friend Filandro has been enchanted and turned to stone."

"Filandro!" gasped his old companion in horror.

"He now stands like a lifeless statue in the forest."

"How horrible! Can nothing be done for him?"

"I've come here to find a certain well that provides something called the water of life," continued Lodovico. "The old village prophet near my cave says it's the only thing that can save him."

The very mention of such a water to a man grieving like Noraldo had the expected effect. "The water of life?" he said, hope blooming in his cheeks. "What kind of water is this? You see, I fear the Prince is dead."

"Ippolito?" gasped the hermit.

"He had intended to come with me. The soldiers of Duke Federigo attacked the palace, and... and to save us, he..." Noraldo swallowed his pain. "Do you think maybe this water of life...?"

Lodovico looked at him sadly. "Breaking an enchantment is one thing," he said. "I doubt if any water can bring a man back from the Afterworld. Tell me, is that what brings you here?"

"No, that happened just as we were leaving. What brings me here is this," and Noraldo pointed toward where his book lay, face down in the corner. "The title is gone. So are the first chapters. Pages are missing. I need to ask the Sfinge what was written on those missing pages." He faltered, too filled with grief for a moment to talk. "Now it doesn't seem so important. I can't get used to the idea that he's gone, that my life in Antichi is over. He will be the one and only love of my life."

Lodovico put a comforting arm around him. "We have both lost our hearts."

"That treacherous Duke Federigo has conquered another kingdom," said Noraldo gloomily. "Soon he'll be calling himself King. Antichi fell with hardly a struggle. We escaped with our lives on the magic carpet. Ippolito wasn't so lucky. My father was visiting us when it happened. He's here, too."

The Devil in Love

"Yes, I found him weeping on the beach," said the hermit. "He told me where to find his kidnapped son. I never dreamed that it would be you."

"Then he's all right?"

"Yes, and waiting for us now," said Lodovico. "Let's gather up your things and go back there."

Noraldo's precious book lay where the giant had tossed it. Noraldo was quick to salvage it and dust it off. Helping him onto the donkey's back, the hermit walked ahead of Placido, leading him back to where he had left Noraldo's miserable father.

"But now tell me," said Lodovico as Noraldo rode behind him, "you say you're going to the Sfinge to ask him a question. I have no idea how to find the well I'm looking for. Do you think the Sfinge might be able to tell me where to find the water that will bring Filandro back to life?"

"The Sfinge will know, for sure," said Noraldo confidently. "But the Sfinge always asks a deadly question in return, and if you don't answer it correctly, you die."

"I'll take that chance," said Lodovico. "Then it's settled. I'm going with you."

Noraldo's spirits were hugely lifted. The moment they came into sight, he could see his father down the beach jumping to his feet with cries of joy and running to meet them. Father and son were tearfully reunited.

"It's a miracle you're still alive," said Petroccolo, holding Noraldo at arm's length and smiling joyfully. "Of all my sons, you were the least likely to survive. You and that book will be the death of me!" Both of them repeatedly thanked Lodovico for all he had done.

"Good Lodovico," said the old shoemaker, "I shall never forget you. You have made future happiness possible for me by restoring my son. I shall make you new sandals every year with my own hands for the rest of your life."

Noraldo was about to say more along the same lines, but instead he said, "I smell something cooking." That was when he noticed, beyond his father's embrace, a campfire crackling on the shore, over which a skinned rabbit on a spit was slowly being turned by Beppo.

"Come on," said Petroccolo to his son and the hermit. "Dinner is almost ready."

"Rabbit?" said Noraldo, following his father to the fire. "Where'd the rabbit come from?"

Beppo looked up proudly from the cooking. "I hit him with a rock," he said. "Almost done, too."

All four of them were famished, and it wasn't long before there was nothing but rabbit bones.

"Thank you for sharing your food with me," said Lodovico. "I can linger here no longer. I must go and meet the Sfinge now, since my heart won't be at rest until Filandro is alive again."

Lodovico rose to his feet, and Noraldo scrambled up, too. "I'm going with you," he said.

"You are not," said Petroccolo firmly.

The Devil in Love

"Father," said Noraldo, "I thought we had an understanding."

"I do understand," said the old man, clutching his son's arm. "I understand that you want to die. You're not going. We need to leave this island. Haven't you learned your lesson yet? We don't belong here. No book is that important, Noraldo, and if you'd just come to your senses…"

Noraldo tried to pull away from him. "Father, I'm not a child anymore. The days of you telling me what I can't do are over. I'm old enough to make up my own mind and do as I choose. I've lost the love of my life – the least I can do is read every word of this wonderful book."

"You may look like a grown man," argued his father, "but you don't act like one. Take a look around you. Happy to be here? We need to leave this island immediately, not linger to talk about books with monsters."

"Father, I've made up my mind."

"And if you make up your mind to take your own life, I'm going to try to stop you. Bad enough that this good hermit is determined to die. You are not dying with him. You've escaped from a giant, now learn your lesson."

"I'm going," said Noraldo firmly, rose to his feet in determination, and then buckled forward, his knees folding out from under him. He collapsed weakly. Lodovico cradled his head.

"My good man," said the hermit gently to Petroccolo, "you need have no fear for me. I have the sword that once belonged to Orlando himself, and it will protect me from harm. As for your son, however, you are right. He is weak with exhaustion and needs rest, not another ordeal. Keep him here with you. I'm going alone."

"But…" protested Noraldo.

The hermit raised his hand to silence him. "I'll ask the Sfinge what happened on the pages that have fallen out of your book, and the book's title, and the missing chapters, too, while I'm at it. I'll repeat to you every word he says."

"But I've got to help," insisted Noraldo.

"Sometimes help is only a hindrance, my friend," said the hermit kindly. "You have a hero's heart, but not a hero's body. You can help me more by standing stand guard beside the bridge, to make sure I'm not surprised by any unwanted company. If you are threatened, you have the magic carpet to escape."

"And I'll be right here with him," said Petroccolo.

"I'll stay here, too," said Beppo. "We'll live on rabbits and berries."

Putting out the fire, the old shoemaker got up on Placido's back and together the four of them set out for the red crag above the waterfall. Sooner than any of them wished, they arrived at the narrow bridge.

"Wait for me here," said Lodovico, "and take care of my donkey, because I'm going to go on foot." He tied Placido's reins to a small, stunted tree. "I don't intend to be long."

The Devil in Love

Then the hermit turned away from them and walked up to the edge of the chasm, where the bridge began.

From the tree where he was tied, Placido nickered plaintively as Lodovico proceeded on his journey without him, taking only the sword Durindana. The hermit looked up at the high red rock before him, across the waterfall. There he could see the forbidding doorway into the interior of the rock.

Beyond that doorway, the Sfinge was waiting for him, with his knowing answers and his deadly riddles. There was only one thing Lodovico cared about now, and that was transforming the statue of Filandro back into his loving friend again. Since the Sfinge could tell him where to find the water of life, Lodovico did not hesitate one moment longer.

He stepped out onto the narrow span which the giant no longer guarded, and began making his way across.

The Devil in Love

CHAPTER 12
The Riddle of the Sfinge

Far below him, the water frothed and crashed among the rocks. The air roared with the deafening boom of falling water. Then Lodovico was across the narrow bridge. Through the ominous doorway he walked, into a dark tunnel hollowed out of the rock. The tunnel coiled upward and then opened into a dark and gloomy cavern, illuminated by a single shaft of light slicing down through a fissure in the rock ceiling. When Lodovico stepped into the light, a shrill scream pierced the air above him, amid the flapping of wings.

Up the rocky side of the cavern he climbed toward the sound, until at last Lodovico reached an upper shelf of rock. There, ensconced between two halves of an enormous boulder that had been ruptured down the middle, lounged the creature of riddles himself.

"Welcome to my cavern, Lodovico," said the Sfinge. "I've been expecting you."

In many ways, especially in the dim light, the Sfinge was profoundly attractive, with the smiling, darkly sensual face of a young man and the lanky, shapely torso of an athlete, where shadows rippled over sensual definition. Only a moment later, when the hermit's eyes blinked, did he notice that the boy's eyes were truly old and evil, his smile cold and indifferent, his legs strangely stunted and twisted and covered with fur and feathers. Huge wings, as brightly colored as a peacock's, rustled and flapped above him, while a long serpent's tail lashed in agitation behind him, striking the side of the mountain and causing rocks to tumble loose.

Though the very sight of the Sfinge was enough to make Lodovico shudder, he walked out boldly onto the high rock shelf until he stood before the blasted throne. The Sfinge folded his wings down behind him, wrapping them around to conceal his grotesque legs and long serpent's tail behind his beautifully-colored feathers.

"What brings you here, hermit?" said the Sfinge in a charming voice.

"As if I didn't know."

"Questions bring me here," replied Lodovico, "for I hear you can answer all questions."

"Ah," smiled the Sfinge, "is that what they say? Well, I shall certainly answer *your* questions, Lodovico. It will be a pleasure. But only if you answer a question of mine in return for each one of yours. If you fail, the penalty is death. Do you agree to my conditions?"

"Agreed," said Lodovico, trembling with anticipation.

"Then, by all means," said the Sfinge, "ask me whatever you wish."

"This is my first question," said Lodovico, taking a deep breath. "Where can I find the healing water that will restore Filandro to life?"

The Devil in Love

"Ah, yes! Poor Filandro," sympathized the Sfinge. "Well, that's not too difficult. Your search is nearly at an end. The water of life can be drawn up from a well on this very island, but it is well-guarded, indeed, by King Polifemo and his two giant cannibal brothers."

"I believe I have already met one of them," said Lodovico. "He tried to discourage me from coming to you. Please finish your answer, and tell me where exactly I can find this well?"

"You must seek it up on the highest rocks of Maligna, in the depths of a natural grotto which resembles the open mouth of a skull." The Sfinge laughed silently. "There you will find the well, whose waters not only heal any injury but restore youth to the body, and make one exempt from the laws of Time. There, does that satisfy you?"

"A grotto like the mouth of a skull," repeated Lodovico.

"And now I have a riddle for you," said the Sfinge, "so listen carefully, for your life depends on the right answer.

"I'm always hungry, yet always eating,
Always running in circles yet never repeating.
I have no wings yet I often fly.
I always grow older yet I never die.
I'm lighter than air, yet stronger than steel,
And though I slay all, I also heal,
Shapeless, yet I'm more than real,
Devouring kings with every meal."

The Devil in Love

The Sfinge smiled and waited for an answer.

Lodovico pondered the strange riddle, but he was a simple and straight-forward man whose mind simply didn't work in devious ways. He couldn't think of any creature that peculiar.

"Do you know the answer?" smiled the Sfinge. Then he burst into a hideous laugh which echoed through the cavern. His huge wings opened and flapped in gleeful anticipation, and up into the air above the hermit he leaped, claws extended. "He doesn't know!" shouted the Sfinge in triumph, and peals of bloodthirsty laughter shook the mountain. "He doesn't know!" Then the creature swooped down until he hovered menacingly over Lodovico's head. "Well, let me tell you then, brave riddler," hissed the Sfinge, "what the answer is before you die. The answer is Time! Don't you see? You were too thick-headed to solve it, and now you have to pay the price. Just like all the others…"

"That's where you're wrong," said the hermit. "I'm not like all the others. I intend to prove an exception to your pitiless rule."

"Oh, do you?" laughed the Sfinge in scorn. "We'll see."

Rearing up into the air above Lodovico, arching his powerful body to the full and spreading his mighty wings, the Sfinge began to beat them furiously while his savage laughter echoed through the cavern. Lodovico could see that the time for questions and answers was over.

The Devil in Love

Out flashed Durindana.

"I warn you," cried the hermit. "Allow me to leave unharmed."

"Unharmed?" repeated the Sfinge in a shriek of mockery. "That's the last thing you'll be."

The wind from the Sfinge's powerful wings was like a hurricane, and knocked the hermit off his feet. Back across the ledge he rolled in that blast, and would have been swept over the edge had he not caught hold of a slab of rock outcropping, where he managed to pull out of that wind. Then he scrambled off the ledge into the crags and boulders which lined the inside walls of the cavern, and began climbing down as fast as he could.

It was not fast enough. The Sfinge's tail writhed down into the rocks and coiled around one of Lodovico's legs. Suddenly he was dragged off his feet and heaved up out of the rocks, into the air. The tail tightened around his middle like a thing with life of its own. He could hardly breathe. Away from the rock wall the Sfinge pulled him, kicking and struggling. The cavern yawned beneath him.

Swing out his sword arm, Lodovico struck upward in a wild, desperate stroke. Durindana sliced the Sfinge's tail in half. His scream caused rocks to slide down the inside of the cavern. Both Lodovico and the half of the Sfinge's tail that was wrapped around him tumbled to the cavern floor.

The tail cushioned his fall. Tugging free of the limp coils, he struggled to his feet. A furious cry screeched above him, and then the Sfinge was swooping down on him, claws extended. One of those sharp talons sank into Lodovico's shoulder, but Durindana was already hissing through the air. Down through the Sfinge's shoulder cleaved the blade, nearly severing one of his wings.

The creature's screams before were nothing compared to the outraged shrieking he now unleashed. Tumbling down onto the rocks, the Sfinge thrashed about, his one remaining wing beating wildly, while the other wing hung limp and useless. Furiously regaining its legs, the Sfinge lunged at him. Rage was in the creature's eyes, and he came at the hermit with all of his strength, hitting him head-on with his full weight and knocking him off his feet. Then the Sfinge seized one of his legs in his talon before Lodovico could get back on his feet and half-flew, half-dragged him out the cavern doorway onto the narrow bridge above the waterfall.

Beating at him with his one remaining wing, scratching at his eyes with his claws, the Sfinge tried to force him off the edge. The hermit clung to the side of the bridge, above the thundering torrent. Then he pulled away from the Sfinge and took his stand in the center of the bridge.

The Sfinge leaped for his throat.

Gripping Durindana with both hands, Lodovico brought the sword down in a mighty blow on the Sfinge's other wing.

The creature's scream rang out over the roar of the waterfall. Tumbling out of the air, the Sfinge clutched at Lodovico in an attempt to drag his murderer with him, but his talons had lost their strength to grip. Down he tumbled into the surging water, wingless, looking like nothing more dangerous than a vicious, mean-hearted boy, to disappear into those turbulent currents where he himself had thrown so many an unhappy riddler.

Lodovico lay there gasping on the bridge until he recovered his breath and his sense of balance. Then he rose up onto unsteady feet, and barely strong enough to carry the weight of Durindana, walked slowly and sorely back over the narrow span toward where he had left the others, where Noraldo and his father awaited him, and his gentle donkey, Placido. He wondered how he would explain to Noraldo how the Sfinge had died before he could tell him where to find the missing portions of his book.

The exhausted hermit had reached the end of the bridge before he noticed. He broke into a run, shouted twice, and then stopped dead in his tracks. There was Placido, his rope broken, his eyes bulging wildly. There was the carpet, rumpled and wrinkled, imprinted with the dusty print of an enormous foot.

Noraldo, his father, and the pageboy had vanished.

Chapter 13
Zambardo's Net

He shouted their names until he was hoarse. He didn't care who heard him. When that didn't work, the hermit began shouting, "Come take me, too" That also failed to get results.

There was only that one footprint across the carpet to cause his alarm, yet it made Lodovico almost sick with worry for his missing friends. He searched all along the shore, thinking they might have tried to escape from the island, but there was no sign of them. On the wild chance that they might have followed him into the Sfinge's cavern, the hermit re-crossed the bridge and called for them until the cavern rang with echoes. But only the hollow echoes of their names answered all of Lodovico's efforts.

Crossing back over the narrow span toward his donkey, the hermit stared down bleakly into the churning water where the Sfinge's body had disappeared. "Today I have brought death into the world for the first time," he thought. No matter how justified he had been, no matter how deserving his victim, Lodovico felt a bitter unpleasantness inside which he feared might never leave him.

He shook the dirt and dust from the carpet, and then rolled it up and tied it on the back of his donkey. Then he journeyed on deeper into the island's interior, searching for some trace of his lost companions.

Lodovico had not ridden much farther into the wild desolation of Maligna when his way was blocked by a river of churning black water which was far too deep and dangerous to cross. There was a bridge in sight, but he could see clearly that it had been broken down, and not by nature, but by the hand of man. Without a bridge, the banks of the river were so steep that there was no way to reach the other side.

Hoping that if he rode far enough he might find a small boat or raft, Lodovico continued to ride alongside those gloomy waters. At last he rounded a rocky bend and discovered, to his surprise, a dark and mighty bridge which reached all the way across. There was a giant guarding the bridge, however, looming over it the size of a tree. Lodovico shuddered. He wondered if this was the brute who had scattered his friends. Making soft, reassuring sounds to his frightened donkey, the hermit rode bravely up until they stood before the towering guard of the bridge.

"Welcome to your fate, wretched man!" snarled the giant scowling down at him. "And it was a sad fate that led you here. This is called the Bridge of Last Wishes, and you must cross it now, for there is no escape. You will not be able to turn around and go another way, but all the roads on this island are twisted and crooked, and no matter which direction they seem to lead, they all lead back to this river again. When you at last cross, as you must, you will have to fight me. Then either you or I will die and fall off this bridge into those black waters, never to rise again."

"And who are you, to stand guarding this Bridge of Last Wishes?" Lodovico called up to the giant.

"I am the mighty Zambardo," the giant replied, "and before I roast you and eat you, I'm going to cut off your ear as a reminder of what you did to my brother."

He was even scarier than his brother, a mountain of muscle, sweating in the sun and waiting for a chance to be malevolent. His forehead was literally two feet wide, and the rest of his body was similarly proportioned. In one hand he held a great iron club from which hung five chains. At the end of each chain was fastened a deadly spiked ball weighing twenty pounds. His only garment was made of serpent's skin, to offer perfect protection, and on his left side hung a razor-sharp scimitar.

"Let me warn you in advance, foolish man," said Zambardo, "that although I am more than a match for you to begin with, my deadliest weapon is not even visible. I am talking about my secret net. Since I prefer beating my victims to death with this iron club and five spiked balls, I use my net only when necessary. But whenever I come up against someone who is inordinately strong or determined, I can always depend on my net of iron to capture my opponent in the end.

The Devil in Love

"Covered with sand, my net cannot be seen. With a mere stamp of my foot in the right place, I can cause my net to spring closed. Once that net closes, the man trapped inside is doomed to spend the rest of his short life being slowly tortured and killed by me, while my iron net holds him in a grip from which there is no escape. Therefore the time has come for you to bid farewell to life, for if one of my weapons fails to slay you, the other will surely succeed."

Lodovico was not encouraged by this information. He could only hope that the giant was bluffing. Slowly he dismounted from Placido's back and walked out onto the bridge, Durindana in hand. Zambardo waited for him in the middle of the span, looming above him, while the five spiked balls dangled menacingly down from his club, swinging back and forth before Lodovico's eyes. The spikes were crusted with gore and blood. They were not a pretty sight.

The hermit came to a stop, facing his gigantic opponent. His head scarcely reached to the top of Zambardo's thigh. Fighting back his fear, in a voice much braver than he really was, Lodovico called up to the giant, "I have listened to your boast, Zambardo. Now do your worst, so that I may continue on my way."

The giant grinned, and then brought down his club in a smashing blow, as though he were swatting a mosquito. Lodovico leaped backward, just barely dodging the whoosh of the club and the spiked balls whirling around it. Then, before Zambardo could draw back, the hermit bounded forward and swung. Durindana rippled through the air and struck the giant's club with such a fierce blow that it was knocked out of Zambardo's hand and crashed onto the bridge, with the chains and spiked balls clattering after it.

The giant roared with anger, and drew back his burning hand. Before he could draw his scimitar, Lodovico rushed toward him. Again and again that whirling blade bit and stung at the giant, but Zambardo's serpent-skin was so tough that the hermit's tremendous blows bothered him no more than the pecking and scolding of a furious bird. Durindana was having no effect on him at all.

Then Zambardo drew out his scimitar, though already he suspected that he was going to have to use his net. Down with a hiss came the giant's blade. The force of that scimitar striking against Durindana was enough to actually bend the immortal sword, knocking Lodovico backward on the bridge, and almost off his feet.

The hermit scrambled up again. He charged back at the giant, his face glowing with the heat of anger, his eyes narrowed in a deadly determination to bring Zambardo's life to an end. He struck the giant in the flank of his leg, slicing upward, splitting the scales of the serpent-skin. Although there was an iron strap fastening the serpent-skin, Durindana cut through that, too. The sword would have sliced right through Zambardo's belly next if the giant hadn't folded over and crashed down on the bridge.

The Devil in Love

Running backward, Lodovico managed to escape being crushed. The giant's body no longer moved. The hermit approached him cautiously. There lay Zambardo, sprawling full-length next to his iron club and spiked balls.

Suddenly the giant's hand closed around that club, and in a single motion launched it through the air again. He had only been shamming long enough to recover his weapon. One of the spiked balls whizzed over Lodovico's shoulder, wrapped its chain around the hermit's neck.

With a brutal jerk on his iron club, Zambardo yanked Lodovico off his feet and down onto the bridge beside him. As he struck the bridge, Durindana was knocked out of his hand and slid away beyond his reach, to hang teetering off the edge of the span. Then Zambardo was on top of him, pinning him under one knee while he unwound the chain of his club from around Lodovico's neck. That done, he gripped the hermit in a crushing hold and lifted him up off the bridge.

Lodovico squirmed desperately and struck out. Though both of his hands knotted themselves in the giant's hair and pulled until Zambardo shouted, it was not enough to stop the giant from carrying him over the bridge and across the black river, toward the place where his net of iron was concealed.

Lodovico beat on the giant's face with both hands.

Just as Zambardo reached the other side and was stepping down from the bridge onto the shore, Lodovico hit him so hard with his fist that Zambardo stumbled backward to collapse sprawling on the beach, nearly falling on the very place where his net was hidden in the sand.

Leaping free, Lodovico dashed past the fallen giant back onto the bridge, where he seized Durindana before it could fall off the edge. Then he turned back, sword in hand, to face his enemy once again.

Zambardo had recovered and was back on his feet, gripping his club, swinging those deadly spiked balls. The fight was renewed on the beach. In order to deal effective blows against such a tall adversary, Lodovico had to take a leap every time he swung Durindana. That blade had already left its mark in red on Zambardo's flank. The fight was brutal, blow for blow. The giant had never encountered anything like the hermit's grim determination. It enraged Zambardo that he was already wounded, while the little man before him still managed to dodge his murderous club.

Zambardo decided to change that. He raised his club, as though he would strike again, and Lodovico leaped aside from where the blow would have fallen – but the blow did not fall there, for Zambardo checked himself halfway through the stroke, and then before the hermit could leap again, brought his iron club down with both hands.

Lodovico was caught off-balance.

Up came Durindana, to stand firm before Zambardo's blow. Against that mighty sword, the iron club broke in two.

Then once more Durindana leaped through the air, striking this time at Zambardo's side, at the place where he had already been wounded once before. The serpent-skin was weak there, for that was the place where the creature's heart had been cut out long ago. Now Orlando's famous sword sliced into Zambardo's side like a knife into butter, cutting through his body from the flank nearly to the navel. His face went white. He knew that his life was over, that he was as good as dead already. He took one last weary step forward, and stamped his foot.

Out of the sand leaped the iron net.

It closed around Lodovico with such sudden violence that Durindana was knocked out of his hand, jerking him up into the air where he hung helplessly suspended from a tree, his arms painfully clamped down against his sides. There he swung, with almost no power of movement at all. Every knot of that net was so thick that all of his straining and tugging was of no avail.

Zambardo grinned up at him, and then shuddered and died.

"Hand of Fate," cried the hermit, "I beg you to help me!"

No help came.

There he hung, as hour followed hour, slowly revolving first one way and then the other, dangling above the net's gigantic owner, who lay cut almost in two on the blood-soaked ground beneath him.

Chapter 14
Spiritual Consolation

What could he hope for?

His friends were either dead or in similar trouble. Maligna was such a remote and deserted island that only rarely did anyone come there. Unable to help himself, Lodovico could do nothing except slowly turn around and around suspended from the tree branch and reflect on the slaughtered remains of the second life he had taken that day.

One hour stretched into the next.

The sun crawled across the sky.

The last flicker of hope was gone. His sense of honor, which always before had goaded him on in dark moments, now abandoned him. A lifeless, unhappy silence hung over the island.

Lodovico despaired.

The sight of Zambardo's cloven body sprawling below him was a constant torture. The guilt of two killings now, no matter how necessary, ravaged his soul. Without eating he hung there an entire day in Zambardo's net, and that night he slept very little, if he slept at all. By the next morning he was only hungrier. Though his body lived on, his soul was dying inside him.

The Devil in Love

He was hanging there helplessly, waiting for physical death to take him, when he was startled by a sound nearby. By rocking his suspended prison back and forth, he managed to turn the net around so that he could see. There before him was Petroccolo, naked except for a few rags, his hair wild, his eyes half-mad, covered with scratches and staring at him from behind a rock.

At the sight of him, Lodovico cried out, though not very loud for he was weak from lack of food, "Petroccolo, help me! I'm starving. If I hang here much longer, I'll be dead."

At first the old man was so alarmed by the sight of Zambardo's severed body that he could not come near. "I have no food," he called from a distance. "There's none to be found on this barren island."

"Please, come closer," begged Lodovico. "The giant is dead, and can no longer harm you. Good Petroccolo, won't you loosen these knots which are binding me?"

Overcoming his fear, the timid fellow approached cautiously and studied the many knots of the iron net, marveling greatly at their workmanship, but not at all understanding how to unfasten them.

"Pick up that sword there," said Lodovico, rolling his eyes in the direction of Durindana, "and strike with all your might against this net."

"No, my son," said Petroccolo, "I'm afraid I must commend you to the Hand of Fate. Though I see why you long to die, I cannot perform this evil deed."

The Devil in Love

"My friend, you don't understand at all," groaned Lodovico. "I swear to you, upon my faith, that the sword will not cut me, but will only slice through the net."

Saying that, and more of a similar vein, Lodovico begged the old man until at last Petroccolo agreed to try, and walked over to where Durindana lay on the ground.

"May the Hand of Fate forgive me if I harm you!" Far from harming him with the sword, Noraldo's old father could barely pick it up. Not only was he getting on in years, but he was weak from the mortifications of the island, and it was all he could manage to get the sword up in the air, and lurch toward the net. Far from bursting the net, the sword scarcely scratched it. The old man wearied himself in vain.

At last he dropped Durindana to the ground in exhaustion. "Some are meant to wield a blade, but not me," he panted, catching his breath. "I'm afraid the only comfort I can give you, my son, is going to be the company of human speech.

"I want to help you die like a true hero, which means not falling into the sin of despair over what has happened. How we face Death defines us. You've been honored with a truly legendary ending. Have faith in the Hand of Fate, my good hermit, since if you can only manage to have patience during this last hour of your death, you can look forward to a glorious eternity remembered as a hero in the tales of men as you dwell in the cool shadows of the Afterworld."

The Devil in Love

Petroccolo continued talking along those same lines as hour after hour of the day passed by. He told Lodovico the story of one hero after another, all unpleasant tales with sad endings (Petroccolo called them glorious) until he had covered heroes for every letter of the alphabet, listing in detail what they had had to suffer, who was poisoned, who was betrayed, who was flayed alive, and who had his manhood torn off with hot tongs.

But no matter how Lodovico begged him, the old man would say nothing about Noraldo, nor about what had happened to them outside of the Sfinge's cavern.

"But what about your son?" Lodovico would persist.

"I have no son," the old man would groan madly, and continue with his catalogue of atrocities.

At last Petroccolo concluded by saying, "And so you see, my son, it is not at all unusual that you should suffer injustice and a cruel death. That is the lot of heroes. There is no escaping your crown. Accept it, and give thanks to the Hand of Fate above. This is the way it is intended it to be, and if you study the lives of other heroes you will see that there can be no doubt about it."

"I thank the Hand of Fate for my destiny," said Lodovico, "but not for sending you here. I need help, not comforting words! If only the Hand of Fate had sent a younger man this way, I wouldn't be starving to death hanging in this net. One more worthless than you couldn't possibly have arrived!"

The Devil in Love

"Oh, dear," said Petroccolo, "I can see I've made you angry now, and that's the last thing I wanted to do. Good hermit, I can plainly see that the thought of your approaching death makes you irritable and desperate. Do not despair, but listen to my words. Since the hour has come for you to leave your life behind, think about your precious soul, and do not abandon it. Such a brave hero as you, Lodovico, can face any enemy. Why allow yourself to be frightened by Death?"

"Yet you yourself," countered the hermit, "know fear only too well."

"Ah," said Petroccolo, "that's different. I'm not a hero. I'm only a child of destiny, and the Hand of Fate doesn't abandon his children. Perhaps I will tell you, after all, what happened to us after you left, a perfect example of the workings of Divine Providence. Listen to the horror from which I was delivered…"

CHAPTER 15
Victims of the Cyclops

You hadn't been inside the cavern of the Sfinge for more than a few moments when something enormous came out of the trees. I remember his shadow more than his face. I try not to remember his face. When that shadow crept over us, we went nearly out of our minds with fear. We fled, left everything behind.

I don't know how we escaped.

Finding our way back turned out to be the problem. Somewhere we must have taken a wrong turn. The red crag over the waterfall was no longer in sight. Neither was the shore. We wandered in circles, and only became more and more lost in the mountains.

Not knowing which way to go, Noraldo said he felt sure the way led through a steep mountain pass ahead, and to save us all exhausting ourselves for nothing, he offered to go on alone, ahead of us, and then signal if we were to follow. Beppo and I waited for him under a rocky overhang, huddled together in the cold. No signal came.

Then suddenly Noraldo rushed into our midst in terror. He was exhausted from running, gasping for breath, his eyes wild. At first we could make no sense out of him. He was sobbing. Then he cried out horribly, "Run for that cave over there!" and leaped away from us.

The cause was soon only too clear. The dark shadow crossed over the ground again. I have never seen a creature so tall. A giant – no, worse than a giant – a walking nightmare, with only one eye in the middle of his forehead. It was King Polifemo himself, and he was wearing the strangest outfit I have ever seen, made entirely of dragons' claws linked together. He was carrying a spear in one hand and a great iron club in the other, but he didn't need either of them to catch us.

In our panic, we followed the advice of Noraldo running before us. Thus we trapped ourselves hopelessly inside that shallow cave. Only too soon we realized our error, and all three of us began to wail. The cyclops crouched outside, and looked in at us through the cave door with his one big eye.

"Do you know the first word he said to us? 'Delicious!' Yes, and his voice alone made that little cave tremble. 'Three tasty men,' he said, 'who have kindly journeyed all the way to my island to join me for dinner. *My* dinner.'"

Then in through the cave opening he pushed one hand, which filled half the cave. It closed around pudgy little Beppo. Screaming and kicking, the boy was dragged out, where the cyclops pushed him headfirst into a large, dirty sack. Back into the cave came that hideous hand. Noraldo began shouting like a madman as the fingers reached toward him. They closed around him. He howled and wept, but what good did it do? He was dropped into the sack on top of Beppo.

I can tell you I broke into a sweat. I was the only one left. I pressed myself flat against the rock wall, but it was no use. In came that hand again! It dragged me out by the legs. None of us escaped. Then the dark sack heaved up into the air, and we all tumbled on top of each other as he carried us away.

The next thing any of us knew, we were dropped roughly onto the rock floor of a huge, black cavern. Another miserable captive like ourselves, gaunt and unshaven, let us out of the sack, and explained to us our grim situation.

Though Polifemo keeps a large flock of goats, he only feasts upon goat-meat when chance does not provide him with more succulent fare. For that grim creature, there is no tastier banquet than the flesh of men. Of course, not many men dare come to Maligna, but of those few who do, none get past him. He ravages the entire countryside. Whenever a luckless pilgrim stumbles into his clutches, he pops them into his sack and drops them into his pit until he eats them, one by one. The bones littered about us had once belonged to other unfortunate travelers like ourselves. The sole survivor was half-mad from witnessing the cruel deaths of his companions, eaten before his very eyes.

Scarcely had his hurried explanation come to an end before he pointed upward and screamed. The single eye of the cyclops was leering down at us into the pit. The four of us cried out and ran to get as far away from him as we could, stumbling over each other in terror, clawing at the steep walls of the pit.

"Well, my little nibblings," said Polifemo, "which one of you would like to be first?"

Down came that mighty hand.

"Ah, this one looks plump," he said. Poor Beppo howled, and was lifted up into the air. We cried out in horror to see the boy being carried toward those open, dripping jaws. At the last moment, I buried my face in my hands. The boy's scream ended with a crunch. When I finally looked up, Polifemo's teeth were red with blood. He had peeled away Beppo's clothes and was chewing on the boy's side, while in the other hand he held a half-eaten leg.

I have never felt more pity for any human being in my life. Soon there was nothing left of Beppo but bones and bloody garments, and the cyclops was reaching for another tasty morsel.

Fate led his hand straight toward me.

I screamed when I felt those fingers closing around me. I cried. I sobbed. And I can tell you, good hermit, at that moment, looking into that bloody mouth which was opening to devour me, I despaired. But then listen to what the Hand of Fate had in store for me.

The cyclops studied me with his one enormous eye, and then said, "I would never eat a stringy old buzzard like you unless I was starving."

The Devil in Love

With that, he threw me with scorn over his shoulder and out the mouth of the mountain cavern. I fell so far I nearly died for lack of breath. But my faith in the Hand of Fate didn't weaken, and the Hand of Fate came to my rescue.

There was a twisted tree growing out from the side of the mountain. I fell into the middle of it. The branches and leaves broke my fall. As soon as I knew that I was still alive, I figured out where I was, and hid myself in the tree, where I remained very quiet, scarcely breathing, till nightfall. Then I carefully climbed out of the tree and began to work my way…

Petroccolo broke off in mid-sentence.

"What is it?" asked Lodovico.

The old man was staring over the shoulder of the hanging hermit, at something behind him.

"No!" screamed the old man in terror. "It's him. Good hermit, I commend your soul to the Hand of Fate!"

With that Petroccolo ran shrieking into the trees, while an ominous darkness blocked out the sun and cast a cold shadow over Lodovico in the net, struggling helplessly to escape.

The Devil in Love

Chapter 16
Dinner Fights Back

By the time Lodovico had rocked the net enough to turn it around to face the danger, the cyclops was almost upon him. The creature was taller than either of his two giant companions, as tall as the Devil himself, and his single eye was terrifying to behold, for it gleamed with fury. Though he gave half a glance in the direction of the fleeing old man, he quickly forgot all about him. All Polifemo cared about now was the dead giant stretched on the beach at his feet, and the man dangling helplessly before him in the net.

With a howl that echoed over the barren rocks of Maligna, the cyclops sank to his knees beside the body of Zambardo, taking him into his arms and wailing in grief, embracing his companion's cold remains. He repeated the dead giant's name over and over again. He kissed the giant's cold cheek. He cradled Zambardo's head.

Then Polifemo looked up from his lamentations. Crouching down by the tree, he brought his single, glaring eye up to within a couple feet of the netted hermit.

"What's this we have here?" he said, grinning bitterly at the helpless prisoner. "I believe I have already heard about you from poor Nazzo. He said you chopped off his ear. Now I find you have taken my other friend's life. Hard to believe a mere man can cause so much trouble."

Slowly his huge hands cupped themselves around Lodovico, who squirmed in vain, his arms pinned to his sides.

"Look at the size of you, and under that robe I can tell you're all meat, firm and tender. You alone should be enough for my entire meal tonight, and that's just what I'm going to save you for, all for tonight – except maybe I'll just take one little bite out of that delicious-looking shoulder."

Then the cyclops tried to rip the net open. He pulled on it, gripping Lodovico with both hands, but the net would not break. In rage, he half-uprooted the tree, but no matter how ferociously he shook the iron net, he could not get the hermit out of it.

"Well, I'm not going to just walk away and leave you here," snarled Polifemo. So saying, the cyclops looked around for some way to get Lodovico out of the net. That single gigantic eye was not long in spotting Durindana on the ground, near one of Zambardo's legs. Immediately the cyclops bent down and took the sword in hand. Leaving his spear and his iron club where they had fallen, the cyclops gripped Durindana with both hands, and swung that immortal blade with all his might against the hermit in the net.

Lodovico certainly felt the blow. His entire body broke into a sweat. But the links of the iron net, which had protected him from the sword, were slashed almost to breaking. With a growl, Polifemo ripped the iron net in two.

The Devil in Love

Lodovico thudded to the ground. So great was his joy at being free and able to move his limbs again that he felt only gratitude for the numbing blow which had released him. The hands of the cyclops closed over him at once on the ground, but now Lodovico could at least kick and struggle between his fingers.

And bite. His teeth sank deep into Polifemo's thumb. The cyclops cried out and loosened his grip. The hermit pried his way out between two fingers.

Scrambling away, he grabbed the cyclops' great club which was leaning against the oak. Polifemo cursed impatiently at the delay. He was not used to so much trouble from one of his dinner victims. That pitiless eye glared malevolently down at Lodovico. He, however, stood ready to fight, raising the cyclops' own club against him.

But the cyclops now had Durindana, and if anything could stop Lodovico, it was that incredible sword. The sight of Durindana turned against him made the hermit grow cold inside. Around and down came that sword like a deadly wind, but Lodovico knew enough to be afraid of it and kept well out of its reach. Since he was able to move about much faster than Polifemo, he managed to dodge one stroke after another.

But the blows coming against him were mighty and determined. Now here, now there he bounded, not daring to stay still, never once taking his sharp eyes off that whistling sword. Though he used the club to strike out fiercely at the cyclops, all his valiant fighting got him nowhere, since the cylops' shirt was made of griffin's claws, the toughest substance known to man.

"At this rate," thought Lodovico grimly, "we're going to go on fighting until one of us drops from fatigue." Continuing to exchange blow for blow with undiminished ferocity, he wracked his brains to think of some way of bringing the fight to a resolution. Suddenly he glimpsed the means to his end.

Ramming the club into the cyclops' belly with all his might, Lodovico dropped the club and made a spring for the cyclops' spear. Quickly he had it in hand, and all in one motion he launched it before Polifemo had a chance to straighten up from the first blow.

The hermit's aim was true. The spear thudded into that huge single eye, right in the middle of his forehead above the nose, and penetrated through the eye into the brain.

With an earthshaking howl and crash, Polifemo collapsed almost instantly dead, half in the black waters of the river and half on shore, dropping Durindana clattering on the rocks. Lodovico folded to his knees in exhaustion beside him. The hermit's whole body was trembling uncontrollably. He knelt there in the red sand, beside the two gigantic beings he had slain. One of Polifemo's arms in death was flung across Zambardo's half-severed side. Lodovico wept, covering his face with his hands, and gave thanks to the Hand of Fate for his deliverance.

He was aroused from his weary stupor by the return of Petroccolo, who no sooner saw the bloody face of the cyclops there before him on the beach than he turned around and fled. Jumping to his feet, the hermit was quick to call him back, reassuring him that Polifemo had eaten his last human being, and at last persuaded him to return, though the old man gave the bodies of the giant and the cyclops a wide berth, as though at any moment he thought they might rise up again.

"How have you been able to defeat such monsters?" said the old man in wonder. "Truly, I should be as afraid of you as I was of them. And you're sure they're dead?"

"Very sure," said Lodovico.

"But the other one – the one with only one ear?"

"Seeing these two here on the beach should be enough to keep him away from us," said the hermit. "I don't think Draghinazzo will bother us anymore."

The nervous old man looked far from convinced.

"Fearless giant-slayer," he said, for truly I must call you so, if you have any strength left it would be the work of a devoted and pious man, indeed, to free from that creature's pit whatever poor souls are still alive and imprisoned there. I know the way back to the monster's cave. I could guide you."

Lodovico smiled weakly. "Lead the way," he said, and with that he reached down and seized Durindana, taking the sword with him.

The old man gave another uneasy glance in the direction of those two titanic corpses, and added, "But if any more of these big fellows should arrive, I'm afraid you won't be able to expect much help from me."

The Devil in Love

"I'll remember that," said the hermit.

Both of them were glad to get away from that death-strewn riverbank. In silence they trudged deeper and deeper into the rocky desolation of Maligna, neither daring to speak what was foremost in both their thoughts – whether they would find Noraldo still alive in that pit of horrors, or only his grisly remains.

The cave was not far off. Petroccolo pointed up toward the place on the side of the mountain, but he was beginning to tremble uncontrollably, and declined to approach any closer. "In – in there," he croaked.

A great stone sealed the mouth of the entrance.

Lodovico cupped his hands around his mouth and shouted up toward the cave in his loudest voice. There was no answer. "Noraldo!" he shouted again. Silence. Then a sound came from the other side of the stone slab that could have been a hoarse voice, very weak, very faint. But perhaps it was only the wind through a crack in the rocks.

"Wait here," said Lodovico to the old man.

"But what if…" began Petroccolo.

The hermit was already on his way, up a crude staircase which the cyclops had carved up the side of the mountain. Slowly Lodovico mounted to the top, the heavy, gleaming sword in hand, clambering up one steep stair at a time, until he stood on the precarious ledge before the stone-blocked entranceway.

The Devil in Love

The massive slab was ten feet high and ten feet across, and it was held in place by two chains knotted across the front of it. The links of the chain were so thick he could scarcely get his hands around them, much less pull them apart. The way was blocked. Only giants could undo those chains. But Lodovico hadn't come all that way to stop now. Gripping Durindana in both hands, the hermit brought down the blade with all his strength on the knotted chains. The legendary blade of Durindana, forged by fairies, centuries old, shattered on impact with those chains, but the chains were also split in two, clattering apart on either side of the stone slab.

Dropping what remained of the broken sword, Lodovico left the pieces where they fell. Setting his shoulder against the side of the slab, the hermit ground his feet into the rocks for leverage and shoved against it with all his strength. Rock scraped against rock with a soul-grating shriek. Inch by inch, the massive stone groaned aside, until with a grinding crash it slid over the edge, dashing itself to pieces on the boulders below.

Chapter 17
From Out of the Pit

Noraldo stared up into the gloom, unable to sleep, knowing that these were the last few hours of his life. Slowly, inevitably approaching was a hideous, incontrovertible fact: Polifemo's next dinner. "And this time it's going to be me," he murmured to himself. Over and over he mumbled those words. The sight of poor Beppo being eaten alive was scarred into his brain, seared into his eyes. He could still hear the pageboy's terrified squeals, cut short so cruelly, and followed by those nightmarish sounds of chewing.

The pit was quiet now. "Outside it must be afternoon," Noraldo thought. The gloom inside the pit changed little during the day, varying only between general obscurity and total blackness. That he could see anything at all – the outlines of a few rocky ledges, littered with human bones – implied that somewhere outside, beyond that hideous pit, daylight still existed.

Noraldo's exhausted, half-mad eyes slowly closed. He seemed to hear his father shrieking again as the old man was thrown over the cliff. "Poor Father!" he sobbed, his head rolling back and forth. Noraldo sank into delirious dreams.

He was searching the island for his book – his beloved, lost book. He was running desperately, peering in all directions. Before him stretched the bridge, crossing over the waterfall toward the cavern of the Sfinge. "It's got to be here somewhere," he whispered, his eyes frantically scanning the ground as he turned around and around.

Something seized him from behind. He felt himself being lifted off the ground. He began to kick and scream. But when he opened his eyes, through his tears he saw, not the leering jaws of a man-eating cyclops, but an enormous Hand reaching out of the clouds, around which beams of light were radiating in a heavenly blaze. Noraldo felt himself floating, falling, into a strange, weightless peace. He was no longer afraid. "I thought I was alive," he laughed. "I thought I was real. I'm only a character in a book."

"You *are* alive, Noraldo," said a familiar voice.

Noraldo woke up with a violent shudder. He groaned as he recognized the stench and rocks of the pit. His eyes hurt from a peculiar brightness. He was wet with sweat. Someone was holding him, wiping his forehead. It was Lodovico.

"I'm still dreaming," said Noraldo, and he started to cry.

"No, I'm really here," said the hermit. "And Polifemo won't be eating anyone again, ever. You don't have to be afraid anymore. I've come to get you out of here."

"My book!" cried Noraldo, remembering. "It must be here somewhere."

At once the two of them hunted all around the pit. Now that the stone was rolled away, there was light, and a breeze of fresh air. Noraldo took a deep breath, and felt faint. He might have sunk back down to the ground if Lodovico hadn't supported him.

"Come on," said the hermit. "There's a rope over here."

"But my book..." groaned Noraldo.

"Just be glad to be alive," said the hermit. "Your father is waiting for you outside."

"Father!" cried Noraldo. "But the cyclops threw him off the cliff. I saw it with my own eyes."

"I'm afraid it will take more than that to get rid of your father," smiled Lodovico.

He led Noraldo to a side of the pit, where a rope hung down from above. "Put your arms around my neck, and hang on," said the hermit. Noraldo did as he was told, and Lodovico hauled the two of them up the rocky wall to freedom.

Once out of the pit, neither of them wished to linger in the cyclops' cave. Soon they were hurrying down that gigantic staircase of rock, at the bottom of which Noraldo was reunited with his weeping father, who hugged his son longer and more fiercely than he had ever done in his life. From that moment onward, Petroccolo continued for the next hour and more to shower Lodovico with his profuse gratitude, promising to pray for the hermit's soul for the rest of his days.

The three of them walked back toward the Bridge of Last Wishes. There lay the two titanic corpses, attracting flies near the slashed and ruined remains of Zambardo's net. Giving the grim scene a wide berth, they slowly trudged back across the bridge. On the other side, Placido was patiently waiting for them, guarding the neatly-rolled magic carpet.

"But no sign of my book anywhere!" sighed Noraldo. "When I came to this island, I had a book with pieces missing. Now I have no book at all. Not only no book, but no beloved Prince, no home I can return to without living in fear."

"For now," said Lodovico soothingly, "my hermitage in the mountains will be just the right place for you."

"Would you let me stay there?" asked Noraldo, a flicker of hope in his eyes. "Yes, that would be perfect. Far away from everything. With you for company."

"My cave is yours," said the hermit, "but I'm afraid you'll have to wait for my company."

"You mean...?"

"I've got to fetch that water of life," said Lodovico. "That's why I'm here. It's the only way to break the enchantment and save Filandro."

"I love Filandro as much as anyone, but Lodovico, we're lucky to be escaping from here with our lives," objected Noraldo. "Let's not test our luck. That water isn't for men to taste. Come with us on the carpet. Now that it's dry, it's sure to work."

Noraldo untied the carpet and unrolled it on the ground. Then he stepped into the center of it, put his foot over the griffin's eye, and creased his forehead in concentration. A moment later the carpet began to rise off the ground, until it hovered in mid-air supporting Noraldo as though he were standing on solid earth.

"You see?" cried Noraldo. "Please, Lodovico. Come with Father and me. This horrible island is no place for us. There's nothing you can do about Filandro. Just as I've had to say goodbye to Ippolito forever. They've crossed over into the Afterworld, and there's no coming back."

"Your beloved Prince has passed beyond reach, Noraldo," said the hermit gently, "but your best friend is only suspended. Filandro can be saved."

"You'll only die trying."

"If that's all I can do," said the hermit, "then that little I must. As long as I can hope, I'm going to try to save him. I've shed too much blood, Noraldo, to let it all be for nothing. Leave now, and take your father back to his shoeshop. Then go to the hermitage. Tell no one your whereabouts. I'll join you there when I've found the water of life."

"But Lodovico…"

"You should go now," said the hermit, "before some other misfortune befalls us."

While Petroccolo joined his son on the hovering carpet, Lodovico stood beside his donkey, scratching sadly between Placido's ears. "I wish I could send you back home, too, my friend," said the hermit to his donkey. "But I'm going to need your strong back and legs to carry me. I hope you don't mind staying."

The Devil in Love

Placido nuzzled one of his master's hands.

"Please be careful, Lodovico," said Noraldo from the carpet. He wiped away sudden, unexpected tears from his eyes with the back of his hand. "I'll be waiting for you at the cave." The carpet had already started to rise when he added, "If you find my book, bring it with you."

Then the carpet was only a shuddering memory as it soared away higher and higher into the sky, leaving the hermit alone to face whatever fate was waiting for him there on the island of Maligna.

The Devil in Love

CHAPTER 18
The Jaws of the Skull

Lodovico climbed up onto Placido's back and the good donkey carried him across the Bridge of Last Wishes and past the slain giants, on toward the sheer slope of the highest mountain on the island, toward the black, skull-shaped rock which Polifemo had guarded.

The wind on the island had died to less than a breeze, the air heating and slowing and thickening into a stifling, waiting hush. All around him he seemed to hear the buzzing of flies. The rocks were baking in the sun. After an hour, Lodovico took off his robe and tied it to the back of Placido's saddle. The sun beat down on his bare shoulders and the back of his head, until the skull inside seemed to be steaming. Sweat ran into his eyes. All the silent hostility of Maligna encircled him, life-absorbing, life-defeating, until Lodovico hunched forward in a daze, his wet shoulders burning, carried onward no longer by his own will but by the steady clip-clop of his donkey's hooves into the relentless, merciless heat.

He had passed the grim mouth of Polifemo's cave when something moved before him on the rocky slope which at first the hermit mistook for heat-waves. He wiped the sweat away from his eyes and squinted into the brightness. When he realized what it was, Lodovico quickly swung himself down off his donkey's back and began clambering over the hot rocks in that direction.

Was it some dry gust of wind that caused the pages to flutter, as though the book were alive and signaling to him, calling to him? Lodovico reached out for it long before the book was actually within reach, suspecting even as he scrambled toward it that his hands would close on nothing, that it was only a cruel prank of the sun, a mirage.

When his shadow fell across the book, the pages stopped fluttering. He touched it. Gritty, warped by the heat, the book was no illusion. It was battered and the cover partly ripped, as though it had been flung or dropped from a great distance, but it was solid and still in one piece. Lodovico patted it back into shape, unfolding bent pages, realigning the half-broken spine. Now he had only to find the water of life, and he could bring both of his friends great happiness at the hermitage. He smiled to think of Noraldo's joy when he saw his lost treasure.

Strapping the book onto the back of Placido's saddle, Lodovico climbed up onto the back of his donkey and they continued on their ascent. It was entirely uphill now. The way became narrow and strewn with difficulty. Lodovico made slow but determined progress until it was too dark to climb any higher. Then he slept like a dead man, only to awaken to bitter discouragement when he discovered by the light of morning how short a distance he had climbed, and how still so very high and far away the skull-shaped rock appeared, with its gaping mouth.

All the long, hot day that followed, with the sun beating down on his red and peeling shoulders, Lodovico rode his donkey toward the top of the rock. His throat became parched. Every muscle and bone in his body was soon aching. His eyes began to blur in the heat. The next day was even worse. He didn't think he could make it. The trail edged around a mound of fallen boulders to end abruptly on the windswept plateau, over which the skull rock loomed like a black, decapitated head.

But at last the terrain before him was no longer barren rock. Lodovico found himself facing a low, fog-shrouded forest of those same root-like trees which he had first seen so long ago, before ever crossing over to this island of terror. Twisting through the roots moved those same tendrils of shapeless gray mist.

Now Lodovico could see that the fog found its source in the skull's very mouth, drifting down through gaps between the blackened stone teeth, dribbling into the root forest like a shallow, irregular waterfall of smoke. Toward those foggy jaws of rock Lodovico guided his donkey. Slowly they managed to wind a way through the twisted trees. Placido's ghostly clip-clop echoed through the mist.

By the time they stood before the cavernous jaws, late afternoon was just beginning to pale toward nightfall. Lodovico hesitated. Caution urged him to wait until morning

The Devil in Love

before entering that mouth. Yet the Devil had warned him that haste was vital, and it had already taken so long.

He groaned in weariness and indecision. Then he scratched his head, and his hair came away in handfuls. Lodovico stared down at it in disbelief. It had turned white. He put his hands up to his face. His cheeks were covered with lines and wrinkles. His hands moved slowly down his neck and chest, down over a body that had become strangely sunken and gaunt. His legs no longer hung down quite so far over Placido's back. He wasn't as tall as he used to be.

"How long has it taken me to climb up here?" he thought in terror. Had it not been a matter of simply three days? His poor, aching body felt as though he had been in the saddle for more like three weeks. "Or three months?" he thought bleakly. "Or three years? Or thirty?"

A shudder convulsed Lodovico's thin body. He didn't have as much time as he thought. He would have to hurry. Clucking urgently in Placido's ear, the old man who was all that remained of the hermit nudged his rapidly aging donkey onward into the dim mouth of the skull, on the last stretch of their journey.

The Devil in Love

Chapter 19
A Taste of That Water

A hollow echo rumbled through the interior of the skull with each step the donkey took. His hooves waded through a rolling carpet of fog. All along the way now, they glimpsed skeletons on the rocky floor beneath the swirling mist, the outstretched bones of other searchers who had failed to find the well in time. Placido shied away from them nervously. Lodovico began to be afraid. There was still no sign of any well, and the farther they went, the older and weaker he became.

From up ahead he began to feel a strange wind sweeping toward them, as though trying to hold them back, causing the mist to scud away sluggishly behind them in billows. The farther they went into that endless cavern, the stronger and colder became the air whistling into their faces. In the icy blast of that wind, Lodovico began to feel older yet. He felt Placido moving slower and slower beneath him. Wheezing, the donkey came to a stop.

"Don't give up, Placido," he whispered in the donkey's ear. "I know you're feeling old and tired, but don't give up. It has to be just up ahead. Keep going…"

The Devil in Love

The donkey took another faltering step forward, but the old leg folded and collapsed. Placido fell. The old man tumbled off his back to the ground.

Pain prevented him from getting up quite as quickly as he expected. When he was on his feet again, ignoring his own scrapes and scratches, he hurried to his donkey's side. Placido's bony ribs were heaving painfully, his mouth hung open for air. He tried to scramble up onto his feet, but no longer had the strength. His breath came in harsh, dry gasps, and his lips were flecked with white.

Old Lodovico began to weep beside his dying donkey. Then his grief and fear mounted up into his throat, and swelled into a cry. "Devil!" he croaked. He had shrunk to scarcely four feet tall, He was bent and bald and toothless. Both he and the skinny animal stretched before him were little more than dry bones and shriveled skin. "Devil!" he shouted again, and when that didn't work, he began to cry, "Hand of Fate, have mercy!"

Every joint in his body ached with arthritis, he was almost blind, and he shivered with perpetual chills. The thought of dying without ever seeing Filandro again agonized him. Yet there could be no doubt that his life was almost over, as surely as Placido lay gasping his last. There would simply be two more skeletons left behind on a journey to nowhere, two more white piles of bones in the fog.

"Hand of Mercy!" he sobbed bitterly. "Don't let it all be for nothing."

The Devil in Love

There was no answer to his cry.

With a last lurch, old Lodovico pushed away from his fallen donkey and began hobbling and doddering forward into the howling wind, alone. Clutching his skinny chest, he was weeping with disappointment. He knew now that there was no well. The Devil had tricked him into chasing his own doom. There was only a mindless wind, roaring through some forgotten hole in the rock.

"But I'm not going to die in despair," he promised himself stubbornly. The few teeth he had left were clenched in determination. "I'm going to die searching for that well, even it if doesn't exist."

That was when he saw it.

An old stone ring, round and three feet tall, rose up from the cavern floor in the middle of a glittering grotto of white rock. On the rim waited a wooden bucket and a coiled rope. Out of the depths of the grotto, from behind the well, roared the mysterious wind, along with a blinding white light. The sight gave Lodovico enough strength to go on struggling against that howling blast, step by step.

He reached the well, and peered down over the lip. It seemed to have no bottom, to be filled with only shadows instead of water. He dropped the bucket down the dark shaft, and began lowering the rope. Down and down it went, clanking against the empty sides. Loop after loop of the rope disappeared down the stone mouth. As the last loop slipped

The Devil in Love

through his fingers, he heard a hollow, plunking splash from deep inside the shaft.

The bucket was heavier now. Old Lodovico tugged on the rope arm over arm, drawing the bucket slowly back up.

It came splashing up over the side, full of a glittering, sloshing darkness. Clutching it eagerly, Lodovico tipped it forward and took a deep, full swallow. Cold and sparkling, it was somehow like liquid fire. A feeling of joyous health and well-being surged through his tired old bloodstream. His arthritis stopped aching, his gums stopped hurting. His eyes opened a little wider, and his sight came more into focus.

Turning with a cry from the well, cupping his hands together and scooping up as much of the precious water as they could hold, the old man broke into a run back into the swirling mist toward where he had left his donkey.

Chapter 20
The Devil's Doorway

Tendrils of fog were wrapped around Placido's still body like the gray, dissolving rags of a shroud. He didn't move. With a weary groan, the old hermit sank to his knees beside his lifeless four-footed companion. A rattling gasp hissed through Placido's open mouth. Quick as a wink, Lodovico no sooner detected that last trace of life than he raised his donkey's head and dribbled some water from his hands over the donkey's parched lips.

Placido twitched. The old man gave him more. The donkey's eyes slowly opened. His cloudy eye lost its glaze. He blinked, and his black eyes gave a faint sparkle. With a cry of joy, Lodovico gave him another drink. His long, furry ears twitched, no longer limp, but stiff again, almost perky. The hermit gave him all the rest. The donkey's four legs gave a weak kick, and then the stronger ones. Placido scrambled up onto his feet again.

With a happy shout, old Lodovico led the donkey to the well, where he had left the bucket still full of water. He scooped his hands into the icy liquid and lifted them cupped and dripping to his own mouth, before Placido gently nuzzled him aside and began drinking for all his was worth.

"Drink deep, my friend," laughed Lodovico. "There's a whole well of it for us to share." The more Placido drank, the younger and healthier he grew, right there in front of the hermit's eyes. Eagerly Placido lapped up the exhilarating water, thrusting his nose deeper and deeper into the bucket, and then raising his head in a healthy, happy bray.

That was what did it.

The crash startled both of them. It was over before Lodovico could stop it, or even understand what was happening. Placido flinched away with a whinny. There before them lay the overturned bucket on its side, and in the midst of the spilled water lay Noraldo's beloved book, dislodged from its place on Placido's back, its pages suddenly sopping.

Lodovico wailed, grief-stricken at the ruin of his friend's dearest treasure. He swooped to retrieve it, then just as quickly forgot all about it, leaving the book where it had fallen. His shame and regret over the loss of the book had changed to stark horror.

The bucket had cracked in two.

"No!" he screeched. He seized the bucket, only to have it snap apart in his hands. In vain he tried to cup the last few splashes of water in one of the bucket-halves, to save it for Filandro. The water ran out onto the rocks, where Placido lapped it up. "No!" he cried, pushing his donkey away. The old man fell to the ground, scraping desperately at the wetness that remained.

The Devil in Love

Then he wept. It was too late. Filandro's fate was sealed. Poor Lodovico and his donkey had drunk just enough of the water to save their own lives. Now his treasured friend would be a statue of stone forever.

The ground trembled beneath him. The hermit looked up in fear. The grotto of white rock behind the well appeared to open before him. Through the gaping doorway stepped the Devil, as handsome and utterly desirable as ever, with the winds howling around him.

"Why are you weeping, Lodovico?" he asked, in an echoing voice which easily rose over the howling winds, "Aren't you satisfied yet? From this day onward, you are beyond the reach of Time. Not only you, but your good donkey as well, are now immortal."

"But there's none left for Filandro," complained the old man. "That was the whole reason I came here. And I only got three swallows – Placido drank almost all of it."

"Placido here will be doing all of the walking," said the Devil, "while all you have to do is ride. Be thankful, hermit, for what you got – most men would give anything for one swallow of that water, and you got three. Now the time has come for you to go back to the cave of infants and start delivering babies. You've been gone for over a year. The cave is already filling up, and there are boys who are ready to meet their fathers."

"A year...?" said the little hermit. "But I thought..."

"Come," said the Devil. "Through this door."

The Devil in Love

"Not yet," cried Lodovico piteously "Not after coming this far. What about poor Filandro? You promised."

"I always keep my promises," said the Devil. "You found the well."

"But Filandro has to have some of this water! I can't just leave him as a statue of stone in the forest!"

"Very well, then," said the Devil. "I'll admit there is one other way to restore him to life. Filandro could also be turned back into flesh and blood the moment that his lips of stone are touched by a kiss of true love."

"A kiss!" cried Lodovico. "Is that all? Just a kiss? But I could have given him that myself. Why didn't you tell me that before?"

"You never asked," said the Devil. "If you had asked me whether there was any other way, I would have told you." He smiled. "I never give unnecessary information. Now, I've told you how to restore him to life. It's time for you to go to work. Through this doorway."

"No, wait," pleaded Lodovico. "Do I have to go back looking like this? Filandro won't even recognize me? A shriveled old dwarf?"

The Devil scowled. "I never promised you that things were going to work out perfectly. You've had a taste of the waters of Eternal Life, and you're still not satisfied. That's more than most people ever get. Just be patient, and your Filandro will soon enough look just as old as you do. Now, come on."

The Devil in Love

"No, please," begged the hermit. "I'll never get this far again. Help me. We've got to make another bucket somehow. Perhaps you could..."

"No one ever gets to draw up the bucket more than once," said the Devil. "I thought I mentioned that."

Lodovico could not have been more miserable. He covered his face with his hands. "And just look at Noraldo's book," he groaned. "Completely ruined!"

"Hardly," said the Devil. Leaving the doorway, he strode over to where the book lay face-open and drenched, picked it up, and gave it a good, brisk shake. The last few drops of water were sent flying. Then the Devil pushed the book into Lodovico's hands. "Take another look."

The hermit stared in wonder, as though he had never seen the book before. Then the Devil snatched it out of his hands, and tied it to Placido's back, on top of the carpet. "There, as good as new. Bring it back to Noraldo. Now, on your way."

"I'm sure he'll be delighted," sighed the hermit. "Well, I suppose things could have turned out worse."

"Very much worse," assured the Devil. "Believe me. Now, are you ready to go?"

"All right," said the little hermit. He climbed up onto his donkey's back. "But tell me this – if I could have just walked through this door in the grotto wall to reach the well, why did you make me go through such horrible adventures on this island?"

The Devil in Love

"The only way a man can ever find this door," said the Devil, "is to climb Polifemo's mountain, just as you did, and enter the jaws of the skull. You will never use this doorway again. Now, follow me."

The Devil returned to the doorway in the white grotto wall. Lodovico nudged the donkey with his knees, and Placido ambled after him. "You mustn't keep their fathers waiting any longer," said the Devil. "The sooner you deliver all those little boys, the better. Isn't this doorway starting to look familiar to you yet?"

Lodovico gasped. "But that's impossible…" The donkey stepped over the threshold, back through the door of burnished gold, leaving behind the well and the mist, the wind and the light.

The Devil in Love

Chapter 21
The Kiss

Often during the long afternoons after he returned from that island of horrors, Noraldo would slip away from the rocky retreat of Lodovico's cave and walk down through the forested hills of Antichi to the grove where Filandro stood cold and motionless. There Noraldo would sit in the grass at the statue's feet and talk to his friend as though he were alive and could talk back.

"Whoever would have guessed, back in Valbrosa, that the two of us would end up like this?" he mused one day. "I've lost everything but you, my friend – but you I'll have till I die."

He had long ago concluded that Lodovico had perished on the dreadful island of Maligna, and that his dear book was lost forever. Though his father still lived and worked in his shoeshop, Noraldo could not safely visit him there. As the lover of the murdered Prince of Antichi, Noraldo's life would always be in danger the moment his whereabouts were discovered in any of Federigo's three kingdoms. From now on, his life would be a secret one in the depths of the forest, guarded by the silent northern mountains.

The Devil in Love

"Still, at least there's always the magic carpet," Noraldo continued to his silent friend. "You know, lately I've been wondering what would happen if…"

Noraldo's thoughts were interrupted by the snapping of a branch. He sat up abruptly, scanning the nearby trees. Then from out of the blaze of sunlight at the other end of the clearing rode a gray donkey carrying an old man. Noraldo had never seen him before, though it was impossible not to be vaguely reminded of his long-lost friend, the hermit. The donkey stopped directly in front of him. The old man smiled benignly.

"Good day to you, sir," said Noraldo. "You're new to these parts. You're probably curious about this statue. He was a wonderful friend until he was enchanted."

"It's taken me a long time to get here," said the old man.

"Can I be of some help to you, sir?" said Noraldo kindly.

"No, I'm afraid not," smiled the old man. "But I can be of some help to you, Noraldo, and together we can perhaps do something for your poor friend."

Noraldo stared at him. "How do you know my name?"

He ignored the question. "But first I have to return something that belongs to you." He reached into his saddlebag and withdrew from it a book which, had it not been so fresh and new, Noraldo might have mistaken for very own lost treasure. The startling similarity between the two books, however, made him gasp and scramble to his feet.

The Devil in Love

"No, you're not seeing things," said the old man. He held the book out to Noraldo. "Go ahead, take it. It's yours. That's what the water from the well did to it."

"Who are you?" asked Noraldo in a trembling voice.

"Never mind me," said the old man. "Take a look at your book."

Noraldo took the book into his hands, staring thunderstruck. Gone was the tattered, soiled and blood-stained old volume, which had endured countless generations of love and abuse even before its violent adventures with Noraldo. What he now held in his hands looked impossibly new, as though each page had just been immaculately written that very morning. He held it reverently, turning the crisp, unwrinkled, freshly-bound pages. "There's not a mark or scratch on it," said Noraldo in amazement. "These pages aren't worn or faded! But it's exactly the same story, the same words, the same writing. Yes, this has to be my book, all right, this could only be my book, except that…"

The old man laughed. "It's your book, all right. The only difference is, your book is now immortal. The binding will never break, and the pages will never pull out. It starts at the beginning, all the story holes are in place, and better yet, the story is now endless. There will always be another chapter."

Overjoyed, Noraldo turned quickly to the places where pages had been missing. The lost chapters were no longer torn out. And now the book had a beautifully lettered title page that it had never possessed before. Though no author

The Devil in Love

was listed, the book certainly had a name, prominently displayed in bold classic script: **The Devil in Love.**

He opened to the first sentence on the first page of the first chapter.

> **Once upon a time** there were three brothers named Piero, Petroccolo and Pasquino who lived in the sleepy, old-fashioned kingdom of Bolgaro and wrote a long epic fairytale together. Piero married into royalty and became fabulously rich. Petroccolo opened a very successful shoeshop in Valbrosa. And Pasquino wrote down the fairytale, shortly before he was expelled from the family for practicing sorcery...

Noraldo gasped. "Sorcery?" That was not the way he'd heard the story. He'd always been told Pasquino had run away from home. He closed the book and clutched it to his chest. Maybe Pasquino's leaving the family had not been so runaway, after all.

"Where did you find this?" asked Noraldo. "How did you know it belonged to me?"

The little old man wasn't listening to him. He was looking up sadly into Filandro's unseeing eyes. "Listen to me carefully," he said at last to Noraldo. "I could answer all your questions about your book, but none of that matters. You'll

The Devil in Love

know soon enough. What matters now is Filandro. It's up to you now. I'm too old. Wait until I've left the grove. And then, listen to me carefully, Noraldo – think about the happiest times you ever spent with Filandro, think about how very much you love him, and then I am asking you to kiss this statue on the lips."

"Kiss a statue of stone?" said Noraldo.

"That's all you have to do," said the old man.

"Yes, but…"

The old man clucked in his donkey's ear to go.

"How can I ever thank you for finding my book, whoever you are," said Noraldo, alarmed that the old man was leaving. "You never told me your name."

The old man looked back only once at the statue. His eyes were wet with tears, but he was smiling.

"Thank you," stammered Noraldo. He wasn't sure whether the old man heard him or not.

Then the clearing was deserted except for Noraldo. He hesitated for only a moment, then he stood before the statue of his dearest friend. He remembered that day long ago when the two of them had gone off into the forest together, and as he recalled their fond embraces that sunlit afternoon he kissed those cold, slightly-parted gray lips.

A shudder passed through the statue.

Filandro's eyes blinked open.

Chapter 22
The Child Bringer

Old Lodovico glanced up at the sky over Antichi. It was clear and blue, swept clean by the wind of any last wisp of cloud. Tomorrow would be sunny, too. Satisfied that Filandro had at last been restored to life, the hermit made his familiar little clucking sound in Placido's ear, and they started out.

All the aches and pains of old age, which had vanished with his first drink of water from the well, never returned. He never aged another day. Though he remained little more than five feet tall and over sixty years old, his skin was no longer so winkled and his gums had teeth again, and the teeth didn't hurt. He could see much better now, too, without blinking and squinting so much.

"Why, I feel like I'm only twenty-five," he told his donkey as they clip-clopped along. "Considering how much you drank, Placido, you must feel like a regular colt."

Leaving the wild hills of Antichi behind, the donkey carried him deeper and deeper into the White Demon Mountains toward the mountain wall. Though he travelled along at an easy and comfortable pace, Placido made unnaturally rapid progress. There seemed to be something magical about his hooves now, perhaps from wading through so much swirling mist. Their simple clip-clopping was now somehow able to elude the stricter penalties of time, so that they made much quicker progress than they should have.

Before long, the donkey was carrying Lodovico across the narrow bridgeway of stone, just as evening began to settle over the mountaintops. Sure-footed and sharp-eyed, Placido climbed up along the dangerous secret path. In the last rays of the sun, he crossed back through the narrow crack in the sheer stone face, bearing the old hermit down and around the winding tunnel, and back to the spell-lit cave, into the presence of the glittering Ice Rose.

The cave was now far from empty. Little boys were nestled everywhere, sound asleep in their mossy nooks and crannies, deep in their dreams. The Devil had clearly been busy in his absence, and now Lodovico and his donkey would have to take over.

The next morning, he found Placido waiting for him in a brand-new harness, which numerous wicker baskets strapped on either side. In the secret land beyond the mountain wall, a dozen infant boys were already waiting for Lodovico on the rock among the flowers. "Placido, it looks like we have our work cut out for us," he laughed. Then he hugged each of the babies, tickled them a little, and popped as many of them into the wicker baskets as would fit. It took him three trips to bring them all to the cave and nestle each one of them into a cozy bed of moss, and by that time plenty of one-year-old dreamers were stretching and waking up in the cave, ripe and ready to go meet their fathers.

The Devil in Love

Into the baskets they went, and together the old man on the donkey took them along the steep underground passageway leading back out into the light of day, toward the trail leading down the mountain into the Devil's Land.

"Congratulations, Giuseppe! It's twins, you rascal."

"Look who's a father again, Antonio. Five is a good number!"

"Oswaldo, I thought I would never knock on your door."

"I know you're in there, Chucho, and I know he belongs to you!"

Every day more babies arrived at the cave of infants. Every day a new batch in the cave were ready to meet their fathers, blinking in the light of dawn, kicking chubby legs and wondering where their dreams had gone. They all remembered forever the same reassuring sight – a smiling old man welcoming them into Devil's Land, transporting them on the back of a gentle gray donkey down from the high cave into the land of men.

Delivering all those little boys was an exhausting, demanding job, with long hours of travelling, dealing with the thousand-and-one emergencies which always arise wherever there are children. He sometimes didn't get back to the cave of infants before dawn, in spite of Placido's magical hooves, and at the first light of dawn he had to leave for the rock to check for newborn boys all over again.

Fortunately, immortals don't need very much sleep. Though Lodovico seldom got to actually lie down in his bed anymore, and never for more than an hour or two, he did manage to catch little naps and dozes while riding on Placido's back.

He didn't complain. The old hermit took his position in the nature of things very seriously. Unlike many immortals, he took great pleasure in each day as it came, and never wasted an hour. He was always prompt, never in a rush, never careless.

As he told Placido at least once a week, "It's all so interesting, this business of fathers and sons." He was proud to be playing such an important role in the celestial machinery.

Whenever his travels took him near Antichi, he always stopped in for a visit at his old home. Noraldo and his best friend continued to live in the hermitage together since the day Filandro was awakened by his kiss.

Usually only Noraldo was at home, with his friend out working in the garden or hunting in the forest. Lodovico would almost always find him reading. Noraldo's pleasure in that endless fairytale had not abated one bit.

"I read a chapter whenever I can," he admitted. "I never know what to expect. There's always some unexpected twist or revelation. And every story has another story inside it."

Lodovico could see that the book had enchanted him, and that the two friends, as different as night and day, were perfectly suited for each other. He never told them who he really was, and no one ever learned his real name. Since

The Devil in Love

everyone thought of the kind old man as their grandfather, he was soon known everywhere as Nonno.

The children of the Devil's Land continued to love the old fellow dearly, long after he left them in their father's arms. Whenever Nonno rode into town to deliver a baby, all the young toddlers would take to their feet and flock to greet him, scrambling out of their cribs, dashing out of doors to flock around Placido in the middle of the cobbled streets with happy cries and shouts, welcoming the immortal grandfather of all generations, as vital and inextricable a part of the Devil's Land as its mountains and rivers, the eternal bringer of all little boys.

*

The Devil in Love

The Devil in Love

Nick DiMartino has had over twenty plays in full-run productions across the United States. His musical adaptations of *Ozma of Oz* and *Rama* were performed by the Bellevue Children's Theatre. His adaptations of *Dracula*, *Pinocchio*, and *The Snow Queen* were performed by Seattle Children's Theatre. His adaptation of *Frankenstein* premiered at the Honolulu Theatre for Youth, was videotaped in 1997 by the BBC and released as a video by Globalstage. His two musical adaptations from the Kalevala were performed by the Finlandia Foundation. He's been the campus book-buyer for the University Book Store at the University of Washington for over forty years, hosts two book clubs, and reviews international fiction online for ShelfAwareness.com. He lives in Seattle. His books include:

Novels
The Devil in Love
Joseph Golem
Women Who Can't Stop Talking
Love in the American Empire
Pineapple Moon
Changes
Dude

Ghost Novels
Christmas Ghost Story
University Ghost Story
Seattle Ghost Story

Memoirs
Mars versus Maple School
Throw Me Among My Own